Earthen Trinkets

Kieran York

Scarlet Clover Publishers

Littleton

Edited by Beth Mitchum
Cover and interior design: Beth Mitchum
Cover photo: Kieran York

A Scarlet Clover book

Published by Scarlet Clover Publisher
www.kieranyork.com
P.O. Box 621002
Littleton, Colorado 80162

Printed and bound in the United States of America, UK, and
Europe

ISBN-13: 978-0692285428
ISBN-10: 0692285423

Earthen Trinkets

Kieran York

Books also written by Kieran York:

Careful Flowers
Appointment with a Smile
Night Without Time
Crystal Mountain Veils (A Royce Madison Mystery)
Timber City Masks (A Royce Madison Mystery)
Sugar With Spice (Short Fiction)
Blushing Aspen (poetry)

DEDICATION:

This book is dedicated to my sister – Karla.

    I'm blessed she's my sister.

    I'm thankful she married my brother-in-law, Bob.

    I'm fortunate for all the happiness they've brought into my life.

Thanks, Karla – I could have never hoped for a better family!

ACKNOWLEDGEMENTS:

At the beginning of this list is my friend and mentor – Beth Mitchum. She encouraged me, she taught me, and she edited, formatted, designed covers, as well as offered expert collaboration on producing *Earthen Trinkets*. She has been there at my side since the very beginning. There is a country-western song that talks about angels among us. Well, Beth is one of my closest angels. Thank you, Beth!

I thank an amazing person and friend – Barbara Oatley. She is a nurse, and has offered invaluable, expert assistance in the writing of medical scenes in this book. I am appreciative of your knowledge, Barbara – and your friendship.

As always, I thank my ever-supportive family and friends. I'm indebted to each of you for your kindness and love.

Chapter 1

Bryana Hays drove her SUV tentatively towards the edge of the highway. She pulled off to the side of the Kansas highway and parked. It was at the corner of the farmland property that had been deeded to her and her partner.

"I need some air," she said. Her words were flat. Her soul matched with a dejection she found difficult to express. She got out and went to the fence that guarded a green, waving wheat crop. Her mouth was parched, but her eyes fought the dampness of tears. She leaned against the weathered fence post.

The heat was heavy, unlike the dry heat of Denver. Just east of the Colorado border, the Kansas rangeland's atmosphere was as thick as suffocation.

Within the pit of her stomach Bryana realized it was more than air she needed. For decades she had put on a pretty good face, but she recognized an unspoken problem, and perhaps her partner was aware. There remained a broodiness underlying her good nature. Bryana had no way to describe it. The word 'forlorn' came nearest. It was an ache buried so deeply, and hidden so precisely. As if it would never be discovered - but it was there. Everything else in life only exacerbated what was forlorn inside her.

She heard the door slam, and then the shuffling on gravel behind her. "Bryana," Michelle Dawson said as she approached. "It will be okay."

"If by 'okay' you mean we're trapped, then it is all okay. Just peachy. We're trapped. That isn't *okay*." She felt Michelle's hand orb her shoulder. They had been together for over thirty years. Louder than her normal voice might have been, Bryana again repeated, "We are so flipping trapped. And you know it isn't going to be okay ever again."

They both had realized the old farmhouse was no pastoral legacy. Although Bryana's parents had owned and worked the farm, she had throughout her adult years supplemented the funds for payment on machinery and an assortment of bills and loans. Both Bryana and Michelle had worked in Denver for three decades. Most of their savings had been siphoned off to pay the farm's deficits over the years.

Michelle was always good-humored about everything to do with Bryana. Always reacting to Bryana's intensity, Michelle knew what to expect of her lover. Now, dumbfounded about the predicament, Michelle only knew that Bryana's demeanor was quiet. As if her mood was being lowered by a pulley, it was a meditative motion of gloom.

Michelle exhaled with a harsh whoosh. "I'll check the figures again, but I don't see how there can be anything at all left in the estate. With current rates, the appraisal on the farm would only pay off the rest of Farmer's Administration loan, and the remaining estate taxes. Property prices have hit an all-time low." After a moment's pause, she added, "I know we'd hoped to break even, but I've discovered a few more bills."

"It's impossible for there to be more. We've been keeping up with the property taxes. When I sold my pottery shop last year, I thought I'd cleared up the loans."

"Bank loans and property taxes, yes. But bills have been accumulating. So not all of them are paid off," Michelle said with a defeated intonation.

Bryana's voice choked up. She commented with remorse, "I'd always figured that we'd save the farm, and when my parents died, we'd have enough to balance out what we've put into it. You even put in the money from your pension fund."

"It wasn't enough. Obviously. Your father had a handful of bills stuffed behind the drawer."

"We truly are trapped. Our options are limited. Walk without a cent, leaving behind a bankrupted estate, or stay with no reserve savings and with bills up the yim-yam."

"If we leave, it will be with nothing. Not enough start-up capital to return to Denver and get an apartment and jobs. Even if we could sell it in this depressed time, the farm sale won't bring what it is actually worth. If we can keep it upright, in a few years prices will bounce back. We can make the Farmer's Administration loan monthly. Pay as we go. And keep paying off other bills, a little at a time."

"Prices bouncing back up!" Bryana's head rested against the top of the wooden fence post. "And then we are solvent. That is if we can keep it afloat until prices go up." Bryana considered their litany of financial woes. "That's iffy." Her words were barely audible, as if they'd gone stale in her mouth.

"We can make this place profitable again. Bryana, I know we can turn it around. A few years of good crops, and we'll have it in the black. Remember the old adage about land being the most valuable thing a person can own?"

"It's an old adage that doesn't fit these times. It's no longer relevant to economics, and certainly not to us. Anyone who said that has probably been dead a long, long time. Earth used to be a treasure. Now it is a trinket."

Michelle shook her head. "But there's also an old saying about it being better to have the living ideas of the dead, than have the dead ideas of the living." She chuckled. "And trinkets are fine."

"Would you really be happy living on this god-forsaken, dilapidated farm? A few years is a long time away from our friends back in Denver."

"Long term we could work the land, build things back up. Then sell and return to home. If we wanted to."

"Long term. Michelle, I'm sixty and you're two years older. It isn't like we're twenty-five again. We're too old to consider taking out a vagabond status."

"Okay, but even short term, if we stay the summer, until after harvest, we'll get funds from the wheat land lease. It will give us some room to maneuver. Some cushion. I know after expenses and bills are paid, that won't really do much more that get us thirty miles to the Colorado-Kansas border. If we keep it going, we could roll crops into the winter."

"We probably couldn't even sell the farm during winter. Much less have enough to leave."

"I know. But we only need one buyer."

"We do have one buyer. Vince Roland will buy it. He isn't willing to pay a decent price. He wants to see me grovel. And I would never sell out to Roland."

"We may one day need to do some first-class groveling." Michelle turned and walked back to the car. "Come on, we've got things to do."

Bryana followed. She started the vehicle's engine. She wondered why she'd stopped. Years ago it would have been because she loved the expanding horizon that the flatlands produced. After pulling onto the highway, she continued driving in silence. "Hell," she mumbled as she heard the police siren behind them. She glanced in the rearview mirror.

Michelle turned. "You weren't speeding."

"It's Pete Myer, the son of one of my schoolmates. Pete's a Tinpsila County sheriff's deputy, slash, bully. The terror of Buffalo Plains, Kansas, would also be accurate. Dad used to call him a room temperature IQ with a pugilistic badge attached."

"I know you weren't speeding, I always glance at the speedometer."

"Pete will just hassle us. Amazingly enough, his father, the sheriff, is a nice guy. People know there's the look of nepotism, but Sheriff Norman Myer keeps Pete in line. Norm jokes that Pete never gets it wrong more than half the time."

As Pete approached, his cocky amble was deliberate. Bryana rolled down the window of her metallic silver late model Honda CR-V. "Miss Bryana Hays," he said feigning surprise.

"Pete, I'll bet you've been waiting all morning for me to drive by so you could play with your siren. Are you pulling me over to harass or arrest me?"

Leaning against the car, Pete scoffed, "I hear you two are the latest residents to the county."

"No decision has been made on that. Look, we weren't speeding," Bryana said with a bristle in her voice. "Everything is in order. I've had my driver's license since way before you were even born."

They scowled at one another with a mutual disdain.

"So you two women may go on back to Denver?" Pete began his fishing expedition to find out her plans.

"Don't hassle me," Bryana's chaffed voice insisted. "I've got your father's phone number on my speed dial. You know your father and I have been friends since grade school."

"My daddy wasn't too particular about who he ran around with back there. Besides, he hasn't turned me over his knee in years," Pete said with a huge, gulping laugh. Looking down at his girth, he added, "I'd never fit."

"You do fill a doorway. Look, Pete, I'm not in a chatty mood right now."

"Maybe Denver would improve your mood," he encouraged.

"We'll be returning to Denver when we're ready. And it won't be too soon for me."

Pete countered, "If it wasn't for town's people caring about your parents, you'da been run out of the county months ago. We don't abide having ladies like you around."

"Obsolete thinking. You know we came back to take care of my mother. After she died, we needed to stay on to care for Dad. We had no intention of moving to this tight-assed, red-necked area. I'm certain the residence of Buffalo Plains would love to see the back of us heading towards the Kansas/Colorado border. No more than we would love going back to Denver."

Sneering, Pete's ruddy face jammed into the vehicle's window. His sandy, walnut-colored hair fell across his short forehead. He brushed the mane to one side with his huge, fire-hydrant shaped fingers. "Gotta give a little sniff to see if you got any grass. Hell, you two need to go on back to Colorado. They abide with marijuana and homosexuals."

Shaking her head, Bryana rolled her eyes. "Do I get any morality points for being born in Kansas?"

He grinned, "You're like a stranger now. We aren't partial to strangers around here in general. Much less *odd* ones like you and your lady friend." His eyes were anchored on Michelle. His smile folded into a lopsided smirk. Turning to Bryana, he rubbed his square jaw. "Your momma and daddy raised you better than how you're living. Bet you embarrassed them."

"Let's not talk about my deceased parents."

"Naw. But you know what I say is true. Your daddy was a crazy old coot, but everyone respected him. And your mama probably taught every kid in Tinpsila County at one time or another. We all loved her. She was much younger than your daddy, and we were all thinking he'd go first. He was over ninety, and still spry as a young twig. Like I say, I can't imagine how they felt about raising someone like you."

"Pete, I've had enough of a chat with you. Either ticket me for some bogus charge, or leave me alone. You can't detain me for driving down a county road," Bryana's words steamed.

"I'm checkin' on your plan. Everyone around these parts is curious," Pete snorted. "Folks wanna see about your farm. What you got, around 500 acres?"

"Eight-hundred and eighty," Bryana answered with an accompanying glare in Pete's direction. The pastoral farmhouse was surrounded by lines of hardwood trees. The land was prime farmland and would yield non-irrigation crops. A few patches remained in native prairie grassland. Within the larger parcel, two lovely ponds dotted the landscape.

"Good farmland. Quite the nice little farm before your daddy slowed down."

Bryana was well aware that after her mother became ill, and then died, her father's love of the farm was extinguished. Bryana responded with descriptive fact, a method her mother had taught her decades ago. Always divert what detractors said with pure fact. "Six hundred acres are leased to Mr. Dreher up north. He's put in a wheat crop. Rolf Jarvis is leasing two hundred acres for both sorghum and alfalfa. About forty acres were left as grassland and leased for Rolf's buffalo herd. The rest is farmhouse and surrounding gardens and an orchard."

"Oh, yeah. Buffalo Bill Jarvis. Got him a good little herd of bison."

"If he could get a loan, he'd buy our spread," Bryana divulged.

"Nobody is lending. Especially to Jarvis. He's up to his eyeballs in bad paper."

"I'm pretty sure you got your information directly from the Rolands. With Vince Roland being CEO and president of our local bank's board it would be impossible for Rolf. Rolf Jarvis wouldn't be lent money because Vince knows Rolf wants to buy something he wants."

"Yeah, but you gotta admit Jarvis isn't any more of a businessman than your daddy was. Or you are."

"Rolf is a good rancher. Through no fault of his own he had to buy tons of feed over the winter," Bryana defended. "I like the guy. He's honest. We exchange baked goods, veggies, and pies and eggs for buffalo meat. And in the bargain, he adds chickens. Then part of the deal we have with him is that he leases land, and pays us, adding hay for our stock. He's never cheated us."

"Yeah. I don't mind him." Pete stutter-stepped his way backward a couple of yards. "And I know for a fact Tank Roland wouldn't mind if his daddy were to acquire your place. Tank would take it off your hands in a blink."

"Tank and his daddy, Vince, wouldn't mind *robbing* me of the land. I'm guessing Vince and Sarah weren't foolish enough to sign their farm over to Tank when they moved to their new mansion in town."

"They haven't given Tank the land yet. They want to see what he does with it. When Vince nicknamed his only son Tank early on, it was because he knew how bullheaded he is. I'm Tank's buddy, and even I can never get through to him. Obstinate, you bet. So they haven't signed any papers over to him. But Vince and the Mrs. would love to snap up your property. Nobody is gonna accuse either Vince or Tank of not trying to swindle a good sale," he said with a cackle. "I'm guessing if you hold out, they'll come up with the price."

"My property isn't for sale to the Roland family at any price. They want it to add to their game reserve. Get weekend hunters here to kill the game they bring in. *Game* is a not exactly the correct word. It's wildlife being shot in a barrel. My father didn't approve of it and I certainly wouldn't blemish his memory by going against what he wouldn't have wanted done with the land."

"Yeah. You got a perfect setup," Pete agreed. "Nice little ponds. The quail and pheasant hunting would be great there. And you got a couple dandy water wells. Tank drools at the thought of adding on to his sporting game reserve."

"Enough of his 'hunters, slash, guests' climb over, or under, the fences onto our land. Last winter I was constantly chasing them off the property."

"Well, Tank hates losing game when the animals escape over to your land. Costs him."

"I don't encourage the wildlife onto the property. And I certainly don't want those so-called sportsmen visiting us. Some of them studied their target practice and gun control at the Dick Cheney shooting academy."

Chortling, Pete admitted, "Yep, they get the rookies in. And they let folks drink alcohol, who got no reason to be drinking. My dad hates it when we get called out there to settle the booze fights. 'Cause I got a gun, Daddy made me all but stop drinking. I get a beer on Sundays, when I'm not working. And my wife reports any second beers to my Daddy. Guns and drinking don't mix. Even I know that. But those hunting farms are like cocktail parties. I seen'em laugh off the near misses. Us deputies hate going out there. Hell, everybody's armed and dangerous. Tank won't listen to me. They make big profits selling booze. Your mama called the hunters "intoxicated novices." Tank's little lodge is licensed to sell drinks, so nothing I can do about it."

"I can't imagine Tank's mother abiding by a slaughterhouse for innocent wildlife," Bryana spoke with cynicism. "Sarah hated cruelty to animals when we were in school. And with all the booze, and goofy hunters, I really worry about those three kids. I've voiced my fears, and both Tank and Alice act as if I'm butting in and don't know what I'm talking about. I'm fearful for my livestock, and our dogs. And us, too. Tank and Alice seem not to care about their kids. I'm amazed Sarah allows that to go on around her grandchildren."

"I 'magine Vince told her not to interfere," Pete offered as if he'd heard the story from Tank. "I 'spose she's worried."

"Having known her in the past, I'm certain she's worried. But she's never been any match for Vince's iron fist."

Pete smirked. "Weren't you and Mrs. Roland pals when you lived here?"

"Sarah and I were friends growing up. Clear through high school. I went away to college and she married Vince."

"There was talk about you trying on your sisterhood stuff with Mrs. Roland. She turned you off like poison."

"Rumors. And none of them your business, Pete."

Pete's eyes always held a malevolent jest. As if playing with mice in a maize, he was wiggling the puzzle just enough to tip those he interrogated off balance. "You ladies have a nice day," he muttered as he tapped his Stetson. He returned to his squad car.

"Fucker," Bryana muttered nearly under her breath.

Chapter 2

Bryana leaned her head back. She felt her blood heat with anger. "Screw these people. Mullet mentality. Pete and Vince Roland's son, Tank, are best friends." She turned the ignition key with a vengeance. Once the vehicle was back onto the road, she sighed as if she might be sneezing. "Damn these people!"

"What was that all about?"

"I came out to Sarah shortly after high school. Her parents owned the farmland just west of us. Where her Tank lives now. So we grew up neighbors, and inseparable friends."

"You told your best friend? Did you have feelings for her?"

Bryana paused then answered, "Yes, I had an attraction. But that was forty years ago. It was a different world. She was engaged, and obviously told Vince about my being Sapphic. She might as well have put it in a banner headline."

"You said you were outted, but you didn't mention the circumstances."

"Sarah has hardly spoken to me since. She barely even acknowledges me. Even at my father's funeral, it was a cool, angry nod."

"Back in those days coming out to a bride-to-be wasn't the way to get an invite to be a bride's maid," Michelle teased. "Now it's no big thing. Back then, whew!"

"You just saw an example of how the majority of the town's people think."

Michelle joked, "Some of them are a little standoffish."

Bryana chuckled. "And you're entertaining the idea of us staying here for the duration of our lives - with these people. With Sarah's son, Tank Roland, and his family living on the adjoining farm to ours. You've now just met Tank's best buddy - the deputy.

They're such narrow-minded assholes! How can we live here inside homophobic *hell*?"

Laughing a deeply rich laugh, Michelle shook her head. "What is so funny?"

"When you curse it is with such decorum."

"Maybe I do it to excuse saying the words you don't approve of. These people bring out the worst in my language." A slight grin appeared on Bryana's face.

"I won't say I'm madly in love with Kansas, but it's where we are. And we're together."

"I love the area. Yes, it's flat and boring farmland, but it's as if a finger is snapped inside my heart when I see the land stretching into a sunset. It's the damned bigoted people."

"Maybe we can get used to them. Or ignore them."

"I didn't want to leave the farm years ago. These prejudiced people know how to make a person feel uncomfortable. I'd considered going to a neighboring college, but after I was outted, I decided on going to Colorado University."

"Four decades may have changed some of their hearts."

"Yes. Maybe some. When I was outted, the dictionaries of Buffalo Plains fanned open. Few of them had even heard of lesbianism. My mother was a school teacher, and it was probably not a word she was totally familiar with."

Bryana had gone away to college in Boulder, Colorado. After graduation, she wanted to settle in a city where she could blend in and be accepted. After purchasing a small shop in Denver's interior, she'd put a kiln in the backyard. She started a small pottery studio and named it Trinkets and Treasures. She was forced to sell the shop because she needed to return to Kansas to take care of her mother and also pay the farm's bills.

"The city has its drawbacks," Michelle inserted. "Remember a couple years ago when you were robbed."

"Maybe that's when I decided I wasn't much good at owning and operating a business. I'm a good potter, but that's about it. It hadn't crossed my mind that danger lurked in owning a little storefront." She recalled the huge druggy that entered her small shop. "A giant with a cannon aimed at me wasn't my idea of an exciting lifestyle. Gunpoint isn't all it's cracked up to be. Yes, even moving back to Kansas seemed an okay alternative after a firearm pokes you between the boobs."

"Why didn't you mention a move then?"

"I figured you would miss your job. Your fellow medics and patients."

"ER didn't give me time to get much of a personal relationship with patients. As a nurse I needed to balance attachments. The pain of loss is so great. I do miss my co-workers. I loved teaching the newbies." Michelle worked in the Emergency Room, as well as being in charge of entry-level ER nurses. "Intercity hospital emergency rooms are now also mop-up areas for witnessing all kinds of absolute abominations. I saw way too much of the negative. Not to mention the terrible risks of blood exchange with all the diseases. I've been lucky not to have contracted something."

"I was glad you were lucky, and cautious."

"But the nuttiness was wearing me down. The disturbed woman who had stuck a kitten fetus up her vagina was probably a huge reason why I'd had enough of medicine. I was so depressed after that happened. You did lift my spirits when you asked if she wanted the doc to deliver Garfield. But things like that have a lasting impact." There was a moment's silence before she added, "I wanted to help heal people. Not see the worst of humanity. With my New York middle class, cosmopolitan background, I'd seen about all the crazy I'd ever wanted to deal with."

"I liked your mom."

"She was way off kilter, but was a good mom. I loved the way your parents were so down to earth. So sensible. Normal."

"Most people would consider them boring."

"They were wonderful. I adored them. They took me in as if I were their own. It doesn't seem like it was over thirty years ago. And now we're completely out of parents."

"Both of us in our early sixties and we're like orphans of the Great Plains." Bryana's sigh was one of desperation. Anger was hidden within.

"But you're from good stock. That old pioneer spirit. Those sodbusters tamed this land. Bryana, we can survive a few bills. As well as outwait a terrible economy. We can," Michelle insisted.

The silhouette of buildings was coming into view. Bryana squinted to deflect the sunshine. She both feared this patch of land becoming her home and wished that it might be.

A cloud of dust followed the CR-V as it turned up the graveled dirt road. Before the women was their inheritance. The century-and-a-half old frame and stone farmhouse had been refurbished numerous times. Surrounding it were several shacks, a silo, barn, and sheds. To the north was choice wheat land being leased by Billy Dreher. To the east was the land planted in sorghum and alfalfa and leased to Rolf Jarvis. Across on the west was a portion of the tract that was a vegetable garden and raw land. Beyond the sturdily fenced property line was the Roland family farm. It was where Tank, his wife, and their children lived. And in Tank's hands it had become a retreat for hunters.

Bryana enjoyed neighbors Rolf Jarvis and Billy Dreher. However the westerly Roland farm-turned-hunting-reserve irritated her. There were snide glances from Tank and his wife, Alice. When Bryana and Michelle first arrived, they were told by Alice to kindly stay away from their children. And them. Michelle remarked that it wouldn't be a major assignment. For months it had been manageable. The women took care of Bryana's invalid mother, Victoria, and slightly later, her father, Bryson.

To the south, across the county road there were no neighbors. For mile after mile, the crops had been sown and harvested by major corporations. Executive farming, Bryana's father had called it. The family-owned farms were becoming a thing of the past. It saddened Bryana when she thought of her father's sorrow at seeing the lands enveloped by corporate farms.

For now, Bryana mused, this farm was all she and her lover had. The women also shared the farm with their dogs and other farm animals they loved. The dogs were an apricot and cafe-au-lait parti standard poodle, O'Keeffe, and a light salt and pepper standard schnauzer named Idgie. Both dogs were about forty-five pounds. Michelle had quipped since she and Bryana were standard Sapphics, they should have standard canines.

As the vehicle rolled to a stop, Bryana felt the weight of her situation. They had believed the farm was nearly free and clear. There were the administration loans, but they were a floating reality, and usually with a string of good crops, were eventually paid back. There were the inheritance taxes. The women had not been hoodwinked into helping keep the farm viable. It had been both women's decision to help Bryana's parents. But it had been based on higher appraisals than realistic. Sadly, the price had not appreciated, but depreciated with the economy.

Her sarcasm lashed as she exited the vehicle. "Home sweet home." She swung back the screen door so hard it slammed against the side of the house. "We promised to follow one another to the ends of the earth. And here we are. At the end of the flipping earth." She felt Michelle's reaching. Then her hand was taken as they entered the enclosed back porch that served as a mudroom. "I'm so sorry."

"Sorry for what?"

"We're trapped. If we wouldn't have met thirty-five plus years ago, you'd be sitting pretty. You'd be where you want to be and doing what you want to do. Surrounded by friends. And your savings wouldn't have been wiped out by my family's debt."

"None of that would have mattered, Bryana. Not if I wouldn't be with you."

The talk of yesteryear lifted memories as if from time's trunk in the attic. She thought about when she met Michelle. At a mutual friend's party, the young women met. Michelle's sweet round face broadcasted her joy. The young nurse's deep blue eyes glanced away from Bryana's stare several times. Her fully formed, sensuous curves had the attention of everyone. She walked past Bryana to freshen her drink. Bryana had first noticed Michelle's eyes. Her face was surrounded by full, dark brown hair that flowed freely, bouncing from her shoulders as if it was a curtain of sheen. Now her hair was partially gray, and usually pulled back. Her face was still pink and joyous. Dimples still appeared when she smiled. Laugh lines on both women's faces reflected their prior contentment.

Bryana's face was still thin, and her build was still wiry and energetic. She had wondered why all those years ago Michelle had given that scrawny girl the time of day. Now, her blond hair was beginning to gray. Short on sides, and longer on the top, the clipped hair was brushed back. It constantly bounced as she moved. Lips opened widely to show her large teeth, and an enormous smile had flashed towards the sweet woman all those years ago. Her smile had announced to a young Michelle that Bryana planned to know her, and perhaps to love her.

The women had fallen in love. Now, after over thirty-five years, both women's mirror introduced a different looking woman. Although years had reconstructed them, they had the same foundations. The reasons they'd fallen in love remained solidly the same.

As Bryana drifted back into the here and now, her eyes closed. No matter what created the chaos, she felt blessed Michelle was part of her life. Guilt about how she'd continued sinking funds into the farm overwhelmed her. And now they were entering a phase of senior life where they should have been comfortable.

A reassuring squeeze of Michelle's hand nearly broke Bryana's heart.

Chapter 3

After a morning at the estate attorney's office, and being pulled over by Deputy Pete Myer, both women's spirits were gliding on empty. In silence, they changed clothing, putting on their denims and work shirts.

By the time the women had ambled outside, and grabbed hoes that were resting against the barn, they had only mumbled a few words about the vegetable garden. Bryana placed the portable radio on the ground. She tuned in one of the few rural stations they received. A country song twanged its way through the airway. She began attacking weeds vigorously.

"That's what I call kicked-in-the-heart wailing," Michelle joked. "But it is music to chop bindweed."

Bryana laughed loudly. "I remember when you despised country, bluegrass, or anything else you deemed dreadful."

With an enigmatic smile, and downcast eyes, Michelle said, "Those decades ago I was an East Coast culture snob. I've mellowed. We've both mellowed."

Bryana paused, wondering how the young woman she met so long ago had converted from a background of excitement to one where the nearest neighbor was a field away. Bryana tried to evaluate the *yesterday* that was located in a quiet section of her mind. But her thoughts continued to be of Michelle Dawson's background. It was so dissimilar to her own.

Nearly the first decade of her life Michelle had spent traveling the country with a circus. Her handsome father had been a circus star. One matinee afternoon tragedy struck. As Milt Dawson swung through the air, he lost his momentum. Then he felt the slap of chalky hands slipping from his brother's grip. From the upside-down vantage point on the trapeze, his brother watched as Milt plummeted to earth – with a low, faulty net beneath him. He was killed instantly.

Michelle's mother, Jersey Dawson, took her daughter back to Jersey's hometown in New Jersey. From there the vagabond mother and ten-year old daughter made their way to an aunt's home in New York City.

All the young Michelle recalled was being held back by several of the circus workers. She lost her breath fighting, as tears swamped her eyes. Jersey had broken free and run to her husband's crumpled body.

Jersey had been a ballerina. Before success had its chance to arrive, she became an aged ballerina with no option other than to give ballet lessons. She raised her daughter, Michelle, to love life. Also she constantly reminded Michelle to be cautious of life's falls.

When Michelle graduated from nurse's training, she begged Jersey to accompany her to Denver, where she'd been offered a job. Jersey declined the offer, but encouraged Michelle to go and take advantage of the opportunity. Michelle hated leaving her mother because Jersey had started to show signs of heart problems even when Michelle was in high school.

A few years after Michelle moved to Denver, her mother's weakened condition worsened. Michelle and Bryana were set to move Jersey Dawson to Denver to live with them. Weeks before that move the former ballerina's heart failed for a final time.

Jersey left behind a bedroom wall filled with ballet slippers that hung decoratively. It was, she had often said, her wall of fame. There were slippers from her own performances, as well as shoes worn by some of her more famous students. In her journal was written how both Michelle and Bryana had brought joy to her life. Also that she was excited she was to be moving to be with them.

Sadly, Jersey's demise left both Michelle and Bryana adrift from Jersey's joyous love. In time Michelle came to terms with her past. She joked how she needed to patch up and get back to life's next production. This was the portion when she was glad to be sharing Bryana's family. It had become her only family.

"I'm thinking about how we've changed over the years," Bryana muttered as her hoe slammed against the earth.

"Yes. We've truly mellowed with time. Or maybe time and adversity has mellowed us. That's sort of inconclusive," she said.

"Farm life is a definite adversity at times. Like now."

"You should be used to farm life. This was your only home when you grew up. I was a wanderer most of my early life. So I find security in farm life. Most of the people living here have been here for generations."

Bryana's gaze across the horizon lingered a moment. "I remember the first time I brought you to visit the farm. You fell in love with everyone from the start. And they fell in love with you."

"Hey, with my background, I was up to my armpits with people who were a tad insane. Grandpa Albert only spoke a few times to me over the years. And he spoke less than that to most other people. He was sweet, but totally antisocial. My grandmother, Fanny, was such a great Broadway wardrobe lady, she picked every piece of lint off my shoulder as it landed. Wacky aunts and uncles. Loveable all, but certifiable. When I asked my merchant marine uncle if I had any cousins, he answered that unfortunately I only had a kitten. He was forever bringing me strays he'd find. Maybe that's why I love cats so much. I always had a stray to care for."

"Now you have a chance to indulge your cat fancy. There must be three or four in the barn. Plus a new litter is on its way. We didn't catch the mommy cat in time to get her fixed. But we did capture those other two females and had them fixed. I'm sorry my asthma has prevented anything except dogs. But now we've inherited a few felines for you."

"Yes, I enjoy them enormously. Gaining their trust is hard won, but worth the winning."

"Putting out food enticements for them to stick around our farm saves them. My parents attempted to keep them in and around our barn so they'd be safe from Tank. When Tank's father, Vince, was courting Sarah, he used to be armed. He would shoot stray cats. Her parents, like mine, objected. When Sarah found out, she nearly called the wedding off. But Vince was always a sleight of hand artist. His smooth talk and handsomeness drew her back to him." Bryana blinked dust from her eyes. "And Tank is Vince's cat-shooting son. Dad used to say the both of them were the meanest fellas ever put down on earth."

"And now Tank operates a slaughter reserve. Men and their guns. What chance do innocent cats have? What chance does innocent wildlife have?"

Bryana again looked away. "Some men find romance in women and war, and not always in that order. Women find romance in nearly everything. Thankfully." After a pause, she returned to the subject. "But we'll keep getting the feral cats fixed when we trap them. And keep food for them to come to a safe haven. Our crusade will continue," she muttered with discouragement.

Michelle gazed into her lover's face, looking for facial feedback. "Bryana, we've got to save this farm. If for no other reason than to protect wildlife and kitties – we've got to stay on."

Bryana examined the concern on Michelle's face. She looked across the gravel-packed lane to see the old barn. And beyond was a teetering storage shed. The plank's gunmetal grey lumber had been whittled down with time. The women planned to pull it down with the tractor's strength. That was on their 'to-do' list.

Crops, sheds, and the barn all needed attention. The garden needed weeding every day. A few rusted implements required being hauled away. Two cows, three goats, two sheep, a flock of chickens, and a well-aged quarter horse needed feed and love. She'd wanted to clean up the edge of the lake and paint the house. At one time in her life she felt she had the world on a string. Now the string had converted into a noose.

Bryana's glance snagged on the top of the barn. "For years I've planned to get the weather vane painted. So much to attend to," Bryana muttered. "It's like capturing confetti in a wind storm." When her glance reached the old kiln, she remembered she needed to fill several orders of pottery for her outlet back in Denver.

"A day at a time."

Bryana said glumly, "L.J. wanted me to get the orders by the time she gets here. I'd better hustle up so I can empty the outside kiln. I've got enough to fill both outside and the one in my studio.

With what I've got on the shelves, and what's in the inside kiln, I'm filling in a sizable order." Bryana's long lashes blinked back tears. "It was so much easier at my shop. I would throw the clay, glaze it, toss it in the kiln, and then shove it on the shelves. Now it's a matter of also driving it to Denver, and hoping I've packed everything carefully enough. It's nice that L.J. makes the three-hour drive every other trip."

"I'm glad you've got the old kiln from when you were in high school."

Leaning against her rake, she watched the slight breeze waving the weeds that were growing against the outdoor kiln. "My parents thought I was crazy, but they realized it might be a way to keep me on the farm and in the area. So they didn't object to me having a little workshop and wheel. I'd have tried to stay on, but too many drawbacks. Too many town bigots for me. I caved in." With a frown, she realized there was so much more to it.

"I understand why your parents wanted you safe and sound in Kansas."

Safe and sound, Bryana ruminated. "If I wouldn't have left, or been socially chased away, I wouldn't have moved to Denver. And we wouldn't have met. That part was the correct part. You are the correct part of my life."

"And also with L.J. taking over your shop, at least you have a terrific distributor for your art."

"She does a great job of selling my pottery in the shop. She's a promoter. And a friend." Bryana thought about how she hated leaving her pottery shop behind. Turning over the keys to L.J. Tracy was difficult. Bryana had built the business from an empty older home in a startup commercial area. She'd built shelves, put in a few furnishings, and carefully arranged the stock of cups, plates, pots, and decorative pottery. She took pride in the shop as revenue grew from barely enough to survive to a thriving business. She knew she would never be wealthy, but appreciated being comfortable. Now the store was still stocked with her pottery, but business belonged to L.J. Tracy.

L.J. had recently turned fifty-five, and decided to settle down. She knew she would keep the business thriving. She teased that there was money in her bloodline, and her wealthy father had passed on his wisdom to her.

When L.J. had decided to become a potter, she started as Bryana's student. For the next two decades the women had all three been friends. L.J. loved the setup. Trinkets and Treasures was homey. It was a place where coffee and tea brewed, and there was a lounge area with a wall shelf of not only pottery, but also books. Bryana always said that the term *customers* should be replaced with the word *guests*.

The living area was on the second floor. L.J. had often stayed with Bryana and Michelle when she bounced back and forth from Florida. Michelle teased that she moved as often as she changed lovers. And that was at minimum of twice a year. A "playgirl," Bryana called her longtime friend, and one-time student.

As L.J. settled, she began to learn more about pottery from her mentor, Bryana. It began as a hobby. As a promising novice, L.J. learned the craft until her work became professional. She had sold her pottery in Bryana's shop. Then she began working there part-time.

She was a natural to take over working in the shop, managing it when Bryana and Michelle returned to help Bryana's parents. There came a day when Bryana's mother's illness required her to have constant assistance. Both women felt moving to the farm on a permanent basis would be more sensible than traveling back and forth. Bryana offered to sell L.J. the shop. Bryana would be able to help keep the shop in stock. It would be her outlet, and she would provide assistance and training when turning the shop over to L.J. It seemed a perfect solution. It became even better during the last difficult year when Bryana lost first her mother then her ailing father shortly after.

L.J. had been raised on a cattle ranch in Florida and loved the Hays' farm. Making several trips to Buffalo Plains, L.J. would pack her small trailer with pottery Bryana had created. She then hauled it back to Denver. Over the weekend, she reveled in helping Bryana and Michelle with their farm chores. She'd tease that she got her "wilderness" fix. Enough to keep her ranching background happily reminisced and enough memories to last her in the city.

"L.J. acts as if she'd gladly trade the shop for this farm," Michelle said.

"Farm life would be bad for L.J.'s love life. Good Sapphics are hard to find anywhere. And nearly impossible in these forlorn parts."

Chuckling, Michelle sputtered, "But if anyone could find one, it would be L.J."

Bryana rummaged through her shirt pocket and pulled out her cell phone. "I promised I'd call L.J. and give her a report on what transpired this morning." She heard L.J.'s familiar voice. "I'm switching to speaker phone. Michelle is here in the garden with me."

Through the phone L.J.'s voice excitedly reported, "Yep, I could tell you're both there. And that you were thinking about me. My inner psychic vibes were pinging. My sensor was going off."

"Financially things are as dismal as we'd guessed," Bryana reported. Dad's will is officially through probate. Between indebtedness and the farm's sunken value, it's a wash. All the monies put towards bolstering the farm, both from my shop and Michelle's savings are gone. Keeping the family farm afloat was an expensive proposition when factoring in years of failed crops and Mom's medical bills from the last few years of her life." Her jaw tightened as she considered how their heritage had dwindled to nothing.

Michelle optimistically stated, "We've still got the farm. And we wouldn't have done anything differently. Mom and Pop Hays couldn't have taken losing this place."

Bryana wondered why Michelle wasn't bitter. Together they had sustained the farm, and she'd not only done it for Bryana – but also for Victoria and Bryson Hays. Her parents had loved Michelle like a daughter. From the moment they'd seen Michelle and felt the impact of their daughter's love, they knew. Bryana's eyes reflected the fact that she considered her lover to be the perfect female template of goodness. That was enough to convince Victoria and Bryson that Michelle was to be loved. And so she was.

"There's no way you can sell now?" L.J. inquired.

"Not really. No." Bryana glanced at her lover's face. "It's going to be a long haul for a couple of sixty-year old women. But my parents ran the place until late in their years. We just need to keep it up until it gets propped up again. And we've got most of the land leased."

"But you could still use help?"

"Sure, L.J.," Michelle said, "But help is expensive."

"Maybe not. Look, I met this kid named Ricki James."

"Kid?"

"Twenty-two."

"L.J., she's a baby. I know you're a cougar, but you're fifty-five!"

"Bryana, darlin', I'm not dating her. She's not one of my sheet-warmer women."

"That's promising to hear. Your usual modus operandi is legal age. Over twenty-one."

"My personal legal age is thirty. Well, I still look at twenty-five year olds. Mature mid-twenties only," L.J. responded. "I can find something loveable in any woman of any age. But I draw the line at anyone under thirty."

"So this Ricki James isn't on your radar?"

"She came by and wanted a job. Wants to be an apprentice potter. I taught her some of the lessons, but you're the best at teaching. You taught me, and I'm better than a Sunday potter. But I'm not as good as you are."

"That's because you've treated pottery as a business, not an art."

"Okay, okay," L.J. acquiesced. "Guilty as charged. Listen, I had an idea. I know you two need help with the farm. And could use a helper keeping up with the pottery orders. I'm thinking since I have a couple friends here to watch the place, I could bring Ricki with me on a quick trip to pick up whatever you've got. We could leave tomorrow morning. Early. If everyone was in agreement, maybe she could stay with you for the summer. Get her out of the city. Teach her a trade. She's a nice kid. And she could help you with tearing down sheds, and rebuilding a couple nice little storage buildings. She's worked construction before."

"Why am I feeling this deal has a few small-print footnotes?" Bryana asked with a chuckle.

"Okay. She's a former juvenile delinquent. Drugs. Bad family life. She has cleaned up her life, and she's a nice kid. She's been here a couple weeks now and been great."

"L.J.," Michelle broke in, "We aren't running a farm for wayward girls. We're in the midst of saving this place. I don't care if she's a graduate of the institute of lesbian manners. It could turn into a babysitting job."

"And maybe she can help. If she's a problem, call. I'll be there in three hours to pick her up." L.J. took advantage of the pause. "Come on, give her a chance. It might be the answer to your problems and hers."

Michelle glanced over at Bryana and nodded approval. "It won't hurt to meet her."

"Fine," Bryana answered. She looked around at the multitude of work that needed to be done. The place had become rundown. Even the weather vane on top of the barn was a midlevel-looking prop needing paint. And that was a constant reminder for Bryana. "But if she is only slightly unpleasant, the deal is off, and back she goes."

"See you tomorrow noon. We'll take off early. Get there in time for lunch. Michelle, how about some of your delicious pie?"

Michelle's rich laugh was issued. The harmonics in her voice was one of the things that first drew Bryana to her. "It's really Bryana's mother who gave me the recipes. I slap the crusts together."

"Well, I've been bragging all week about those pies. It helped convince Ricki to give Kansas a try."

"Terrific!" Bryana's voice indicted, "You coerced her. She didn't want to come here anymore than we wanted her. You bribed her with pie!"

"Baa," L.J. quickly said her Southern 'baa' for goodbye.

As Bryana slipped her phone back into her pocket, she shook her head. "As if we don't have enough problems." She turned, walking towards her pottery studio.

"Bryana, are you okay with this?"

With a sigh of resignation, Bryana trudged away. She mumbled, "Not really. I'm going to see how the glazes came out."

"I hope they're perfect," Michelle uttered. "If not, I'd better pour you a cool wine to drink with dinner."

Bryana looked back over her shoulder. "Like a little social lubricant would make up for babysitting a fledgling *and* a ruined batch of pottery."

"You're snappy as a crabby terrier. I'd better bake your favorite rustic blueberry cobbler. And L.J.'s apple pie."

Bryana chuckled. "That might take care of the pottery. But taking on an ex-juvie would take an entire bakery full of pies."

"Trust is a currency we need to spend once in a while."

As if putting on the brakes of her legs, Bryana turned. Her head lowered. "We certainly don't have any actual U.S. currency to spend."

"Your parents used to say that making do with what they had was how they made it through the tough times."

"Michelle, I am not a materialistic person. But we've both worked hard to become comfortable. And now we're broke. Besides, I'm not as strong as my parents." She saw Michelle's eyes appear wounded. "I wish, for your sake, I was."

A chunk of nearly flat, barren land and a small frame farmhouse had become their empty empire. Bryana glanced down at her patched denims and her splattered t-shirt. They would never have been rhinestone ranchers and possibly could never even be financially solvent. She glowered at the farmhouse. Self-confrontation was never her strong suit.

Chapter 4

Time on the farm was filled from morning until night with chores. Between exhaustion and never-ending work, Bryana usually didn't have energy to be overwhelmed with the financial concerns. Sunday mornings were different. There was time to think. On Sundays, traffic along the country road increased tenfold. Bryana's parents had often sold their produce on Sundays. It was, Bryana and Michelle decided, an opportunity to plump up the coffers. At the edge of their driveway the women set up a makeshift veggie stand.

Bryana always loved mid-summer's bounty. Mostly beans, squash, tomatoes, onions, cucumbers, and herbs were sold Sundays. Some Saturday mornings, later in the season, they would also pick enough produce to sell at the small farmer's market in Buffalo Plains.

Although there wasn't much traffic on the old highway that had become a frontage road, the weekend traveler often enjoyed the fresh produce. The new freeway was busier, so local traffic opted for the quiet of the small surfaced road of old highway.

When Michelle baked, she would place an additional wooden sign under the larger produce sign. That sign announced that pies and homemade breads were also for sale.

Early that morning both women arranged a few small bushel baskets of the produce that was available, and Michelle's dozen pies and two dozen loaves of herbal flavored, multigrain breads. She had saved back the two pies for L.J. One was for dinner and one for L.J. to take back to Denver with her.

Bryana was happy that Michelle took such pride in recreating the famous Victoria Hays pie recipes. Although Michelle had watched Victoria as she baked, and picked up a great deal about the countywide, award-winning pies, she had no accurate guide until after Victoria died. When Michelle found the index cards, with Victoria's careful printing, she was overjoyed. And the stack of cards had Michelle's name on it. She worked diligently until she had perfectly recreated several dozen pie and pastry recipes.

Bryana was glad that the morning was busy. It left little time for her to consider their financial constraints. Nearing noon, the women had sold most of the produce, and all but two of the pies. Bryana found it comforting to allow her gaze to cover the area that was becoming her home once again.

The two-story farmhouse, with an exterior base of limestone and wood above, was surrounded by flowers and herbs. The corridor of mint always smelled fresh. Cottonwoods grew from one side, as a wind shield. There were corrals, stock pens, sheds, and a small silo placed on native grass pasture land. She eyed the two wells, and the small ponds with their worn paths. Reinforced fences edged the entire property.

Bryana smiled back at Michelle. Sunday mornings were always a relaxing, tranquil time. The women always had a Saturday night date with a special meal, wine, and sometimes a few dances. It was important for both women, in the dynamics of their relationship, to have visible love. Although seniors, their kisses were what L.J. described as kisses hotter than a full-lit iron. Bryana and Michelle's evening began when they stepped into the embrace of one another's arms. Sensual and erotic love had never been a problem for their relationship. In the morning they were hemmed tightly together.

Bryana heard the crinkle of the grasses across the grazing acreage. There was the covey of quails snapping the thicket's branches. These sounds, this place - was not what she'd expected to experience again. So many times plans are interrupted by the unexpected, she mused. Through her mind streamed the phrase about eternity owning each person. And it was true, she decided.

Bryana heard tires crunching gravel. She glanced up at the road. With a moan, she complained, "It's Tank and Alice Roland. Looks like they're going to grace us with a visit."

"They're obviously on their way home from church, and probably need a pie or two for their paying guests. The hunters."

"I don't think the term 'hunters' applies when the game is anything but game. They fill the fields and let the *sportsmen* have their target practice. It's obscene."

Michelle grimaced. "Now, be nice. A sale is a sale. And we're relying on this surplus money."

Tank Roland's luxury van came to a stop with dust swirling beneath the tires. A metallic sign on the doors was impressive to novice hunters arriving on the Buffalo Plains airstrip. Roland's Animal Reserve was in bold letters.

At thirty-three, Tank seemed younger, however looked older. Dark close-cropped hair matched his piercing, angry green cobra-like eyes. Tall and stocky, he was muscularly built. He had his parent's good looks. Even in his church clothing, he seemed thrown together. Although sloppily dressed, he applied the same strut as his father, Vince, to his walk. Vince, however, wore expensive suits as if he was an immaculately clad magazine model.

The commonality of father and son was their pious haughtiness. They were both men of hazardous intent. It was understood. Tank's lazy smile was issued with the intent to warn. No one doubted that his was a stalling moral compass when it came to integrity.

Tank's wife, Alice, was twenty-nine. They'd been married for seven years, and each year seemed to have taken an emotional toll on her. She was a blond, ex-beauty queen with exquisite features. After three children, she appeared pained. Her gaunt expression was one of unhappiness. Her motion was quick and sharply performed. Blue eyes darted nervously. Although tall, she was beginning to stoop.

Both car doors fanned open as they exited. Approaching Bryana and Michelle, their air of arrogance rose. "Selling pies to pay off your bills?" Tank questioned. His smirk lifted slowly - deliberately.

"Selling veggies and pies isn't as lucrative as slaughtering captive game," Bryana countered. A side-glance told her that Michelle disapproved of antagonizing a paying customer. "We only have two pies left. Both apple. And there's three loaves of bread."

"We'll take both pies, and the bread," Alice snapped. Usually the rest of what she had to say needed to be thought about before she began. Her jaw bobbed as if it were unlocking her mouth to talk. "You must really need the money to be selling on the roadside on a Sunday morning. But you women don't attend church on the Sabbath anyway."

Bryana's eyes flared. "That's right. I've never been pious. But I'm certain your congregation members will set me in the dunking chair if I get into heaven."

"Not much chance of you ladies getting anywhere near heaven," Tank muttered, before a laugh bellowed as if he'd unbuckled it from his throat.

After a quick, edgy laugh, Alice resumed her dour scowl. Bryana always thought Alice's laugh was like an uncontrollable elevator going up and down, and finally sinking to a stop.

Michelle's eyes squinted as she blurted, "I'm not certain about this heaven business, Alice. My mother taught me both Christian hymns and Buddhist chants. That's probably where I over-dosed on liberalism. I'm certain you'd have thought Mom came from another planet."

Tank sucked his stomach in. He spewed, "You may not have had good training. But Bryana here, she had her God-loving momma and daddy."

Michelle defended, "My mother, Jersey, taught me not to be close-minded and opinionated. She taught me respect for people and animals. She wasn't a soul adrift in hatred. She was a loving woman. And yes, Bryana's parents were wonderful."

Tank straightened his posture. "Bein' raised up by them didn't do her much good. My daddy has always been a church-goer."

Bryana's laughter bellowed. "Tank, that doesn't make him any wiser or kinder. So I wouldn't use your father as being an exemplar of the church." She added quickly, "And I do believe in a creator. But mine is a no-name creator. Once a name is attributed to a deity, laws, rules, commandments, and edits begin. From there it slides into mythology and cultism. After which there are prejudices, bigotry, and ultimate ugliness of the human spirit. There's my pulpit Sunday in a nutshell. She handed the boxed pies to Tank, and the sack of bread to Alice. Bryana said tersely, "That will be thirty-two dollars."

Tank's ice-cold eyes narrowed. He grunted, "Didn't you used to give a five buck discount when someone bought two pies?"

"Times have gotten considerably harder," Bryana answered with a pronounced squint. "Twenty for the pies, and twelve for the bread."

Tank cackled as he handed her a twenty, a ten, and two flagging tattered ones. He and Alice got back into their vehicle. He shouted back, "And my bet is they're going to get a whole lot harder."

As the Roland's vehicle sped away, the women glanced at one another. Bryana's voice was brittle. "He's such an ass."

"Almost noon, and we're sold out of bakery. And nearly sold out of produce. Time to shut down," Michelle spoke. She gathered the signage. "And yes, he is an absolute jerk. I'd like to pound him to jelly for his shooting cats."

"His time will come. And every cat in the county will purr a symphony."

Michelle added, "I know I'll do a string of cartwheels." Her pause was contemplative. "Do you think he'll get his just rewards?"

"Someday both Vince and Tank will. Both of them pride themselves on their precious reputations. One day they'll find out what everyone around here really thinks of them."

"Tank doesn't act as if he gives a darn about what others think of him."

"But I believe he does. Vince and Sarah spoiled him rotten. Still are. Sarah couldn't have more children, so Tank was their one shot at populating the world."

"You sound so bitter when talking about Sarah."

"Yes." Bryana looked away. Her queasiness flared. She was baffled by still caring about Sarah. Some relentless foreboding blurted out from her soul. She should *not* care. The gossipy climate of Buffalo Plains insisted that she and Sarah ignore one another.

"Bigotry is the very cauldron of intolerance," Michelle said ambivalently. She placed the last of the produce into a large basket.

Bryana answered with irascible sarcasm, "The haters have impoverished souls, so they believe depravity abounds. They also think it's their business to clean up the world."

"I'm betting most people don't believe we've depraved." With an impish flicker from Michelle's eyes, she then grinned. "But then, I don't breathe a word about what we get up to in bed."

Bryana's smile spread across her face, and her eyebrows lifted. "And it's best you not tell anyone."

Chapter 5

"This is a perfect time for L.J. to arrive." Bryana pointed towards the county road.

When L.J. turned into the driveway, her Jeep skidded to a stop. Behind the fire-engine red Jeep was a small trailer. "Y'all want a ride back to the house?"

"Meet you there. We can still haul a few vegetables to the end of the eighty-yard trek," Bryana teased.

As Bryana and Michelle each took a handle of a bushel basket. They walked briskly behind the Jeep. Michelle commented, "Hope this Ricki works out. We can use the help."

L.J. nearly leaped from the driver's side to gather both women into her arms. Slowly, cautiously, a young woman exited the passenger side. There was the sound of a slamming door.

Ricki's rough demeanor gave her an aged appearance. Bryana knew she was only twenty-two, but her soul seemed ancient. Dressed in tattered denim pants and with a matching thin jacket over her muscle shirt, she was stick thin. The jacket's collar was lifted behind her neck, as if it were an act of defiance. Her wiry frame shrunk into a posture of complete dejection. Short brown, closely cropped side hair lifted into a longer top faux hawk. The tip was dyed bright red. Her head seemed to be only slightly resting on her neck. Her coloring was dull and pasty. Enlarged smoky, light-brown eyes narrowed as she approached the older women. She mumbled a quick greeting.

L.J.'s emotions always brimmed over. With large, animated features, her face snapped with periodic smiles. Blue eyes squinted behind her sunglasses. Dark blond highlighted hair was stylishly trimmed and the waves were in perfect rows. Slightly stocky and short in height, she stood proudly with large breasts protruding outward. She loved the title of playgirl.

Loud, boisterous, L.J. was generally thought to be likeable. Some women considered her gregarious, and a few called her abrasive until they knew her. She nearly always charmed them over.

"Bryana Hays and Michelle Dawson, meet my new friend, Ricki James," L.J. introduced. "She's promised to be a model dyke."

Outstretched hands crossed. It was as though both Bryana and Michelle could immediately sense Ricki's somber soul. "I hear that you want to help me load up the kiln with a treasury of stoneware?" Bryana questioned.

"I'll do my best, if you give me a chance." Ricki's words were stones falling. Her expression was a fortress.

Bryana wondered if there was a hidden bridge for Ricki's moat. "All we require around here is an honest effort. Right now let's get you settled in. We have L.J.'s favorite pie in there, and the grill will be going soon. We'll have lots of grilled veggies, and Michelle has buffalo steaks marinating already."

L.J.'s laughter spewed. "These women can grill a buffalo steak that even Michelle's deceased vegetarian mother would have done a pirouette to gulp down."

The women joined in her joke. Bryana explained, "Michelle's mom was a ballerina."

Michelle added, "And we get the buffalo from our neighbor. We do some trades to keep our freezer filled with his prime buffalo meat. We lease out some of our land to him for his crops to feed his livestock and ours."

"I never ate buffalo before," Ricki said self-consciously.

"Better than beef," L.J. explained. "Actually it's better for you, too. While dinner is grilling, why don't we get the trailer unloaded and filled back up with stoneware? I'd like to take off right after lunch so I can make it back to Denver before sunset."

Bryana led Ricki to the studio workshop. The new electric kiln inside the workshop had been filled. This kiln had been a recent purchase so Bryana could keep up with orders. The outside brick gas kiln had been emptied. This was a large brick and stone kiln she and her father had built years ago. Through windstorm, snowstorm, rainstorm, and attacks by wayward hunters from the farm across the field, the kiln had remained sturdy.

Bryana slid the studio doorway open. She took out the key to her small, aged front-loader and slid it into the ignition. As L.J. pulled her trailer strategically into the loading area, Bryana aimed the front-loader towards the trailer. Soon the half pallet containing eight fifty-pound boxes of moist clay were lowered, and placed in her workshop's corner. Buying the clay in Denver, then transporting it, was much less expensive than having it shipped directly to the farm.

"Enough for a while," Bryana commented. "Did I have enough sales to pay for it?" she tentatively asked L.J.

L.J. gave a quick affirmative nod. "More than enough. I've brought a check for the difference. And I have an interior designer interested in a couple of your artworks. Also, I'm talking with little art shops. The hand-built art works seem to have created interest. We're talking some high end prices - artwork prices. If I can get them sold, it will be a nice little profit for us both."

"I welcome filling the cash register. It's looking as though we're going to need all the cottage industry money we can get. And thanks for picking up the clay."

"No problem. They've got a couple of adorable ladies at the warehouse."

"Has L.J. always had harems?" Ricki inquired with a bemused chuckle.

"As long as I've known her, fans have flocked to her. And that's been decades," Bryana answered.

As the women loaded the trailer back up with earthenware, they chatted. The stoneware's crates nearly filled the trailer. Their banter continued until they returned to the BBQ patio area where Michelle was preparing the meal. The aroma of grilling buffalo seemed to bloom through the airway.

Bryana noticed when the dogs left Michelle's side to greet them, Ricki suddenly became tense. "They won't bite or jump up. They're both well-behaved," Bryana promised.

Ricki moved back slowly. Her steps were protectively taken. "The dogs - they're so big," she excused her fear.

"O'Keeffe is the standard poodle," Bryana introduced. "And Idgie is the standard schnauzer. Both are about forty to forty-five pounds." She surveyed the dogs. O'Keeffe was nearing seven. Her apricot and tan-colored parti mixed fur was trimmed very near her body. Idgie had turned four, and her light silver coat was also neatly trimmed short. Both dogs seemed interested in the newcomer, however sensed Ricki's reluctance to befriend them. "They're clipped short because of the weather. Winters they look more like their poodle and schnauzer breed. They aren't traditional farm dogs. When we got them, we were city folks. Not even thinking about a farm."

"I'm not great with animals," Ricki muttered. "Growing up in an intercity slum in Miami didn't help. Most of the dogs were pissed-off pit bulls."

"So many are trained to fight. Their owners, or trainers, make them mean."

"Yeah, well, I hate those little fuckers." She stalled a moment. "I apologize for the language," she amended.

"No problem with me, but Michelle isn't excited about cursing. She believes there are enough words in the English language to find alternatives."

"I'm not wild about the f-bomb either," L.J. added. "But to give a little emphasis, I am sometimes known to pitch a few skyward."

Bryana reached over to give Ricki's shoulder a quick hug. "We'll try to all get along with each other. My daddy was a wise man. He often said to try whatever keeping the peace takes. Kiss ass, or kick ass. Different people respond differently."

As they closed up the studio, Bryana felt a slight camaraderie building. She hoped it would work out, for all their sakes.

With a loping stride the dogs suddenly jounced back across the garden towards the west field. The women followed. As they reached the property line, Bryana saw the youngest child of the Roland family. Five-year old Jon often escaped his mother's nonchalant care. The little towhead was sliding beneath the fence. He quickly grabbed a branch. The boy began to hit the curious O'Keeffe with a long stick. O'Keeffe backed away, but the boy gave chase.

Bryana screamed, "Jon, stop!" The boy continued until he reached her. O'Keeffe continued to run past Bryana towards safety. Bryana grabbed the small boy's arm. "Easy, Jon. That dog is no threat to you. You're not supposed to be on my property." Quickly dialing the Roland residence, she heard Alice's supercilious telephone greeting. Bryana spoke into her cell phone. "Alice, this is Bryana. Jon is over here."

Hysterically pitched, Alice's voice boomed. "He's not supposed to be over there." With her acid tongue, she continued, "Not with you women."

"Well, he is. And he chased O'Keeffe with a stick. I'm not best pleased. Your kids try to emulate the hunters. Your kids also throw stones whenever they get a chance. And they're always hungry. We give them sandwiches. They act hungry enough to eat an elephant in one bite. Don't you feed them?"

Through the phone Alice could be heard impatiently sighing. "They can get our hired lady at the lodge to feed them. I've told them to stay away from you."

"We don't mind feeding them. They're little kids. But they need to know they should be kind to animals."

"I'll send Tank over immediately." Her shrill inflection added, "Immediately, he'll be there." The phone slammed off with a thwack.

"Come on, Jon. I'll see if I can get you fixed up with a piece of pre-luncheon pie."

Bryana took the small boy's hand and the three women and boy walked to the backyard where Michelle was grilling.

Looking up from the grill, Michelle laughed. "Jon, did you escape?"

"Have a slab of pie," Bryana said as the boy was seated. She sliced the pie and plated it. "Give him a sugar high and send him home to his mother," she joked. "But the rest of you will need to wait until after lunch for your glucose overload."

Hungrily, Jon ate. He had almost finished the pie when Tank's camouflage-painted truck sped up the driveway. He was shouting as he jumped from the high driver's seat. "Jon, what did I tell you about wandering off?"

"Just as importantly," Bryana spoke, "what didn't you tell him about hitting dogs with sticks. And rocks."

With compressed lips, Tank squinted down at Bryana. He sneered before saying, "To hell with your dogs. They rile my hunting dogs. Bother our clients." Between his clenched teeth, he warned, "And you better keep outta my way. And stop moaning about the hunters."

"To hell with your hunters!" Bryana spat back. "And I don't want to hear your yammering about my dogs. My dogs are always on my property. Which is more than I can say for your *clients*. And for that matter, your children."

He roughly scooped his son into his large arms. As he drove away, Michelle said with concern, "We should watch O'Keeffe and Idgie even more closely. Always be with them. Not just to watch they don't tangle with a coyote or a snake. I don't trust Tank. And certainly don't trust the *damned* drunk hunters."

Ricki's head popped up. To Bryana she half whispered, "I thought you said she doesn't curse." She sluggishly coasted down to a squat as she tied the laces of her tennis shoes. "Sounded like cussing to me."

With a laugh Bryana answered, "She does cuss selectively. The neighbors to the west deserve any words they get. As you can see, they're the neighbors from hell. I feel sorry for the kids though."

When Michelle went in for the fruit and Jell-O salad, Ricki mumbled, "She must rule the roost."

"Let's put it this way," Bryana explained with a sparkle in her eyes. "I believe in karmic endings. Sometimes what seems like defeat leads to emotionally pleasurable endings. They are far better than pretending not to buckle under for the love of a woman."

L.J. roared with laughter. "That's her way of saying after thirty years Bryana has learned about salacious give and take."

Bryana explained, "Loving is a pilgrimage that doesn't begin with pulling down the bedcovers. The journey begins with the sensuality of minds meeting. Believe me, there is plenty of soft responsiveness in the embrace of agreement. I realized that long ago when I traded being right for a touch of Michelle's glistening skin and the taste of her moist lips. Rule the roost. I suspect she does. She's always been the more emotional. Dramatic. You'd have to have known her mother. But whoever rules the roost makes little difference. Michelle makes my desire meter go right off the edges. I don't want a silly argument to unhook our hearts."

"Bryana has always had a gravitational pull in Michelle's direction," L.J. teased.

Bryana began plating the buttered, well-seasoned vegetables, and the smoky bison steaks. L.J. poured the iced teas. A strong aroma of mint from the tea lifted.

Bryana thought about the multiple delights of Michelle. There was the honeyed aroma of her skin, the petal softness of her shoulders, and the luxuriance of loving her. When their flesh wrapped, love became tuned perfectly. There was agility and perfection in the women's orgasms. They ignited when pleasing one another. The touch taking them through a portion of the night was an aphrodisiac borne of the goddesses, Bryana believed.

She likened women to some lovely pastoral lullaby. The earth seemed to stop when she and Michelle shared love. Arousal came in two varieties, Bryana considered. One was sculpting earth, and the other was caressing the woman she loved. For Bryana there was arousal and reverence in the lock between both earth and her woman.

When Michelle returned, the women began eating. L.J. lifted each forkful as if she was paying tribute to a hierarchy of angels. Ricki pushed food into her mouth as if it either was her last meal, or she was frightened there may never be another delicious meal. She suddenly, between gulps, said, "That kid reminded me about why I hated being a kid. He's all tensed up and helpless."

Bryana explained, "Jon's the only boy and a little rascal. The little imp is the youngest. He's the lineage prince. His older sisters are slightly milder versions. The oldest sister is Nita. She's seven. Mouthy, she bullies her younger sister, Letty, and is manipulative. Letty is six and shy. Of course, you're aware how spoiled Jon is. I feel sorry for the middle girl. She takes a lot of abuse from the older girl, and from the baby of the family. If I had a favorite, I can't imagine it not being her. She's sort of lost in the mix."

Ricki observed, "The rotten little guy sure shut up when the pie landed in front of him."

"Pie," Michelle agreed with a lilting laugh, "is the great equalizer when it comes to children."

"And me," said L.J.

Bryana's laugh blended with the others. "Michelle said *children*, didn't she?"

L.J. bellowed. "One difference. Kids are hungry for pie. I actually get horny for pies."

"Pies and women," Michelle said with a playful indictment.

L.J. gave a quick wink. "Oh, yeah. I can find something to love in all women and most all pies."

Chapter 6

Bryana and Michelle extended the usual warm hospitality to their new guest. Ricki slept in the guest bedroom upstairs. Ricki awoke early the next morning. Greeted by bleating goats, and a rooster's revelry, she was still bleary-eyed as she rose. The aroma of bacon, eggs, and freshly baked biscuits wafted up the stairway. When she reached the main floor landing, she still wore the clothing she'd arrived in.

With a motherly concern, Michelle had pulled a few of Bryana's old shirts and denims from her closet. She presented the armload of clothing to Ricki. "Okay, give these a try after your shower. Bryana's worn clothing will be great for farm chores, and clay splattering from the pottery wheel. L.J. said she purchased a few outfits for you, so change out when you go into town this afternoon. You'll need to look presentable."

"Go into town?" Ricki repeated.

Bryana put down her steaming biscuit and nodded. "I have some pottery accounts there. I usually take deliveries in twice a week. A little gift shop, the bar, and the café. Buffalo Plains is only about five-thousand population. Add another thousand surrounding farmers, and it includes the entire county. And it's probably best that you dress in a manner presentable to our neighbors."

"Less like a dyke," Ricki replied as she lifted a biscuit to her lips. Michelle placed a plate filled with breakfast in front of her. "Thank you."

"You're welcome. And we don't have fashion requirements. But we don't want them mistaking you for a man gone punk. We're all for the right to be as we are. But we don't want to kick the beehive." Michelle poured coffee. Squinting back at Bryana,

Michelle added, "Bryana dresses fairly androgynously, but her hair is a tad longer and a tad more farm-town fashionable."

As Michelle passed by, she lifted some of Ricki's top hair then pushed aside her bangs. "You'll be very attractive once we can get you cleaned up, and Kansas-styled."

Ricki was silent a moment then grunted, "Sounds like this is going to be worse than jail."

"We don't have fire-flare prison orange," Bryana replied with displeasure. "It isn't a good idea to live in a community and rub their noses in something they don't approve of. We're attempting to coexist. Think of Buffalo Plains as a different version of life."

Seeming frail, Ricki mumbled, "I've always dressed this way."

"And you've never lived in small-town Kansas," Michelle said. "But you're here now, and we're not going to become your wardrobe mistresses, but we do want to help you assimilate."

Bryana rummaged through the kitchen's small drawer her mother had called the clutter drawer. She pulled out a cell phone. "Here, Ricki. Keep this on you so we can communicate. It should be charged, just plug it in every night. The landline is number one. Michelle is two. And I'm three. You can reprogram the rest of the numbers if you like. No overseas calls," she chided.

Expelling a huge sigh, Ricki then continued eating. "Good breakfast. You're a terrific cook."

Michelle laughed heartily. "Bryana can brew coffee."

"And tea," Bryana added.

A blaring horn beeped from the side of the house. Michelle looked through the curtains. "It's Rolf Jarvis. Our neighbor to the east. Come on out when you've finished breakfast," Michelle directed Ricki.

Ricki shoved a final gulp into her mouth. She obediently followed the women out to the driveway where an old navy blue, battered Ford pickup was parked. Rolf Jarvis examined her as they were introduced. "Hell, I figured you were a guy at first," he said with a huge grin.

Bryana's eyebrows lifted. "What did I tell you about your hardcore dyke outfit?"

They all chuckled then Rolf said, "Can't wait until Tank Roland, neighbor on the other side, gets a load of you. He'll think there's a lesbian convention over here. He won't be laughing. Hell, if he ever tried to laugh, he'd probably fart a lung out."

"We're doing a free make-over on Ricki," Michelle said quickly.

Rolf took out a bandana then lifted his hat to blot sweat from his forehead. "You'll be getting all dainty for the judgmental blabbermouths in this county," Rolf said with a husky bassoon-voiced laugh. The buffalo man was balding, with his longer side hair pulled back into a pony tail. The roped pony tail was a mixture of black and grey strands. Mutton chop sideburns, bushy mustache, and grizzled wiry eyebrows made his face appear shaggy. Rolf's dark eyes, and lashes blinked multiple times as they followed Ricki's movements. "Folks are all global roommates, but some want to be everything from housemother to imperial ruler."

"Yeah," Ricki agreed self-consciously.

Rolf's large, sturdy body was quick and powerful. His chest protruded, and his hands rested on his belt. Wearing worn western boots that were caked with clods of earth, and with his aged Stetson in one of his enormous hands, his occupation was rarely mistaken. He was a man of the land. "You'll get along fine, kid. Don't let 'em hassle you. I'll send a herd of bison to stampede any and all Rolands if they mess with you."

Bryana chortled, "I think it's safe to say we are being messed with around here. The Roland clan is in high gear."

"I'm sure they're sending the hunters over to poach your waterfowl. Birds love your larger pond. And the hoofed animals love the native blue stem grasslands. They're poaching your habitat. Hunting camp, my ass! It's abysmal."

Bryana agreed. "The problem is, trying to catch them in the act."

"Get your daddy's old shotgun out and give 'em a taste of buckshot."

Michelle shook her head. "Don't even think about it, Bryana."

"No." She recalled what her parents always said about violence. Hatred wasn't in their hearts, and she didn't want it in hers. Her mother always said that the empty heart is the heaviest.

Hers was already lumbered with responsibility. "You take it easy, Rolf," she said as he made his way back to the pickup.

After Rolf left, Bryana showed Ricki around the farm. She executed the morning chores of feeding the animals first. Scattering chicken feed to the laying hens, she also explained how to collect eggs. Then hay and other nutrient-filled feed was delivered to the larger animals.

When the potters at last entered the studio, Bryana said with a laugh, "After chores the real work begins. But for me, it is my chance to express myself. After finishing morning chores, it's clay throwing until evening chores, which are at twilight or before. We can go through them at that time. For now, we'll toss a few pots and then make deliveries."

"Feed and water the animals twice a day? You want me to do all this stuff? By myself?"

"Yep." Bryana's eyebrows lifted. "Unless you're not up to it. Maybe L.J. can find someone who might be more *able* to handle it."

"I'm able. I need to be somewhere safe. I'm not crazy about being here. But at least I can learn some stuff, and then get out of here. I need to be somewhere I can dress as I please. Do what I please."

Bryana was silent for many moments. "Doing what you pleased hasn't given you much in the way of safety, respectability, and easy living. You've been incarcerated, and nearly starved when you were released. Doesn't sound free to me."

As soon as she'd uttered those words, it occurred to Bryana that she was in a similar predicament. She saw no way she would ever be freed of debt. That meant she wasn't free to return to Denver. Although she'd never felt the restraints of prison, she and her lover were trapped by fate. An encumbered old farm had become a ball and chain. She took a deep breath. Then she attempted to translate Ricki's gaze down at the floor.

"I've messed up," Ricki acknowledged. "But I hate rules."

"There are always going to be rules and regulations because we live in a society. Some societies aren't as rigid. Being part of a community means attempting to get it right. Your garb isn't really going to get you anything but trouble around here. And trouble is the one thing Michelle and I don't want. And we can't afford trouble of any kind."

"That buffalo man, Rolf, he didn't mind how I look?"

"Rolf is one of the dandy human beings here in Kansas. But they aren't all like him. You're working for food, room, and pottery lessons. Every job has dress codes. It isn't as if we are dictating uniforms. Only that you look neat, clean, and less noticeable." Bryana could read Ricki's eyes. The young woman would conform, but not willingly. "Ricki, here's the deal. Michelle and I can't afford to antagonize people around here. We all eventually end up needing one another. You're still free to make a fashion statement. Just not an overly rebellious statement. And I dress pretty darned androgynously. That's acceptable. But looking as though you're a punk Hell's Angel in rags and accompanying dirt isn't going to fly."

"Whatever you say," Ricki muttered with a mixture of minimal trepidation, and resistance.

"For now, yes. It needs to be what we say." Bryana had noticed Ricki's demeanor was without either ebullience or appreciation.

"Yeah." Ricki nodded again.

With a mischievous grin, Bryana added, "Gert-the-Goat currently has the honors of being the farm's most smelly occupant, and she wants to keep it that way. If you cross her, she'll eat your bra off the clothesline. Her pals, Alice and Paris, come in second and third in the stinky contest. And Gert could ravage an entire clothesline filled with our wardrobe. Including your bra."

Ricki chuckled. "I don't wear one."

"Your socks could be pulverized."

Ricki frowned. "Gert and Alice, the goats. Did you name them?"

"Yes, and Paris was where Gertrude Stein and Alice B. Toklas lived, so the youngest goat was named Paris. Stein is one of our literary lesbian high priestesses."

Ricki paused. "Yeah, I've heard of them, but I didn't know they were French."

Bryana grinned. "They were only French by association." She figured she could bring Ricki up to speed about Stein later. She continued with the barnyard tour. "My dad named the cows Milkshake and Buttermilk. The sheep Dad named Lippy and Speedy. And the old horse is Pierre."

"Crazy names."

"Yes, naming didn't come naturally to my family. Now, acquaint yourself with the studio. After that, toss your body under a sprinkling showerhead, dress, and by that time I'll be done with some bill-paying. Then we'll roll into town and I'll show you about delivering orders."

"You got collapsing buildings around. Instead of going to town, I'd rather pull down those weak shacks. I can even build new structures."

Bryana rubbed her chin. "How long do you think that job would take?"

"A couple weeks if that's all I had to do."

"Okay, how about working on it for two or three hours every day for a week or two. That gives us time to go in to town when we need to." Coaxing, she added, "That sort of intersperses the things you like best with what you like least."

Ricki's shrug was compliant, but not whole-heartedly so.

Bryana entered the farmhouse. In the kitchen, she sat for a quick cup of coffee before attacking the mound of bills on her father's oak roll-top desk. Michelle eased down into the chair beside her. "Bryana, the bills frighten me. I've never in my life been behind on payments. Even when I started out, I'd taken a part time job to stay afloat. Now, we're shuffling payments. Writing apology notes on the statements."

"When the wheat is harvested in a couple weeks, we should be able to catch up. And L.J. left a check. Rolf said that the alfalfa crop looks decent. He'll mow it this week. So we'll have hay for the animals, and a lease check from Rolf. Until then, it's pottery sales, pastry sales, and whatever we can get from the veg and herb crops."

"This is a role reversal. I'm usually the optimistic one."

A smile started then Bryana's lips moved back to a straight line. "Maintaining surveillance over Ricki will keep us too busy to be pessimistic. She needs to conform. But I can tell she harbors a quiet resistance. Thankfully, when we get to throwing clay, I have a minimally harsh lesson plan. Whatever gets the job done is the road we take. But I hope she isn't problematic about learning techniques. I'm from the pragmatic school of pottery."

"She's not going to sabotage a chance to learn from the best. She's young; she'll learn."

"Youth shoves problems from one slot to another. When you get to be our ages, there are fewer slots, and less energy."

"Bryana, we're both blessed to have energy. We'll be fine."

Bryana's hand covered Michelle's fingers. "At least, with all that's wrong, you're right. We're right."

She finished sipping the coffee then silently went back to shuffling the stack of bills. The implement bill for the tractor three years ago was way behind. It would need paying first. A partial payment, she corrected. After she had finished paying the most important bills, Bryana went upstairs to check on Ricki's 'cleanup' progress.

As she stepped onto the landing, she noticed that the wallpaper was lifting. The threadbare carpet needed replacing, and the entire second floor needed a coat of paint. Both upper bedrooms, and bath were aged, and paint was chipping. Just like the sheds, and other fix-up projects, there was limited time and funds.

As if an emotional army was marching on her, Bryana realized Michelle had wanted to redecorate the old house and there hadn't been funds. Michelle had given up everything. A nice home in Denver, Their friends. All the familiar places were left behind. And it was now all so precarious. Recently, her bright eyes of optimism were so often dulled with the shine nearly extinguished. With a demoralized lift of her eyebrows, she would then smile back at Bryana.

Neither of them, Bryana considered, had known the price tag would have been so high. Her outrage was within, and her soul noise made fists. Mutterings directly from her heart were flooded with rancor. It was only having Michelle near that allowed her to smile. Realizing then how seldom the hidden epithets of hope surfaced, she hoped her nerve center would compensate.

Bryana stood, stretched, and walked to the window. She saw the panorama of their land. In front of the rising globe of a sun was the land filled with growth. The small lakes were in the center of meadowland and were surrounded by serene trees. On the flat land fields were striped with green. There were the yellow tassels of corn silk beginning to flag in the mild wind. The old windmill against the skies was rotating a circle. Bryana could almost hear its familiar whirr. That was followed by the sound of dripping water as the trough filled. It competed with the window air conditioner's vibrating pings.

Some of the land was matted with brush and stubbly pastures. Ruts, like gashes, ran perpendicular to the rim of the horizon. On the huge barn was a once-gilded weather vane. Each time she viewed it, she was depressed beyond belief. Bryana had promised her father she would restore it to its former gleam. But years passed, and she came to feel uncomfortable about climbing onto the sloping roof. Steeply pitched, the barn cover was a nemesis. It would probably never be climbed, and the weather vane would never again gleam in the sun as it once had.

A volley of birds thrust themselves across the skies, breaking into her thoughts. Their sounds were scolding as if they wanted to riot. She also felt a riotous soul. Her mind rattled with problems. She couldn't put her confusion into words. She lamented her plight. It was a throb of time where there was no good way to turn.

The bedroom door was open, and Ricki sat on the bed. She was holding the Martin guitar that had belonged to Anthony Hays. The visitor had taken the prized guitar from its case and was tightening the gears to tune it.

She looked up, defensively she began, "Bryana, I wasn't going to play it. Only tune it up. If you don't, the bridge can warp...."

"It's okay. It belonged to my father. Do you play?"

"Yeah. Well, kinda. Self-taught." She strummed a moment. As she did the G-string snapped. "I'm sorry, I'll buy another one. I shouldn't have even touched it."

"Don't worry. The strings are ancient. We'll get another set when we go into town. My father always said there should be music in the house. When he hit mid-eighty his fingers became arthritic so he stopped playing. We can replace the strings. A little music filling the house would be welcomed."

"Hey, thanks. I promise I'll take good care of it. I had to sell my guitar a few months ago. But my guitar wasn't a Martin. This guitar is incredible. And it's worth a lot of money."

"Music is worth a lot. Now, let's get into town. I'll show you around - then we'll pick up some strings." Bryana noticed that Ricki was wearing a clean outfit, and her hair had been slicked to the sides. "You look much better."

"It'll take a few rinses to get the color out of my hair."

Bryana reached over and lifted the center of Ricki's hair into a barely visible spike. "We don't want to completely convert you to *establishment straight*," she said with a smile. "Wearing ratty clothing is appropriate for working in fields and in the pottery studio. But town clothing needs to be a little more planned. You look great."

Ricki quickly retrieved the denim jacket that had been wadded up and thrown in the corner. "Sorry for not keeping the room neat."

"Michelle is head of the housekeeping unit around here, and she likes me to pick up after myself. So imagine that holds true for you, too. You'll do fine."

Chapter 7

After boxing orders of pottery, Bryana and Ricki went to the small town of Buffalo Plains. Rows of houses fanned back from the main street. Mostly the homes were white frame, and neatly groomed. Picket fences lined many of the homes, and hollyhocks lifted from their snug fit next to many mailboxes. Shrubberies were trimmed, and muted colors of charcoal-grey, green, blue, and brown decorated the shutters, rainspouts and eaves.

The small downtown area included rows of older buildings. On the corner of one was a blinking neon sign with its name: The Brass Rail. The most popular bar in Buffalo Plains, The Rail, was owned by a woman named Charlotte Gottschalk. It was large, as small town bars went. A long brass rail rounded the base of the oval serving bar. Booths and tables were off to one side. The stale smell of cigarette smoke and beer fumes were reminiscent of most of the other bars and taverns Bryana had visited over the years. There was a quiver to Ricki's voice, "This is the best bar in town?"

"Yep."

"It's a dive. It's like some of the city gay bars. When you said *best* bar, I thought you meant a classy place."

Laughing, Bryana explained, "Charlotte, the owner, thinks it *is* the classiest joint in Kansas. Let's not discourage her opinion. They sell lots of mugs for us."

Bryana introduced the new recruit to Charlotte. The woman was nearing fifty, with large, pretty features and a sensuous figure. Her enormous breasts were plumped high and partially exposed. With face cosmetically enhanced, and a huge mouth and violet eyes, she flirted with every man who entered. Her hair was long and dyed dark black; she swung the ringlets as she talked. Her speech seemed to be from a megaphone, and her laughter was pronounced and rhythmic.

Her bartender was a handsome man of thirty-five named Sylvester Dinkel. The town talked about him being Charlotte's toy boy. He was about an inch or two shorter than she, and always wore the highest of western boots to compensate. His eyes were light green, and his features were ruggedly handsome. With a clean-shaven head, and muscular build, he was appealing to most of the younger female patrons.

Mornings and early afternoons found mostly elderly regular patrons in the corner booths or at the bar. A haze of cigarette smoke lifted, and an occasional cackling laugh pierced the barroom's quietness.

Charlotte pointed to the corner group. "My base clients," she explained. Then she called to Sylvester, "Syl, free draws all around at the sweet old geezer tables!" They cheered, and as she approached Bryana she whispered. "I just love 'em."

Bryana joined her laughter. "You are an outrageous flirt."

Charlotte grinned. "Yep. And there's not a one of them I can't outrun. Bless 'em."

"I'm a pre-geezerette, so I don't plan to challenge any of them to a race."

Charlotte's laugh filled the bar. "And they seemed interested in you. Want me to break the news to 'em?" She ruffled her bonnet of hair as an accompaniment to her laugh.

Bryana's lips churned. "I'm sure they have the hint already. Are you needing more mugs and tankards?"

Ricki lifted the cardboard box of pottery onto the bar top. She scanned the room while Bryana and Charlotte discussed finances. Charlotte had a check ready for Bryana, and a hastily scribbled order list.

"Tank brought a troop of thirsty hunters in from last weekend. Half of 'em bought those high tankards you made. So I need more whenever you can get to it. Tank may be my cousin's kid, but he's a total prick. Tried to talk me into ordering tankards so he could buy 'em from me then resell those for a profit. I told him to go direct to you. Hell, Bryana, the guy claims he gives you enough business buying pies off of you."

Vince Roland was Charlotte's eldest cousin. She was the youngest and got a great deal of family attention. Vince always resented her, and she was aware of his jealousy. Tank was an extension of Vince, so Charlotte considered Tank nearly as bad.

Bryana took a deep breath. "He and Alice love our mini-bakery, and they pretend to make their purchase on the spur of the moment. Like their cook didn't make enough. Or had an accident and burned the pies. They'll run out of excuses before we'll run out of pies. Michelle has nearly all of Mom's pie recipes down to a science."

"Your mama was the best teacher in the country. And pie baker. She could have opened a shop. But when I asked her, she said it was a hobby only. She took her baked items around to people to make hard times better."

"We sell them now to make *our* hard times better," Bryana joked. There was a deep pang of dejection. Her jaw band twitched and she inhaled deeply. Sorrow caught in her throat. "I miss Mom and Dad."

"The whole damned town misses those two," Charlotte agreed.

"Yes," Bryana repeated. As if the word spun off from her heart, she added another *yes*. "Well, we'd better get going. We have a couple more stops to make."

Bryana directed Ricki across the street to the town's café. Ricki seemed relieved to be in the Buffalo Plains Café. While she sat at the counter, Bryana delivered the order for cups, mugs, and saucers to the café owner, Tess Walters. Tess was thirty-eight, and had been widowed in her mid-twenties. Her life revolved around running the small café her parents had given her when they retired, and attempting to run her attractive daughter Gloria's life. Having recently turned twenty-one, and in college at a nearby college town, Gloria had the same coloring as her mother.

Both had auburn hair, green eyes, lightly freckled complexions, and thin builds. Gloria's frame was filled with more curves than her mother. Tess lectured her daughter on the woes of marrying early. Tess had married young and immediately became pregnant in her teens. She preached to her about staying away from the boys. Gloria's dates were few and far between. And there was usually only one date before Gloria found something wrong with the young man.

Townspeople would remark that Gloria was such a pretty girl. They wondered why she didn't have a love interest. Or "suitor," as her mother said. Tess would explain her daughter's love of church instilled her with caution. Religion had been carefully taught Gloria throughout her young life. "No room for sin," Tess declared. Between college classes, Gloria worked part time at the café.

Gloria was pouring the women coffee. Its aromatic steam wafted through the café. "On the house," she said as she smiled down at Ricki. Behind the counter her mother's agitated stare at her got her attention. "My mother always says we should treat the vendors good. Right, Mom?"

Tess handed a sheet of scratch paper to Bryana. "A new order. Those coffee mugs with the buffalo stamped onto it sell like wildfire. Some of the truckers have bought those. One wanted six of them. Cleaned me out. So if you have extras, I can use a couple dozen."

"I do have some extras, and I'll get more made this week. Now I have Ricki helping me out. She can bring at least a dozen by for you tomorrow."

Tess gave Ricki careful scrutiny. Under her breath she asked Bryana, "A little severe, isn't she?"

"She's a good kid. And she wants to learn to throw pottery."

"Looks like she's probably already learned about your other proclivities."

Bryana laughed. "Well, the sisterhood movement is improving. A year ago you would have called those proclivities 'sins' from the devil in hell."

"We're supposed to love the sinner." Tess's blinked piously upward.

"That beats being incarcerated, institutionalized, or stoned to death by the church," Bryana replied with a teasing sarcasm.

"Mr. and Mrs. Hays were always fine, upstanding folks," Tess declared. "Why your mama not only taught school, but she baked those pies. Baked like an angel."

"My spouse, Michelle, is a great baker, too. She retired from a nursing career when we came back to take care of my mom. Mom taught Michelle some of her secret recipes. And recently Michelle found the rest of the written recipes. Remember Mom's rum pie? She can make that. And you always liked the peaches and cream pie, if I recall correctly."

"For a fact, that is my favorite pie. How I do love that pie. You say Michelle can make it?"

"Yes. Well, they were on the recipe cards Michelle found. We've been selling pies at the farm. So if you'd like to try out some for the café, I'll have Ricki bring along a couple samples for you. You might need some extra bakery items."

"Tastes exactly like you mom's, does it?" Tess questioned incredulously.

"Nearly exact."

Tess examined the empty display cases where pastry was sold. "That would be fine. Yes. Have this Ricki here bring some samples for us." She glared back at Ricki. "She okay? Trustworthy?"

Bryana lowered her voice, "Yes. You have my word that she won't give you any trouble. I'll keep her on a short leash. If she wanders off the reservation, I'll send her back to Denver. I trust her, and I hope you and the rest of the town learn to trust her."

Tess sniffed loudly. Her eyes narrowed. "Trust is something I seldom give. It's earned and hard won."

"You've got my word. And I've got hers. I trust her because I don't want my soul to go dark with cynicism. I want to believe in people." Although she'd been let down before, Bryana hoped this time would lift her belief in the goodness of others. She'd stated her case. There would be no problems, she'd assured Tess.

"Bryana, your word is good enough. If she don't give out trouble, I won't bother you."

After Bryana and Ricki left the café, they picked up a packet of guitar strings. Strings, sheet music, and other musical items were sold by a music teacher in his small store front.

With the guitar strings purchased, the women trekked back to the vehicle. On the return trip to the farm Bryana and Ricki discussed how pleased Michelle would be. A possibility of having an actual outlet for her bake goods would thrill her.

Then Bryana brought up a conversation about Gloria. "I saw you take plenty of interest in Gloria. She's a deluxe woman."

"You can say that again." Ricki issued a semi-embarrassed grin. "She's hot."

"Take my advice, I learned the hard way. You don't want to inflict the ire of the community on you by making a pass at Gloria. All the guys want to date her and she's the frost princess. Believe me, I'm still feeling the scorn because of a mistake years ago. Times may have changed, but some of the folks haven't. And never will. So tread lightly."

Ricki rotated her head towards Bryana. Her eyes held a meditative stare. As if computing words, she uttered, "I was getting vibes from Gloria."

"It's easy to be taken into another woman's heart. But believe me, you've got to be careful." She recalled locking off a corner of trust in her heart years ago. "Not all people are accepting."

"I got a theory about people, Bryana. Actually from someone I was incarcerated with. She told me, and I make it my own. People are broken down into percentages. Fifty percent of the people in the world are okay. Twenty-five percent are nice. The last one-forth are evil. The evil people keep getting the fifty-percent to be on their side."

"Then you've potentially got seventy-five percent becoming evil?" Bryana questioned. "Right?"

"Yeah, right, exactly."

"That's what I'm saying, too. Easy to get a crowd riled up, and against you. Ricki, be careful." Bryana's own life had become semi-stranded years ago. She felt her lashes becoming moist. Exasperated, Bryana said, "It's easy to end up wrecking things."

"Yeah, but Gloria was looking me over, too."

"I'm cautioning you." Bryana's words were launched at the younger woman. "L.J. would not be pleased if you called her to come get you because of an altercation about a woman." She pulled the vehicle into the space beside the farmhouse. "Even a tasty looking one like Gloria."

Ricki was amused. "For your age, you're pretty cool."

Those words, Bryana considered, required no additional verbiage. "Time to feed the livestock their evening meal. In the morning you can muck out the barn, feed the livestock, and then we'll throw some pots."

"Aren't you going to help me?"

"I'll be weeding the garden, gathering eggs, and emptying the small kiln. Then throwing pots. Want to change chores?"

Silence answered.

Chapter 8

The early morning's raw heat had indicated it would be a scorching hot day. Bryana recalled her father warning her that the scalding sun was a Kansas furnace. "An iced tea day if ever he saw one," he would say. This, she thought, would be such a day. She missed her parents, and wished their lives would have been easier. Her current situation might mean her life could also be one of continuing seasonal obstacles and never-ending work.

She wanted to have farming's happiness and reverence for life. The joyful farm life now presented nothing but difficulties and uncertainty. For a quick moment she wondered if sleeping on park benches might not be far less stressful. She exhaled a discouraging moan.

Bryana entered her studio. She saw the plastic-wrapped, damp, raw clay cubes along the wall. Lifting them, along with working the clay, had allowed her weight to be maintained. Pulling up the walls of clay in one strong motion was critical. And her wiry, athletic body helped form the clay. However, in her youth, it had been less tiring.

Sculpting was an intersecting of her spirit with the clay. The colors and shapes had the opportunity to become amazing. The way alternating colors would bleed across the clay never ceased to surprise her. She recalled watching her mother carefully making quilts, and piecing the colorful designs together. One quilt she recalled was her favorite because its edges were bright yellow. Her mother had said that the quilt had a rim like a Tierra of sunlight.

That thought had inspired Bryana. She examined the florid, stretching sunrise. She wanted her next batch of glazes to capture the brilliant colors across the horizon. She wanted to create her own Tierra of sunlight. She considered some variant mixtures of the colors. She needed to find that perfect facsimile of sunrise. She would try to get an exact glaze for her next firing. Or perhaps firing at a slightly different temperature might be the correct formula.

There was the pale violet sky she'd gazed at earlier that morning. It might be a warning that the day's weather could be a problem. She wanted to capture that color. For a moment, she tamped down the fear of a stormy day.

As if trying not to tempt fate, she switched from the Tierra of sunlight pots, to the wall décor projects. She felt a power that the cranberry underglaze represented. Inspiration was humanity's best technique for creation, she believed. The voice of passion needed to be inserted into the clay. It needed to enter and contact the core of art. Interpretation had always seemed to dictate its own vocabulary. She smiled as she thought about being accessible to such a euphoric feeling. Each project was a vehicle to express a story. Told without words, perhaps, but told.

Her studio was a station of serenity. In her mind she formulated designs to cover the walls of vases and other vessels. She envisioned the blistery cracks of sod in a dried creek bed. With fluting tools she swirled to replicate the land. She carved chunks with dental picks. On a bas-relief piece that was leather-hard, she made a feathering effect on the background. Wads of clay conformed into pleasing images.

Bryana's experimentation added to her bundle of new techniques. She loved attempting to research different glazes, and rather than guarding her recipes and clay techniques, she often wrote down instructions for any interested potter. When Michelle said that she'd inherited her mother's teaching ability, Bryana added her father always assisted young farmers in learning to predict weather patterns, planting, and harvesting.

Unloading the kiln's treasury of ornate work was a joy. Even when the temperature was wrong, and the glazes were imperfect, she jotted notes to improve. After unloading, and reloading with a new batch, Bryana stretched.

She'd made several fishing rod racks. Those were quickly reordered by the Brass Rail. Fishermen loved them. She had first made one for her father. She glanced up at the template and smiled. It had pleased her dad so much that she made a few to sell.

And these trinkets, along with other gift and specialty items had been a staple at her shop. Although they were improved through the years, they stayed similar to the first she'd created.

However, it was the more creative, free-spirit decorative works that intrigued her. They were larger, more difficult, and much more interesting. There was always a minimal market for them, but never a solid enough financial reward.

Midmorning found her joining Michelle in the garden. "I have a few more rows to weed," Michelle said.

Grabbing a hoe, Bryana began attacking the soil. "Glad we have air-conditioning units on both floors, it's going to be a hot day and hotter night."

"And I'm going to be baking later. The pies from last night look terrific. They ought to entice Tess to sell them in her café's bakery. And that bubble bread I made certainly impressed Ricki this morning. I think she ate half of it herself. When I said bubble bread, she wrinkled her nose. But after she saw what it was and tasted it, she dug in."

Bryana chuckled. Bubble bread was sweet bread dough chunks rolled into circles, dipped in butter, then covered with cinnamon and sugar. From there they were placed into Bundt pans, allowed time to rise, and then baked. When they were done, the bubble bread was cooled then tipped over to show the mound of small delicious rolls. Sometimes icing blended with cream cheese, and chopped pecans capped the bread. Other times a thin layer of lemon juice frosting was drizzled on top.

"I used to love it when I was a kid."

"Your mother's recipes never miss."

"Glad you found Mom's recipes. It was her gift to you. Might not be a bad idea to include some bubble bread for Tess to sample."

"I've got an extra bubble bread ring. I'll include it with the pies. I nearly always make two because I have two Bundt pans."

Bryana leaned across the table and coaxed a kiss from Michelle. "Well, judging from Ricki, the bubble bread was a hit. And she offered to take the pies to town. I think she wants to see Gloria. Thankfully, Gloria is probably back at summer school in Payton. She spends weekdays in her dorm. Works weekends."

Payton Community College was twenty miles to the east of Buffalo Plains. Bryana thought about the small college town of Payton. Several times larger than Buffalo Plains, the population, including the college, was about twenty-two thousand. Her parents often shopped there when they couldn't get an item in Buffalo Plains. And all residents of Buffalo Plains went to Payton when they needed medical specialists.

Michelle's eyes lifted as did her smirk. "We need to teach Ricki impulse control. A twenty-minute drive to Payton College won't shut down the urge for romance."

"I teach pottery, not impulse control. And particularly when the impulse is gynecological yearnings," Bryana said with amusement. "Time will shake her around to learning all kinds of controls. She tore down the shack, and said she'll begin setting up the new shed in a couple days. She even poured a concrete floor. Looks like she knows what she's doing. When I told her we couldn't afford lumber, she said she'd use some of the wood from the shed, and from the lean-to we tore down last autumn."

"You told her to watch for teetering boards? And particularly for snakes?"

"Yes. She took a shovel with her, and must not have encountered any reptiles under the rubble. She probably has encountered more danger from her past drug life than snakes."

"Fortunately she got out of that world unscathed." Michelle sighed then spoke, "However, with a background like hers, one wonders if that's unscathed. The kid is a terrific worker."

"She also got the livestock fed this morning, mucked the barn, and she's at the potter's wheel now. L.J. said she's a pretty decent potter, so I'll check her work out after we've finished the garden. I told her to make her mark on the base of the mugs she's throwing. So L.J. can pay her directly for her work. At any rate, Ricki scratched her initials with large and decorative letters. She takes pride in her work. That's always good."

Ricki waved as she pulled out of the driveway. Bryana was happy she didn't need to deliver the order. She preferred gardening. There was a moment of contrition when Bryana thought she was sending the poor kid into the heat of battle. She then realized that she would enjoy not walking through town. She shook her head a moment – the difference was that Ricki didn't seem to give a rat's ass if they made fun of her.

It always bothered Bryana.

Chapter 9

When O'Keeffe and Idgie left the women's sides, Bryana's body twisted around quickly. Her heartbeat was rapid. The dogs weren't after a rabbit; their barks were warning yips. She looked across the field to see the long strides of the poodle and schnauzer. Beyond was a small figure throwing stones at O'Keeffe and Idgie. The women dropped their hoes and rushed after the dogs. Stones were thumping the ground as the women approached.

Bryana yelled for the dogs to retreat. They were both shrinking with fear. Yet their trepidation was mixed with curiosity. With her hands cupping her mouth, she screamed in Jon's direction. "Stop that right now!"

When Jon was in clear sight she saw a large cairn of rocks beside him. Defiantly, Jon threw another sharp stone in the direction of the perplexed dogs. They barked as if they knew trouble was near them. Michelle had pulled her cell phone from her breast pocket and was dialing Tank and Alice Roland's number. When the phone was answered, she exploded. "Jon is throwing stones at our dogs."

From the speaker phone, Alice's voice sounded muffled. "Is he on your property?"

"No. He's on your property."

"He's got a perfect right to be on his own property."

"He hasn't got a perfect right to hurl dangerous projectiles at our dogs."

"Get a life. You two old maids, or whatever you call yourself, are nitpicking bitches. He's a boy. Boys throw rocks. You're either screaming about my kids, or our clients, or something. Leave us be."

The phone went dead. "She hung up on me."

The boy grinned devilishly then turned and ran towards his home where his mother's voice boomed.

"Damn!" Bryana cursed. "He's exactly like Tank was when he was a boy. Tank's mom, Sarah, said he was ornery. But there was more. He was cruel." Bryana looked wistfully away. "Now the world will need to worry about two Tanks. And we'll need to really worry about our dogs and our livestock. It's like living in a war zone. Even the child has artillery. A stash of jagged stones."

Michelle looked back over her shoulders as they returned to the garden. "Bryana, it's more than that. Alice sounded sloshed. Maybe Jon hasn't got a chance because she's not working with him."

"Sloshed!" Bryana mused. "It's only midday. Maybe she'd taken medication to help her sleep. My dad said she takes medication for her migraines."

"At the hospital it was a big joke. When one of the alcoholic workers would call in sick, it was always a migraine."

Concern covered Bryana's face. "I have always wondered about the kids. The little girls seem unhappy. Nita and Letty don't have much to do with Jon. Maybe they've been told he is the little prince. Hands off. He rules the roost. Not nice to say, but Tank even acts as if he would trade his trophy wife and daughters in before his son. And certainly his daughters are going to be raised like his wife. Trophy women."

"A healthy conclusion since it's how the mentality seems to be around here. Male oriented. It's important to procreate males. Some of the older people give their property to the oldest male. When your mother once told me about that, I was in complete disbelief. She said if they'd had more children, it would be given equally."

Bryana recognized the diversity between heirs in days gone by. She felt a stab of sadness. "Much of the world is like-minded. Yet it's changing here more rapidly than I thought it would. Thankfully. But there's no denying, there's often a difference."

With a subdued response, Michelle's voice was almost without volume. "I feel sorry for the little girls. And even sorry for Jon. He learns a terrible lesson when he gets away with harming animals.

If Jersey would ever have been told I'd tried to harm an animal, she would have been furious with me"

"Your mom loved animals. And loved you enough to encourage your love of animals."

"Exactly."

The strange uneasiness accompanied both women through the rest of the gardening. Both the stalwart O'Keeffe, and the trusting Idgie, stayed near. They normally followed one or both of the women. They'd been trained to stay near from when they were puppies. Now, at the farm, it was for their protection from predators - snakes and coyotes, Roland's hunters, and now, a five-year old with a stash of rocks.

A quick montage of memories made Bryana even more sullen. She thought about growing up in the relative isolation of a farm. She and her best friend, Sarah, were seldom separated. They would meet midway between their farmhouses at day's start, and be with one another throughout the day until nightfall. They spent time working on one another's chores together, studying together, and spent leisure time with one another. They shared their plans for their futures. Now, Sarah's grandson was tormenting Bryana's pets. Sarah's son was a major annoyance with his industry of killing birds and animals, and killing cats for sport.

Sarah voiced her views that Bryana was a lascivious freak of nature because she had become a full-fledged Sapphic. And if Sarah had expected that the Bible belt would recruit her onetime friend back to religion, she was mistaken.

Mockingly Bryana suggested, "Michelle, think if we put up a little white picket fence, they would stay away from us?"

"Their intention isn't to stay away from us." She flavored her conversation with a snicker. "Nope, they want trouble to erupt. Or they wouldn't allow their child to harass our dogs."

The women were taking an iced tea break when Ricki arrived back at the farm. She burst into the kitchen announcing how Tess Walters loved the bubble bread. She handed Michelle a check and two pieces of paper. Gasping from her run inside, Ricki exclaimed, "Tess said back in her day bubble bread was also called monkey bread, and also pull-apart bread. She loved it. I told her the bread also came in flavors. She said that food is an art form. I remembered all the available flavors. Butterscotch, orange, and herbs. She was excited. Said to call her right away about costs. And she sent an order for pottery, pies, and bread."

Michelle pulled out her phone and hit the number for the Buffalo Plains Café. As Ricki sat at the kitchen table, across from Bryana, she muttered, "Sounds like Tess is gonna be ordering her socks off."

Bryana asked Ricki with a tease, "Was it the bread, or your newly acquired sales skills that closed the sale?"

Ricki glanced away. "I learned street sales years ago. It's how I lived. Drugs."

"Must have been tough out there as a teen alone on the streets."

"Yeah. I don't ever want to go back."

"Keep throwing pottery with the relish and enthusiasm you have now, and you won't need to return to the streets. And it also looks as if you're good at construction."

"It's easy to get a construction job in most cities." Ricki frowned. "You really think I'm a good potter?"

"I looked over your work. You show great promise."

"I'm better at the guitar than I am at the wheel. But I love throwing pots. It's like a therapy for me. I like building things, too. Like a shed, and a greenhouse."

"You can do both. Pottery and music." Bryana paused. "And building a greenhouse, and a shed or two also."

"I worked one summer constructing sheds for one of those prefab companies. So I know the basic structure."

Bryana paused for a moment before asking, "Was Gloria there?"

"Naw. Tess said she was on campus. But you're right. I need to get other things done right now. I don't need the problems of having a woman."

Michelle ended her phone call with a yelp of joy. "She wants to order half a dozen pies to start. And she wants a standing order of a dozen bubble breads every other day. Thinks she can sell them that quickly. The question is, can I make them that quickly. I'll need to order some new bundt cake pans."

Bryana finished her iced tea. "If you order them online you can have them sent right away. And as far as baking enough, you can do anything at all. You amaze me. I'm going for a walk down to the pond. Relax before I get back to work."

As she walked along on the knitted sod, she listened to the crunch of earth. She felt the breeze that was beginning. The ripple of the Plains, she thought. Chips of earth and the crinkle of dried grasses were part of the scenery, and nature's sound system. A fan of light sprayed out across the patchy land. Turning, she noticed the clouds gathering and darkening. A leaden gray wall of sky was encroaching quickly.

A moment later, the breeze converted into a howling wind. Those clouds were moving rapidly towards the farm. Bryana began sprinting across the field. A sudden tension burned her body's muscles.

When she reached the farmhouse's door, she screamed, "A storm is on its way. Ricki, we need to get the animals in the barn. Cows inside and in the corner stall. Pierre, the horse, move him into the farthest stall. We need to get the goats inside running free." She rushed her instructions. "Michelle, I'll take the dogs to the storm cellar now. I don't want them getting spooked. Then I'll corral the chickens and lock them into their henhouse. And is the vehicle in the garage?"

"Yes. What's going on?" Ricki asked.

"A storm is headed this way. Careful to watch your feet when you lead the cows inside. They sway as they trudge. We need to house the livestock safely." Bryana stepped back outside. She pointed towards an angry horizon. Within moments, dark billowing clouds had become a wild vastness of pouring black sky. She saw the churning winds beginning at the bottom of a whipping, accelerating slap of the sky. "Hurry with securing the animals. We need to get into the storm cellar fast. And Michelle, don't forget to bring the radio, flashlights and the lantern, and your cell phone.

As she ran, she witnessed the flashing, illuminated sky. It was thunderously vibrating as it muscled over the landscape. The pond's stitched embankment was receiving winds that lifted the water several feet. She saw Michelle and Ricki heading for the corrals. With nerves fringed in stark terror, she looked back upward. Wind and dust unfurled in small wind funnels, and sprouts.

The faint sound of the tornado alert became louder. A whistle sliced the airwaves. The sky's stillness meshed with a chill. A strange hush seemed to lull the moment as the alarm siren lessened. A rush of wind approached.

Off to the horizon an ashen sky poured its way towards the farmhouse. An inky blackness dimmed the sky's light. Bryana's skin rippled in currents of fear. Thunderous vibrations continued pressing through the air, stabbing at Bryana's back. She yearned for safety.

After herding the hens, and taking care of the last minute emergency measures, she made a dash towards the shelter. Heavy stone steps led down to the shelter. She then pulled the horizontal door closed and secured it.

When she tucked into the protection of the underground sanctuary, she continued to feel insecurity. If anything, she was now confined and claustrophobic. She felt Michelle's hand grip hers. "I forgot to turn off the oven. The pies...." Michelle murmured.

Bryana patted her arm gently. "Don't worry, I turned off the gas lines. Also, I shut the electrical current. The pies probably won't even burn."

An ominous moment preceded what seemed like the earth being thrashed. The three women and two dogs sat around the battery operated lamp. Both O'Keeffe and Idgie hadn't stopped shivering since the women entered the underground shelter. Beneath the house, the shelter was thickly cemented.

"I saw several funnel clouds," Bryana said. As she protectively hugged the dogs, her throat felt constricted. She switched on the radio. It was forecasting what the women already were aware of - impending tornadic conditions. "Tornadoes sometimes come in bunches, so we may get more than one wave."

The women shuddered when sudden pulverizing rumbles were heard and felt. Ricki's voice quaked, "I'm frightened."

Bryana had been through wind storms and nearby tornadoes many times. "Me, too. Storms are terrifying." She patted Ricki's arm. "We should be safe here."

Michelle closed her eyes as the ground shook. Winds were seeping through the hatch. Clattering sounds surrounded them. Crashing thunder, and the deafening roar of winds had overtaken the wail of alert whistles and sirens.

Ricki's voice trembled. "I wish I was back in Denver."

Bryana's nervous laugh escaped. "Sometimes when I was in my shop back in Denver, I would dream about this homestead. How relaxing it was to watch the tops of wheat as they wagged like metronomes across the field with afternoon's wind."

Michelle's face hinted at her set of dimples. Her eyes by dim lighting became the color of wisteria. "I haven't lived in New York for years. But there are times when I think of the traffic blenching puffs of carbon monoxide. I miss the corner stands. Warm pretzels with mustard slopping down the sides. The obscenities called out. I don't think we ever grow too old to reminisce about life as we knew it. I wouldn't mind being away from Kansas right now." Her ashen face constricted tightly as a howl of wind blustered.

Ricki hugged her own arms tightly. "Florida only reminds me of running, chasing, getting caught dirty with drugs. Ah, for fuck sakes, I don't want to think about how terrible life was then. Even this is better. If we live."

"We're safe down here," Bryana reassured her. "As safe as we can be. See all the braces on the ceiling - and the many posts holding them. My father reinforced this cellar." She thought to herself about her father. He used to say nature bats last when it comes to storms. But her mother believed that all existence is a pageant. Bryana was tired of this part of the parade. Dreams had come and gone and she felt totally used up. Wincing, her eyes closed, she wished this part of time would flow through eternity quicker.

A vacuum inhaled the air as squealing winds battered the shelter. Bryana's stomach lurched when the light flickered. The three women's hands reached for one another.

The sudden quiet from outside provided a pause, and the radio signal lifted the volume. The tornado was directing itself towards the southern portion of Buffalo Plains. These furious winds were only the preliminary to what would soon be smashing a next victim.

Chapter 10

The women weaved slightly as they exited the shelter. Shivering hands wiped away the dust that covered their faces. Words were few as they examined the horizon.

The crops and surrounding farmhouses had been spared. Wheat stalks leaned from the wind's battering, but had not been pounded into the ground. Thankfully, Bryana thought, rains had not accompanied the storm. However, as she scrutinized the storm while it pressed through the skies, she could see dark, angry clouds beginning to unload rains as they neared the town.

Remaining on the farm was a low moaning breeze that shook leaves, and lifted waves on the rippling pond water. The old rowboat's stern bobbed with each whoosh of wind.

Michelle cringed as she choked the dust from her throat. She uttered, "The storm skirted our farm." As she whirled around to the south, she commented. "But the corporate farmland across the way got hit."

Across the road, Bryana saw the debris strewn. Leveled were the out-buildings. The fence posts were crumpled like aged twigs. Although their own property had taken a beating, to the south much had been leveled. "Lucky we didn't get a direct hit. Are you two okay?" Bryana questioned with twitching pale lips.

"Yeah. Jez, I've never seen anything like this." Ricki made a complete wobbly turn as she surveyed the damage. "Everything on your property is still standing, but all the small stuff is all over." She walked towards some of the farm's debris. A few of the screens had been pulled from the house. She began picking them up. Dazed, she turned back to the two older women. Her mouth trembled then shut as if she was grinding her teeth. "Jez!"

The following moments of quiet were welcoming. A voice on the radio suddenly jarred the women back to the moment. Bryana had retrieved the radio from the shelter. They heard pleas for emergency first responders to go immediately to the southern part of Buffalo Plains to evacuate those trapped. They requested all medics to report to the small local hospital.

"I'll get the utilities turned back on," Bryana said quickly.

Michelle nodded, "I've got my Kansas certification. I've got to help. Bry, can you move the SUV out? I'm going into town."

According to the radio reports, the southern part of the town had been badly hit by the wind storm. The tornado had not directly hit, but had caused enormous secondary damage.

Michelle ran to the kitchen to get the vehicle keys. Knowing Bryana would be turning the utilities back on, Michelle would also turn off the oven.

Bryana yelled back to Ricki, "Get the dogs inside. And stay there. Michelle and I have to go to town and help."

Ricki glared as she grimaced. "The people around here hate you. Now they holler 'frog' and you're jumping to help them. Why bother?"

Michelle was coming out from the kitchen, she answered tersely, "Ricki I'm a nurse. It's my duty."

Bryana backed the SUV around for Michelle to enter. Ricki leaned against the vehicles' window and asked, "Can't I go, too?"

"Ricki," Bryana ordered, "you'll need to take care of things around here. As soon as the wind dies down, make sure the fences are okay before taking the livestock out. Then feed and water them. You might try and pick up some of the debris, too. I'll call later with more instructions."

"I don't understand why you're going. Look, the window screens are blown off. Things are all over," Ricki argued. "We have work to do here."

Bryana glanced back at her. Insistently, she spoke, "People are hurt, maybe dying. Some are undoubtedly homeless now. This place just needs tidying up. Please, just help us."

Begrudgingly, Ricki turned. She gave the gravel beneath her a kick of anger.

As Bryana drove towards Buffalo Plains, she muttered, "I understand the way Ricki feels. When you asked for a job at the hospital, they turned you down flat. With all your credentials. And you passed the State board. They told you to piss off. They needed staff, advertised for staff – and then kicked you to the curb. Now you're going to assist."

"Your pal, ex-friend, whatever," Michelle answered with contempt. "Sarah Roland. She's on the board of directors. I'm certain she had my application nixed. It was all fine until she explained to the hospital administrator that I was the woman with you. The lesbian."

"Do you want me to turn around?"

Determined, Michelle said, "No. If they need my help, they've got it."

"You're a better-hearted person than I am."

"I'm not. I'll bet that after you drop me off at the hospital, you'll be going to the southern site of destruction to see if anyone needs your help. And they've done a hell of a lot more to you than reject your employment bid."

"Michelle, some of the past months have seemed long. But if we stay, time will seem longer than either of us could have ever imagined." She glanced back up at the dust-filled sky. "Maybe we should keep driving."

Michelle allowed a moment's silence before she responded. "When we've had rough times before, you always said as long as we were together we could make it. When we lost our parents, our previous pets, our home and business, as well as our entire savings, you always said we'd make it. If the people want our help, we'll help. Not because we haven't been hurt in the past and won't be vilified in the future, but because it's what we need to do. Together."

They passed by people straggling out from their basement confines and other hiding places. Their faces were masks of weariness and confusion. Some held bloodied areas of their bodies.

Bryana's glance tugged away from the scene back to the street. As if in a hypnotic trance, she stole looks back at the disaster areas. Planks were driven through homes, the foliage had been stripped from trees, posts uprooted, shutters ripped and dangling, and sheds were missing. The survivors were in shock. With disbelief, they craned their necks, peering suspiciously up at the skies. What hadn't been blown away had been well beaten with hail and rain. Paint was stripped, windows were blown in. A metallic smoky haze veiled the land. And this had not been a direct hit.

Bryana swerved the SUV, turning on the street where the hospital was located. Through the mud and puddles the town folk sloshed as they walked towards the hospital. When one of the men's legs buckled, he fell clutching his legs. Michelle instructed, "Let me out here. I'll see if I can help him get to emergency. Please try to get to the ones injured and help transport them back. It's best to prioritize by bringing any life threatening injuries first."

"I love you, Michelle. See you later." Bryana heard the door slam. She then drove away. She was aware that as pummeled as this section of town was, it would be worse chaos the more southward she drove. The dusky clouds ahead began showering the landscape again with another pounding. As streets filled, swirling winds carried galvanized trashcans and other debris. Trash forged a conglomerate of dotted specks throughout the air.

The interlude of calm was followed by a peal of thunder. It was definitely worse as she drove south. The SUV threaded through water and floating litter. Bryana was glad when the rains were shutting down. The charcoal shadowed sky began to lighten slightly. Bryana knew the school cafeteria was always an evacuation center. She would take the uninjured there.

The drive was slow as Bryana maneuvered around the downed trees and power lines. Mist clouded the vehicle's windows. The storm passed through the southern-most fringe of Buffalo Plains with a vengeance. Behind were left huge puddles of water and steam. There were numerous automobiles that had been left behind when the rains flooded. For several blocks, she cautiously drove through the battered area.

Without warning she heard the shriek of a voice. From the side she saw a woman waving to her. "Can you help?" A woman with two toddlers strung from each of her arms was running towards her. She opened the SUV's door. "My car sits low and was nearly washed away. It won't start. Could you take us home?"

"Get in, I can attempt to get you as near as possible," Bryana answered. "There are lines down."

The woman gave directions as they drove. "I've never seen anything like this." The young woman trembled. Her eyes were hysterical, and her damp stringy hair made her appear even more so. As they turned the corner, she saw her home. Trees were uprooted, and most of the windows had been blown out. Screens were twisted and mangled.

"At least it's still standing. It's uninhabitable though. Do want me to take you to the shelter? You can't stay in there."

"My neighbor is elderly, and she can't drive."

"Let's get her and then I can take you all back to the high school gym or cafeteria. They are always shelter areas." As Bryana exited, she instructed, "You stay with the little ones, I'll get your neighbor." She rushed to the door and knocked loudly and impatiently. When the tearful woman got to the door, Bryana said, "I have your neighbor and the two little ones in my vehicle. It would be a good idea to get you all to the shelter." Bryana glanced inside. Broken glass, and the frothing waters had rained in on the woman's living room. "You probably won't have electricity here."

Nodding, the woman asked, "Do I have time to get my prescriptions?"

"Yes."

By the time they'd started back, Bryana picked up a few more people. Crammed into the SUV, they clasped one another. After they unloaded, Bryana made several more trips as she ferried the wounded. The water level had lowered, and now many of the people were being evacuated by buses, and emergency vehicles.

Although she'd picked up some people with abrasions, they all had wanted to stay with family members. Knowing they would have first aid services at the shelter, Bryana took them to the cafeteria. She knew the hospital was probably swamped. After delivering a final load, she took out her cell phone to call Michelle.

"Hi, just pulling in the hospital parking lot."

"No deaths so far, but lots of serious injuries. Some are in critical condition," Michelle reported. There was a pause. "Bryana, the supervisor asked if I could stay throughout the night.

When she recalled that I'd been an emergency room nurse, she told me the patients were stacked, and even though they have responders and medics from some of the towns around here, tonight is critical in getting everyone one patched."

Bryana examined people still entering the hospital. Wrapped in blood-soaked blankets, they wandered.

"Yes. You've got to stay. I can go back to the farm. See if Ricki is okay. Then when you're ready to come home, I'll come get you."

"I'm ready now, but I've volunteered for as long as they need me."

Bryana sensed a problem. "What's wrong?"

"That sheriff deputy, Pete, made a fuss when he saw me. Started yelling about not wanting me to work with blood. Said something about AIDS."

Bryana's jaw clamped. "For god sakes, we're in the lowest possible risk group. Tell him to go to hell. And don't let it bother you."

"One of the ER doctors already told him to stay out of our way. After Pete's remark, he said that as a medic he was certain I'd been tested for everything imaginable – repeatedly, as well as recently. And he insisted Pete get out of the ER." There was a pause painful to both women. Michelle questioned, "Is that what people think?"

"Not people who are able to think. I want to go back to Denver," Bryana uttered.

"There's hate all over. I'll call you when we get caught up here. Try to get some sleep."

"Yes. I've volunteered to help mop up tomorrow. It's a mess. Lots of repairs. I'm glad there aren't any fatalities." She heard Michelle's hasty goodbye.

It was becoming dark when Bryana drove onto the gravel road. As her headlights hit the farm house she saw that most of the trash and strewn items had been carefully picked up. The kitchen light was on, and Ricki was wide awake.

"I thought you'd be in bed. You must have worked all day on clearing the debris around the farm. And you fixed the screens. And fed the livestock. I'm impressed."

"Busy day. I didn't have time for pottery. I kept wishing I could help with the people in the middle of this storm. You're right. No matter how they treat us, we need to show them we're not shits." Ricki pulled a plate with a sandwich and French fries from the warming oven. She then poured a cup of tea as Bryana sat. "I didn't cook anything because there were leftovers from last night. So I just made a meatloaf sandwich for you."

Bryana's smile was faint. "Thanks, I appreciate everything. The cleanup. Taking over the animals. And this looks great. I'm starving." Her mouth wrapped around a huge bite."

"Michelle called to tell me you were on your way. Said she's staying over. If you want, I'll go get her in the morning."

"I want to go in and help."

Ricki asked, "Can I go with you in the morning?"

"Who would take care of the livestock? The farm." As if on cue O'Keeffe gave a whining moan. "And watch the dogs?"

"It's because of the way I look. You're ashamed of me."

"No. Ricki, I took you in when I made calls at the tavern, café, and introduced you to everyone we saw. I'm not ashamed of you. Okay, how about if we both take care of chores early tomorrow morning, then we can both go help. Carpenters are going to be needed, and you're good with odd jobs. Then tomorrow evening we can both come home and feed the livestock. How's that?"

"Yeah. Did you know they got Buffalo Plains on the national nightly news?"

Bryana stopped eating a moment. "If you want to help tomorrow, you better not have any outstanding warrants. There will be cameras."

"Naw. I'm clean," she answered with an embarrassed grin. "I left all that bullshit behind me." Her eyes clamped tightly. Tears were left when they opened. "Bryana, I can't stand to think about how terrible it was then. How terrible I was then."

"You're not terrible now. If we want to talk terrible, Pete was at the ER. He accused Michelle of having a communicable disease. He was obviously thinking of gays and AIDS. But druggies need to be careful, too. Have you been checked for AIDS and Hep C. Things like that?"

"Yeah. I guess that was one of the things most scary. See, when you're doing drugs, there's an automatic denial about any risk or trouble. When you're high, you aren't thinking. Your brain is numb and dumb. Well, when I went into jail, I was tested. After a while my mind cleared up. I realized I was blessed I hadn't gotten anything. I promised never to expose myself to death again. A new lease on life. And I never have had a single drug since. And I've never had too much to drink. I keep my mind available for fighting any stupidity that might be knocking on the door." Ricki chuckled.

"Turning over a new leaf. I'm glad. I wouldn't want you to throw away your life. And I'm sure you're also frightened of returning to prison."

"Yeah. But I'm most terrified of L.J. She said she'd wring my scrawny little neck."

The women shared a laugh. "Everyone is terrified of L.J. You'd be a fool not to be."

"I may be lotsa bad things, but a fool ain't one of them."

"You aren't a bad kid, Ricki. You just need a little tweaking. You'll be fine. I believe that. Now, get some sleep. Tomorrow we've got a full day. Together we'll first tackle the chore war. Then help our neighbors."

Chapter 11

The next three days seemed too rushed to have even existed. But they had. The storm placed a curtain of gloom over the area. Each day the three women worked tirelessly throughout the day and into the evening. Michelle had been at the hospital nonstop. Bryana and Ricki had boarded windows, pumped water out of basements, and gathered scattered lumber and debris.

Thankfully, Bryana reported to Michelle, Ricki's actions were exemplary. She worked hard, long hours. The townspeople stared at her, but soon became accustomed to her. And she to them.

Ricki had climbed into a battered home to rescue an elderly woman. She also had attended to a young teenager when brickwork fell in on him. She soothed his mother when the woman's dolorous sobs became ear shattering. Ricki assured her that he'd be fine. Bryana and Ricki took the mother and son to the hospital emergency.

At the hospital, Bryana was happy for the brief interlude. She'd given Michelle a quick hug in the hospital's hallway. When she turned, she saw Ricki talking with Gloria Walters. She motioned in their direction. "I don't want to encourage that."

"Bryana, they're just being nice to each other. I know you explained the danger of getting too cozy. Ricki is well aware she can't touch Gloria."

"These people already believe we're perverted. And Gloria's mom would totally freak out. Tess is *very* much into the church. She wants Gloria to reach her wedding day chaste as a frigid virgin. We don't need problems."

"So Tess spouts scripture. And she wants her daughter to be completely innocent. I don't think Gloria would cross her mother. And Ricki might have the hots for Gloria, but she's wise enough to know it wouldn't do any of us any good. Maybe she's just talking with her about bakery orders. My pies and bubble bread. When I saw Tess earlier she asked when I was getting back to my little baking business. They're here to see Tess's father. He hasn't been well. So it isn't like Ricki and Gloria decided to meet up here."

"God forbid - to borrow a term from Tess. I know I'll impart as much embossed wisdom as I can. And when are you going to be able to begin baking again?"

Michelle covered her eyes for a moment. Her mouth pursed. "Not soon enough. I have a ping of conscience about wanting to stop being a nurse. Is it wrong for me to have become overwhelmed when it comes to the business of healing? I want to bake. I can't wait to get back to the kitchen."

"Have they been making difficulties for you?"

"Not at all. I've become friends with most of the staff, and the supervisor. In fact, she confirmed my suspicion about Sarah Roland declining my job application. She told me there isn't much that Sarah and Vince don't have influence over in this town. She seemed to be frustrated by the Roland's bully mentality."

With a beleaguered side-glance, Bryana spoke with a crusading voice, "Maybe Sarah was told by Vince to insist you not be hired at the hospital. She was once my closest friend. I would never try to sabotage her life. Yet it's pretty apparent she no longer remembers our youth."

"She ruined your reputation around here."

"Michelle, that was a long time ago. Things were fragmented. I should have read the warning labels. Things were complicated - multi-layered."

"Look, it's great you have this undying loyalty to her. I admire your magnanimous spirit. She not only outed you, she made certain it would change your life forever."

"As I said, that was decades ago. Around here people believe when you're born and raised here, it was by God's special invitation to Kansas. I was part of what the sanctimonious call 'right-side up living.' I should have known better than be who I am."

"It seems as though everyone has reservations about us."

"If it bothers you, let's walk away now. I wouldn't do anything to mess up what we have, Michelle."

"Sorry I'm being miserable. It hasn't been a good day."

"Things are getting back to normal. Tomorrow we should stay home and catch up on *us*. On the farm, the animals, baking, pottery - us."

The corners of Michelle's lips lifted. "Now volunteers from other communities are overrunning the place. You're right. It's time we concentrate on home."

When Michelle was called away, Bryana approached Ricki and Gloria. "How's your grandfather?"

"We've been told its terminal, but I think he'll make it a little while longer," Gloria answered. "He's back to pulling quarters from behind my ears. And he told me a dozen very corny jokes this afternoon."

"Good to hear he's improving. Ricki, you ready?"

Ricki followed behind. When they got into the SUV, Ricki asked, "How well do you know Gloria?"

"Not very well at all. I know her family, but she wasn't even born when I left for college all those years ago. And as I've mentioned before, it would be best if *you* wouldn't get to know her too well."

Ricki glanced down at the floor. "She's the only one who seems friendly to me. Everyone else acts like I'm some foreign devil."

"I understand completely, Ricki," Bryana commiserated. "I've been a stranger in the town I grew up in since college. But if we antagonize them, they'll hate us even more. So we need to do the best we can, wait it out until logic and science catches up with ideological hatred and religious bigotry. At one time churches held the notion that it was a sin for a black to marry a white. It was a law, too. Now it's viewed as prejudice in unhappy people's hearts. For now we've got to make a good impression as we live our lives. If not, we're lost."

"And we're supposed to play goody-goody in lockstep with their dictates?"

"We supposed to be good, not *pretend* good. And that's not lockstep with anyone's dictates. It's what our heart tells us to do.

Heart talk is what the past three days have been about. Not helping for any reason other than it's what our heart tells us. It makes us better human beings."

Ricki's laughter escaped. Sarcastically she muttered, "It's made me a much better lesbian."

Amused, Bryana added, "Only in theory, not in practice. In practice, I'm hoping you're not going to hone your Sapphic skills around here. And especially on the town's most eligible beauty queen."

"I promise you. I won't touch her. Even if she begged. You have my word."

"From the gossip, I don't think she wants anyone to touch her. That includes the local Lotharios."

With a dramatic twist to her voice, Ricki joked, "What chance have I if the local studs have struck out?"

"Not much, probably. But events in even the lower end of the probability charts sometimes happen. So please behave."

"I told you I wouldn't mess around. You have my word. If I break my word, I'll go back to Denver. And," she hesitated before asking, "do I have your word that we're done with the cleanup crew?"

"There are enough crews and people on the hospital staff to take care of everything. Enough volunteers from all parts of the country to rebuild. So yes, you have my word. Back to the farm work."

"And you think Michelle is okay with staying home?"

"She's ready to get back to baking. And for us, pottery and taking care of the garden, and livestock. As well as your out-building construction."

"Funny," Ricki said wistfully, "after the last three days, getting back to the farm will be a vacation."

Bryana walked nearer the young woman. Her hand reached to give Ricki's shoulder a playful shove. "I guess it must have seemed like you'd been thrown into the deep end when you arrived."

"I'm getting faster with the chores now." With an inner sagacity, Ricki began to hum a tune Bryana wasn't familiar with. "I'll even have time to finish the song I'm writing."

"Glad you're getting some use out of Dad's guitar. That would have pleased him. And knowing songs are being written on his guitar would've made him even happier."

By the time the three women made it back to the farm, they were exhausted. Twilight was well on its way. The sunset was spectacularly unfolding across the horizon. Turning into driveway, they spotted L.J.'s Jeep. Behind it was a horse trailer.

"What the…" Bryana exclaimed.

"Horses?" Michelle questioned.

As they neared, they spotted horses inside their carrier. L.J.'s door opened quickly when she saw them driving up. The women embraced, as L.J. explained, "No pressure. You don't need to keep them here if you don't want."

"Of course we'll be glad to keep them here. Who do they belong to?" Bryana questioned.

"Me. I mentioned your farm to my brother, and he drove them up to me. Can I board them here? Then when I come to visit you, I can ride them. If that's okay. I'll pay for their feed, and any upkeep. In exchange for your watching them, maybe I can work here a couple days a week and pay a boarding fee. Just like right now, I know you're behind with orders. So I can feed the livestock, and do other chores, while the two of you attend to the pottery. I figure in a couple days, you can have enough pottery for me to at least fill the Jeep. The horse trailer can stay here, in case we need to take them somewhere."

"But who is watching your shop?" Michelle asked.

"A nice couple staying with me. Look, I miss my ranching background, so a couple days a week here would be terrific. Ride, work, enjoy."

"L.J., are you sure?" Bryana questioned.

"Hell, yes."

"We can definitely use the help. And taking care of the horses wouldn't be much more than taking care of Pierre. We have extra stalls in the barn," Bryana added. "I don't see why it wouldn't work. Michelle, what do you think?"

Michelle responded, "An answered prayer. We could get caught up. Yes, of course."

"Right now I'm needing pottery to keep the store filled. And I want to get plenty of stock before the weather gets bad. Weather will make trips more difficult. Plus I'll need to work in the store over the holidays."

"Wintertime work on the farm slows down, so I could easily make some delivery trips out there. It would all work great," Bryana offered.

Ricki rocked from foot to foot. "If L.J. is doing the chores, do I still have a job?"

Bryana affirmed, "We need you here. Of course. It would give you time to finish the shed you're working on. And then begin the greenhouse. As well as make more pots. And those little silver-dollar-sized necklace ornaments."

After unloading the horses and allowing them time to graze, Bryana, L. J., and Ricki fed the other animals their evening meal, and cleaned the stable areas. Michelle had volunteered to put together some dinner.

Ricki had returned to see if Michelle needed any assistance. As Bryana and L.J. coaxed the two lovely horses into their stalls, L.J. hinted at a question. "Things going okay with Ricki? She's not a problem?"

"Nope. Everything is fine. She's been working hard, watching her language, wearing suitable clothing, and toning down her hair."

"How about toning down her libido?"

Bryana enticed one of the horses into its boarding area. "This horse seems to be taking to her new digs nicely. What did you say her name is?"

"The brown mare is Brandy, and the black is Sherry. My brother named them. His wine and whiskey cellar is jam-packed. He likes his hooch. Expensive hooch." Her laugh was raucous. "Now, let's get back to my interrogation. Is Ricki chasing?"

"She's given me her word she won't mess with anyone."

"Don't try to snow the snowwoman. Remember me, the woman known for having a variety of women. A six-pack of lovers on both arms. And I know Ricki. I'm not trying to snitch. But so you'll be aware, I'll mention it. She's called me a couple of times and told me about this girl named Gloria. Ricki claims

Gloria is coming on to her. The woman is purportedly straight. Her mother is a hawk, and the town would not appreciate Ricki trying to bring her into the fold."

"Okay, she may be taken with Gloria. But as we both know what I learned years ago, in a small town it's perilous to try bringing anyone into the fold. You know the old straight question. How old were you when you realized you're straight. Ricki couldn't recruit Gloria. People can't be converted to be what they aren't. And for all I know, Gloria *is* taken with Ricki. But they both know it wouldn't be a good idea." Bryana closed the barn door. "I'm not the heterosexual security cop, so the best I can do is warn Ricki about it. I have. And I've got her word."

"Come on, Bryana, if they have the urge, no one is going to be able to hose them down. But she's aware she can't make things harder for you and Michelle. You've helped her. She owes you that loyalty. Ricki told me she learned to be deceitful at a young age in order to survive. It's not only second nature to her, but her past made it mandatory. The question is, can she stay away from Gloria? I can't give you a guaranty."

"So take her back to Denver with you." Her calm mood had evaporated. "L.J., I have reservations, too. I'm aware she's a throw-away kid. Trusting her may be the only thing that keeps her right." Bryana felt beleaguered. She scowled. "But on the other hand, I can't keep her under house arrest. And I can't stop the runaway bulldozer of love."

"You okay?"

"It's just that I fought the same battle decades ago. Most of this town believes the raging fires of some eternal abyss awaits my soul. And still, to this day, they are determined to show me that rotten spot in my heart. Get that perversion out of my soul. After all, my parents were God-fearing, decent, law-abiding people. The town people believe they're playing tug of war with my spirit. Think about your little town in Florida. It was the same. A no-sin zone. And being Sapphic is a sin. And redemption is time-consuming. These folks haven't given up on me. For my parent's sake. They'd love to cure me." Her deadbolt stare at the wall redirected to L.J.'s face. "Well?"

She flashed a mellow smile. "Ricki fucks up and she hasn't even got the parent connection. They'll tar and feather her. Leave her on the side of the road for the creator to cure. Let's hope Gloria keeps her ice-goddess reputation intact."

"I don't want to give up on Ricki. But Michelle and I are no longer young. There aren't many do-overs left. I remember in youth we never believed age was following us so closely. It's right behind us, waiting to roll over us. And mistakes take longer to correct, if there is time to correct them."

With a sullen glance back, L.J. bantered, "You've got time for lots of mistakes. But don't make a crazy mistake of trusting too much."

Bryana itemized the various problems she faced. "Unfortunately, even tons of time don't leave enough time for stepping into some traps."

The women walked towards the farmhouse. Glad for the luscious fragrances of Michelle's meal, they hurried to the table. While digging into a feast, Bryana considered she'd always had a search for life's meaning. Trusting one another, loving one another, and being the finest human you can be was part of it. Life's significance - that was the real question. Even the meaning of love sometimes eluded her. When there is love, it seems as though love itself is the most significant part of existence. Yet, she deliberated - one is so easily mistaken about some loves. The gnawing questions poured. Answers weren't confirmed either way.

By the time the women were ready for bed they'd sorted out the details of work schedules, had many laughs, and talked about friends in Denver. Each woman was exhausted, and ready to shut down the evening.

Already on the bed was O'Keeffe. With her fuzzy, apricot and tan coloring, she perched as if she were a queen. She yawned when Bryana and Michelle entered. O'Keeffe's front paws crossed, as she placed her head down on them.

"Come on, girl, we need some room to sleep," Bryana said as she scooted the poodle over. "Where's Idgie?"

"I know both of the dogs are inside. I called them in not fifteen minutes ago. My best guess is she's with Ricki. She spent most of last night MIA, and followed Ricki around this evening." A smile creased across her face. "For being so anti-social, and frightened of dogs, Rickie has gotten along with the animals splendidly. And for being what L.J. called a punk kid, she's worked great around here."

Bryana recalled, "And with the cleanup crew, she busted it. She looks scrawny but her muscles are strong as teakwood. I think she's withdrawn because of her past. She's had a worse background than we know. I see it in her eyes. She has empathy for those in pain. When she'd help with injured people, she touched them as if she knew their misery and their fear."

When Michelle slipped into bed, she agreed, "Yes." When the women kissed, Bryana felt the dampness from Michelle's tear against her cheek.

"Are you okay?"

"Yes." Michelle squeezed Bryana tightly. Her embrace warmed with a sensual flush of womanhood. "I'm glad she's here. I think we can help her. I know L.J. has helped. She brought those horses for Ricki. She believes the kid is worth saving, and helping with horses has been known to turn hearts. I agree she's worth saving. She plays your father's guitar like a professional. Your dad always used to say it usually takes a good person to play good music."

"And here I was thinking you liked having Ricki around because Idgie bunked with her. We only have to share the bed with O'Keeffe."

Michelle lulled in Bryana's ear, "That, too. It still leaves one less dog on our bed to be kicked off."

Even O'Keeffe knew that wasn't going to happen. The women cradled together in one another's arms. The tremble of excitement never ceased when their flesh melded. Nesting closely was as blissful as it had ever been.

Michelle touched Bryana's face. "Ricki can be our chance to help change the indifference of today's youth."

"I'll be there in her corner as long as she doesn't jeopardize our future. And she understands how firm I'll be on that."

Michelle thought a moment then said, "I don't think she'd betray us."

"I'm hoping she won't. Now then, do you want to toss O'Keeffe's toy towards the corner so we can scoot around the bed and get comfy? And before she jumps back up here with a drooled-on toy."

Michelle chuckled. "Shhhh. Or she'll hear you. She could get back up here and poop on the bedspread."

Bryana joined in the first therapeutic laugh she'd had for days. "Not if she doesn't want her new address to be the barn."

Chapter 12

Tawny daybreak crossed the skyline. A glance to the east showed large quantities of sunshine would belong to the day. Bryana's first look when she exited the farmhouse in mid-summer had always remained the same. As a child, an adult, and now a mature adult, she loved the fluidity of dawn and the Plains. The stream of time hadn't changed that.

Mornings on the farm always provided an emotional way of huddling with life. Time had coasted its way across Bryana's life taking her to her senior years. But the rim of earth always looked to be only an extender of things beyond. The horizon caught the light and suspended time. Or perhaps became a brief second of infinity realized.

Cows had been milked, eggs gathered, and two pots of coffee had been served to the quartet. After a scrumptious breakfast of eggs, potatoes, bacon, and homemade herb bread, the women set off on their assigned work. Both Ricki and Bryana began throwing clay while L.J. finished the morning chores. Michelle started her day of baking.

In her studio, Bryana stretched after creating an unusually large pot that L.J. had ordered for a downtown Denver art shop. They requested a variety of uniquely shaped decorative vessels, with an assortment of wild colors. Ricki glanced over, noticing the work. "It's going to be great, Bryana," she commented, transfixed. "I love the way you work. You feel about pottery the same as I feel about music. Everything."

"I like doing these wild artsy pieces. Composition is a celebration for me." Her eyes crinkled with a half-hidden smile of remembrance. "My mother made quilts – some with her own wildly imaginative style. Free-form and brazenly colored, they were. One of the women in her sewing club remarked that my mom must have been hitting the cider jug. I remember how Mom's usually quiet titter would go full force into a huge laugh when she told that story."

"It sounds like your mom was wonderful."

"She was. She loved creating. She was nourished by sewing. I loved sculpting."

"Pottery is fun," Ricki agreed.

"You don't get the same excitement when you create pots as when you create music?"

"Naw. I love working with clay, but it isn't the same as when I'm playing music. Clay is relaxing, and fun. Like a good time. Music tears my heart out, and it's required to be torn out with each chord. It's like I'd die if I couldn't ever play music again."

On Ricki's face was the expression of total truth. She would even, Bryana guessed, overcome any obstacles and hardships so that she could play the guitar. Looking back at the young, wayward musician, Bryana conceded that it wouldn't be people that would keep Ricki on the right side of the street. It would be a song.

Bryana examined her clay-stained hands. "Loving what you do is important. As long as you have something, or someone, to live for, you'll be okay. And you're talented in lots of areas."

"I guess," the young woman said. She looked down and her hair strung across her forehead like a curtain.

For Bryana there was never any question about her love of pottery. She'd used the lake mud to shape toys when she was a small child. She found the emotion of fulfillment by creating ceramics. The colors were added flavors. When she grew, it was a continuum of experimentation. She was at the epicenter of each piece of pottery she threw. There was the mystery and tension of designs on the mosaic shapes. There was a certain divinity – an inside delight, when she crafted. She could imagine that Ricki's sound of strumming was the same as her own visual experience – wonder intensified.

After throwing an assortment of pots, mugs, and artistic vases, the women worked on packing small shipping crates, and filling and firing the kilns. When the work had been completed, they exited the studio. Skies were darkening with evening's approach.

They walked to a corral then leaned against the horizontal fence planks.

Bryana commented as she gazed into the sky, "Looks like the moon is going to be howling-beautiful tonight."

"Yeah." Then Rickie quizzed, "You aren't upset because I love music most, are you?"

"Not at all. Seems like everyone has this pivotal place called a heart, and it moves around. Eventually it takes its rightful place where it belongs. You may belong to music, but you're an excellent pottery student. There doesn't need to be an emotional entanglement requiring the choosing of either. It can be a love of both. Your legitimate passion will pick your path. And it will be time-selected."

Ricki frowned then stated, "Music makes sense to me. I reflect my feelings with songs."

"And when you play, most of your music makes sense to me." Bryana failed to say that some of Ricki's music eluded her. The young songwriter didn't bring Bryana into the orbit of her soul with a couple songs. There was a disconnect, as if Ricki intended to hide out. As fine as the music, and eloquent as the lyrics were, Ricki's songs were not always emotionally shared.

Bryana gazed up at the great shawl of the clouds that hung above. That evening, she admitted, the sky was lovely. A burnished ocher sunset crossed the horizon. There were no sinister rumblings from the skies. There was only quiet that the vast, blue day had issued. "I hope L.J. got her riding done this afternoon," she mentioned to Ricki.

"When I went in to get us lunch, she had finished with the garden, and raking livestock poop. She said she couldn't wait to plunk her behind on the saddle. So I think she was planning on saddling up soon. She knew she needed to get back for the animals' final feeding this evening. So I'm sure she's back by now."

"Lots to do on the farm. Is it as bad as you thought it would be?"

Rickie rubbed her eyes. "Worse. But I'm happy." When she got to the door, she looked back at the sunset. "Yeah, it's okay."

"In Kansas vernacular," Bryana said with a chuckle, "you're getting Kansasized."

Going through the back porch, she inhaled the fragrances of herbs that had been picked, washed, and hung, or spread on large screen frames. When she turned and saw Ricki sniffing, she commented, "Herbs. Michelle dries them and packages them to sell."

"Smells good."

"Yes. After they've been dehydrated they can even become fragrant potpourri mix for sachets, or delicious cooking additives and teas. Food for the stomach or the soul, no matter, they're great curatives. Michelle always puts herbs like mint in her iced tea."

"That's her secret. I knew it tasted better than teas in restaurants."

"Herbs. That's what Michelle wants the little greenhouse for. And if you get it built before winter, she can continue selling herbs to our merchants."

"I'm pretty fast," Ricki offered. "You've seen how quick I am at tearing things down when we were working after the tornado."

Once inside, Bryana greeted O'Keeffe, "Hey, girl, how you doing?" She glanced around. "Where's Idgie?"

Puzzled, Michelle turned. "Isn't she with you?"

"No. I haven't seen her all day."

"I saw her mid-afternoon," L.J. said. "She was following Ricki back to your studio."

"But then she turned around again and went after you," Ricki said.

The women quickly ran outside, calling her. "I'm not sure where she could have gone," Michelle exclaimed. "She always stays near someone. The house or barn. The studio. Idgie's the timid one. She needs to be near someone."

Ricki rushed back into the house, over her shoulder she said, "I'll check the bedrooms upstairs."

L.J. hurried towards the barn. "I'll saddle up and search aboard Brandy. I heard shots coming from the next farm before I came inside about half an hour ago. But no one would shot a dog."

Michelle's voice cracked, "Both Bryana and I play the radios, so we wouldn't have heard the shots. But the hunting farm to the west isn't known for discriminating between dogs and deer. I'll get the all-terrain vehicle and my medic's kit."

Bryana immediately ran towards the western perimeter. As she ran, she prayed no one had harmed Idgie. Soon she heard the hooves of Brandy striking the ground and the engine of the ATV. The threesome called for the lost dog.

"Cut your engine," Bryana instructed. "Listen." Intently the women listened, cupping their ears. The nearer to the fence, the louder the whimpering was. "It's Idgie." She dashed wildly across the furrowed land then spotted the downed dog. Idgie's front leg was bleeding. She tried standing then fell, buckling back to the ground.

Michelle bent to inspect the lower leg. "I swear it's a bullet wound." She grabbed her medic's bag. Inside was professional medical and surgical equipment she had purchased so that she could keep it in her auto for emergencies. It had served her well in the past.

"Tank's drunken hunters."

As she donned the medical vinyl gloves, Michelle snapped them as they were secured on her hands. Carefully she pulled back the cuff of torn fur then took small forceps, hemostat, and scalpel from her bag. Bryana poured an antibacterial solution over the wound and alcohol over instruments and Michelle's gloves. With precision, Michelle extracted the bullet from the lower right leg of Idgie. The moaning dog let out a yelp.

L.J. and Bryana held the dog tightly in their grasp. Michelle put numerous sutures in then turned back to Bryana. "We've got to get her to the vet to have him look at her tendon. She isn't able to stand, that's for sure. She lifted the bloodied bullet from the ground and handed it to Bryana.

Bryana's fist balled around the bullet. She felt an anger that made her eyes water. "Those crazy fucks!"

Ricki sputtered, "I thought you didn't curse around Michelle."

"At times it's more than fitting. Come on," Bryana countered. "Michelle and I are going to get her into the vet. And the two of you go back to the house and stay with O'Keeffe. No backstreet cowgirl justice, Ricki. After we've taken Idgie in, *I'll* deal with it. Do you hear me?"

Ricki brooded. "I could have a meeting of minds in no time if you let me have five minutes with that flipping Tank."

Tenderly, and with care, they lifted the dog onto the ATV. Her body was limp from the blood loss while trying to crawl back to the house. As Bryana carefully directed the ATV to the driveway, Ricki had raced to the garage to pull out the SUV. They loaded Idgie into the backseat then Michelle crawled in beside her mate.

When they arrived at the animal clinic, the veterinarian quickly responded to the emergency. Carefully, he examined Idgie's leg and paw. He'd noticed that a small part of her paw pad had also been clipped by a bullet. He attempted to find the range of mobility in the leg. X-rays would be needed, but he would not attempt to re-suture the dog. The stitches were holding, and he said the wound shouldn't be bothered further unless there was excessive seepage. Although the bleeding had been stopped, if it were to begin again, they were to bring Idgie back to the clinic. In three days he wanted to re-examine the wound, to check for tendon damage and infection. He fitted Idgie with a leg brace, so she wouldn't put pressure on the leg, and it would help to keep her from toppling.

Before the women left, he indicated to them this wasn't the first 'accident' that had happened near the hunting reserve. Although he didn't know these women, he didn't hide the fact he was perturbed. He looked away, adding it probably wouldn't be the last accident. He strongly suggested making a call to the sheriff about their complaint because he planned on reporting the incident to both Animal Control and the local humane society.

The return trip to the farm seemed like forever. When they arrived, Idgie had happily ingested the antibiotic and pain medication that had been wrapped in a small square of cheese. Her head nodded drowsily. Ricki begged for her to be allowed to sleep in her bedroom. Bryana objected, saying she didn't want the schnauzer on the bed because she might forget and attempt to jump off. In fact, she said, the dog needed to be on the ground floor to get her easily outside. Ricki said she would put blankets on the floor and lay down with her in the living room.

Bryana asked Michelle to call the sheriff and tell him to meet her at the Roland ranch. She was going alone to talk with Tank about Idgie. The three women disagreed with Bryana's decision to go alone. Finally, she looked at Michelle. "Michelle, maybe L.J. should go. Idgie needs one of us with her. And you're the nurse. You should stay."

"What about me," Ricki protested.

"Nope. I doubt if I could hold you back from a fistfight with Tank. You stay with Idgie and Michelle."

Bryana admitted to herself that she'd love to see Tank get beaten to a pulp by a scrawny, young woman.

Chapter 13

Bryana and L.J. drove to the neighbors. She glanced at L.J.'s expression. "Ready?"

"Why bring me and not Michelle?" L.J.'s frown was deeply carved.

"I'll do better on my own. It's my hometown. And I went to high school with Sheriff Norm Myers."

"And?"

"And he's a good man. We were close friends. I specifically requested Norm, and not his son Pete."

"And?"

"And nothing else."

As she pulled into the driveway, Bryana was immediately followed by Sheriff Norman Myer's vehicle. She introduced Norm and L.J. as they walked towards the large farm house. Off to the side was a lodge that worked independent of the farm house. Room and board were offered to the hunters. Behind was a larger barn, and garages.

Norm suspiciously eyed L.J. The very tall, slim sheriff was uniformed in his neat, well-pressed beige twill. Unlike his son Pete's messy appearance, the gray-haired, blue-eyed man looked immaculate.

With a soft-spoken manner, his well-modulated voice began, "If Tank's clients are giving you trouble…."

"My dog was shot by one of the partying clients," Bryana interrupted. She pulled the bullet from her pocket. With her hand outstretched, she spoke, "This came out of the front leg of my dog. The vet will be reporting it. What those hunters do is Tank's responsibility."

"And I'm sure he'll take care of it."

Tank had slammed shut his backdoor and was stomping towards them. "Norm, they're causing trouble. Always picking." His puckered face was brimming with rancor.

Bryana stabbed him with her glare. "My dog was shot. Shot! I just took her to the vet. She is wearing a brace so she can stand. She could have been killed," Bryana's voice rose.

"Tank, here," Norm pointed in his direction as he spoke, "is going to take care of it. Vet bills, pain and suffering, and any additional therapy the dog will need. He's going to be taking care of everything." Norm's shoulders lifted as his head tipped. "And Tank is going to assure me it won't happen again."

"Norm, they're hassling me. Making trouble. It could have been anyone." Tank's sinister lips curled, yet anger shaped his taut face.

Norm put his hand up, with palm facing Tank. "Easy, Tank. It wasn't anyone, was it? We've got the bullet extracted from the dog. If you want I can have every weapon on this farm taken in to have ballistics tests. And I'm betting we'll have a match somewhere," Norm speculated. "Now, you're going to give me the name of the hunters at the lodge."

"I don't want them bothered."

Norm's back went even straighter. "Tank, I don't care what you want. Someone from your property shot a gun and injured a family pet."

"Okay," Tank quickly acquiesced. "I'll take care of it. One of the hunter's bullets might have gone ricocheting onto her property."

"And you'll take care of the costs, and promise to keep your bullets off, and away from the Hays property. Compensate them for time. And apologize."

"Yeah, sure." He glowered at Bryana. "Sorry. Send the bills to me, and I'll have Alice drop by money in the morning. How's a thousand for pain and suffering?" His swagger had returned.

Bryana remarked, "Fine. I'm more interested in knowing my pets and livestock are safe. And Tank, you have three children running around. What if it happens to them?"

"We take care of things here," Tank blustered. "Alice watches them."

Bryana and Norm traded glances. Norm scratched his head. "Okay, I'm not gonna take you and your hunter in. I am going to write up a report. Document it. But it better never happen again. And you see that Bryana gets money tomorrow, and the vet sends you all the bills. You call the vet and tell him you're paying. All charges. Follow up treatment - the works. Paid for by you. Got it?"

"Yeah." Tank whirled around and stormed back to the house. The screen door slammed with a thud.

"Case closed," Norm said with a smile.

"He should have been hauled in. And the shooter needs to be reprimanded, and if alcohol is on his breath, needs to be jailed," Bryana insisted with a glower. "Tank got away with it again."

Norm's head sunk as he looked at his roper boots. "There's not much I can do about an accident, Bryana. If the hunter is drunk, Tank will pay one of his hired hands to take the blame. You know that. The best I can do is what I'll do. I'm making a report. So it will be documented. If it were ever to happen again, it would make my job easier. I would be able to see that he didn't get away with it. As it is, he could have denied it, refused to pay. Then you'd be waiting months for a court date. Pay a lawyer. Probably end up with nothing. This way you'll at least have your vet bill taken care of. The vet is expensive. Could be several grand before it's over. Unless you have that kind of money on hand."

"You know I don't."

Norm's gestures were uncomfortably wooden. "Then Tank didn't completely get away with it."

She squinted, examining him. "And if Tank wasn't Vince Roland's son?"

"It isn't easy living here. It's Vince's town. You know that. Everyone is beholding to him. For jobs, for loans, everything."

Bryana's jaw clamped tightly for a moment. "And he's a contributor to your election coffers? He backs you. Norm, when we were kids we wanted to do good things. The right things. That's why you went into enforcement."

His glance skittered sideways. "I keep the town safe. I do what I can about Vince's sharp elbows." Norm turned and walked towards his vehicle. Over his shoulder he muttered, "Good seeing you, Bryana."

L. J. gave a punch into the air. "What a gutless wonder friend. You got the old el paso on that deal."

"He's got a lot to contend with. Norm's daughter and her kids are back living with them. His youngest son is still in college. He's got responsibilities."

As the women got into the SUV, L.J. exclaimed, "That's no excuse for not jailing both Tank and the offending hunter."

"Norm is a good man with constraints on him. He knows the deck would be stacked against us if it did get into court. And he's right. I'd never see a penny. At least Idgie will have the best medical attention. I won't skimp on my pets, and that vet didn't sound as if he would cut a pricing deal for Tank."

"What was your relationship with the sheriff? School days, my ass. He had the hots for you, didn't he?"

"Norm had a crush. My emotions were confused. I didn't know who I was." She watched the sheriff's vehicle slowly crawl away from the house, and edge onto the county road.

"That's why you wanted Michelle to stay home. She would have picked up on it."

Bryana started the engine, and directed the SUV towards the farm. "There is nothing to pick up on. We ran around together. When he started acting as though we were sweethearts, I skedaddled."

L.J. snickered. "I believe you, but Michelle might not have. As I see it, if you would have put out for him, he might have arrested the hunter responsible for the shooting."

"L.J., if I would have allowed the romance to continue, and hurt him, he probably would have let Tank shoot me."

The women laughed together. Then L.J. bantered, "He might have encouraged Tank and his six-guns to shoot an entire tribe of lesbians."

As they pulled up to the farmhouse, Bryana's mood became more serious. "L.J., I once thought Norm was the most gallant person I knew. We were about six or seven. We'd play swords with dried, stripped sunflower stalks. He always let me win. Any game, he enabled me to feel I was just as powerful as a man. Even when he was a child, he was sensitive."

"He should have pistol-whipped Tank. *That* would have impressed me."

Bryana chuckled. "L.J., thanks for helping. For coming here and helping."

"We've always been around for one another. And I'll do what I can. Well, I'll do everything but slaughter the livestock. This city girl isn't into beheading fowl."

"You've met Buffalo man."

"Sure. Rolf Jarvis. Saw him this afternoon and he loved Brandy. He seems to hold you in high regard. What's Rolf got to do with chickens?"

"When chicks are born, we keep some to become laying hens for eggs, and send the others to Rolf. He raises them, executes them, and his wife dresses them. Sells them, and give us as much freshly dressed chicken as we can eat. Like the trade we have allowing him to grow hay and he gives us buffalo meat. A good trade. And I don't need to slaughter. But Rolf and his wife are much more pragmatic."

"I like the guy. And he isn't just another townsperson beholding to Roland."

"That's why he's having so many money problems. He can't borrow money from Roland's bank - or anywhere. I guess Norm is right to worry about crossing Vince Roland."

"And your chances of joining the safety of the Roland tent were lost when you and Sarah Roland had your fight?"

"Sarah told the town I'd made a pass at her. He isn't likely to do me any favors. And my father's loans were with astronomic interest rates attached. That's why we got what loans we could from Michelle's credit unions. It took everything we had. So here we are." Bryana got out of the vehicle. "Let's go in and see how Idgie is."

"And devour some vittles and pie."

"That too," Bryana answered. Indicators in her voice showed how exhausted she'd become. She never minded the physical work. It was the emotional tension that leveled her. "It might be best to walk away from all this. I always thought I could depend on Norm."

With total candor, L.J. replied, "Leaving would mean the Roland family wins again. Just like when you were falsely accused all those years ago. You turned tail and ran."

"The situation was filled with emotional content I barely remember now. And if I were able to run from this, I would."

"Bryana, you know what a contentious bitch I can be. I've been your friend for centuries, and I like a fight. I'm at your side. Don't even consider running." She delved, "You aren't going to give up, are you?"

"Let's have some chow."

L.J. moved more quickly. "Hell, yes. This lusty woman has a hole-in-the-tummy hunger."

Bryana inhaled deeply. "And I can tell from one sniff, the air is being perfumed with Mom's award-winning pies. Produced by Michelle." Bryana's shoulders hoisted upward as she led the way to the kitchen. "Michelle is making a bourbon with pecans special. Maybe I'll just have the bourbon."

L.J.'s head flew back as she laughed loudly. "After today, I'll try as much bourbon as you can pour, and as much pie as you can slice. And slathered with whipped cream."

Bryana's eyebrows lifted in amazement. They danced for a moment before she asked, "I'll bet you never dreamed country life would be more exciting than the city?"

Slapping her leg as she giggled, L.J. answered, "This excitement I can live without. You should have given Sheriff a little. He might have insisted on upping Tank's offer to two grand."

Embarrassed, Bryana answered, "It wasn't like that."

"Sure. I remember taking an art course in college. One lecture was about a colony of artists. They had this event called *exquisite corpse*. It's where different artists each add element of their own individual slant to the painting. The canvas was filled with dozens of additions by different artists."

Bryana turned to her friend, "And this relates how?"

"It seems like the town people around here are only participating by filling their own canvas in their own way. That Norm had it bad for you. It wasn't just a crush on his part. You gave him the hards."

Laughing loudly, Bryana then shook her head. "When are you going back to Denver?"

Chapter 14

Bryana and Michelle sat silently as they ate breakfast. Upon waking they'd both claimed they were famished. Yet, by the time they sat to eat, they had lost most of their appetite. Their usual morning chipper chat had been switched off. The kitchen seemed as vacant as their hearts. The house itself seemed naked of joy. The shooting of Idgie had taken up their conversation.

From the kitchen table they saw Ricki on the living room floor with her arm wound around Idgie's midsection. Michelle whispered, "Ricki was up twice letting Idgie out last night. I doubt if she had much sleep."

Bryana slapped down her toast, "None of us did."

"In spite of what happened, I got some sleep," Michelle disputed. "Idgie is alive, and she'll be taken care of. We have that to be thankful for."

Bryana's words hammered with anger. "She may never walk properly again. She can't stand without the brace. And can barely stand with it. Idgie is such a good dog. She's never put a paw wrong. O'Keeffe is more adventurous. I remember when we got her I used to call her Calamity O'Keeffe. But Idgie has always been cautious and sweet."

"She limps with the brace, but at least she's moving." Michelle smiled. "I remember when you called O'Keeffe that. I remember when we got her and you wanted to name her Basket because 'Basket' was the name of Gertrude Stein's standard poodle. But I insisted on O'Keeffe. Your pottery colors remind me of O'Keeffe paintings. Then we got Idgie, and I insisted we name her Idgie after the main character in the movie, *Fried Green Tomatoes*."

"You were always better at names than I was. Seems like a lifetime ago."

Bryana's thought retreated into the past. She recalled watching the movie and hearing the theme song. She'd thought of Sarah when "I'll Remember You" played. So many times Sarah would enter her thoughts. Even now, confusion was like a mechanical puzzle. Bryana knew she loved Michelle. But there were remnants of her love for Sarah. She dared not admit that Sarah had always been on the edge of her love. Making certain thoughts of Sarah pointed in another direction, Bryana wondered if she'd ever allowed herself to examine it all that closely. Or if she ever would be able to objectively observe her own emotion.

"Yes. Bryana, Idgie will be okay." She stood. "I've got the pie and bubble bread orders for the Buffalo Plains Café ready. And you've got the tankard orders for the Brass Rail complete. Maybe you can deliver everything, then drop by the bank and deposit those business checks. Oh, and the cash Alice brought over here first thing this morning. Why do you think Alice brought cash rather than a check?"

"She probably gave us a thousand in cash so it wouldn't come to the attention of Vince. I'm sure he rides herd financially on Tank's business. Vince would have questioned what the check to us was for. Tank doesn't want his father involved. My best guess. A check or two for vet bills he can cover by saying they were for one of their hunting hounds."

"If Sarah was this wonderful person you grew up with, why doesn't she object to her son running an animal shooting gallery?"

"She's being a good little wife. Vince runs the show. She became subservient to his wishes when they were married. Before they were married. She changed." Bryana took a final swig of coffee.

"A person's heart usually doesn't change."

"That's what I thought until last night. Now I'm convinced people do change. My friend Norm has changed, too. Power corrupts."

Michelle studied the gold glint in her lover's brown eyes. She'd always thought of the gemstone tiger's eye when Bryana's eyes sparkled. But that twinkle had turned to a flash of anger. "Bryana, you sound so bitter. Maybe it's time for us to pack up."

Bryana flushed "And do what? And go *where*?" Bryana asked too loudly. Her fist unclenched. "L.J. thinks we should battle on. Ricki has been a tremendous help. She's even getting started on building you the greenhouse for herbs. But you're right, maybe we should leave."

A timer bell interrupted her thought. Michelle got up to take steaming pies from the oven. "Between our bakery orders, selling veggies and herbs, and your pottery sales, we can survive here."

"Maybe."

The cinnamon fragrance from the apple pies steamed. "I love baking. I think it's because it reminds me of your mother. Always taking something out of the oven. She was always so happy. And your father, always so jovial. When we came here last year, I had this dream about our lives becoming like theirs. Difficult times once in a while, but a sweet freshness about the life. I thought our life could be a duplicate of theirs."

"We're together. That's about as much resemblance as I see."

Ricki rolled over, yawning loudly. She jumped up. "Bryana, sorry I slept in. I'll go get ready and make the deliveries in fifteen. I just need a quick shower to wake me up."

Bryana stood and walked to where Idgie was sleeping "Ricki. Have some breakfast first. I'll be outside packing up the tankards and getting bakery goods ready to take in."

Ricki rushed up the stairs, two at a time. Michelle joined Bryana. She knelt to pet Idgie. Idgie gave a slight moan when she tried to get up. "She isn't standing with any stability," Michelle said. Examining the brace, she added, "Could be the brace isn't right for her. Looks a little too tight. Rolf is terrific making leather goods - and all from his buffalo hides. Maybe he could work on a brace with a padding that wouldn't hurt Idgie. Maybe he might try adjusting this brace. I'll give him a call."

"Good idea." Bryana stood. "I'll be out packing the order."

"The pastry order is ready." She paused. "Bryana, it will be okay, won't it?"

Bryana picked up the stack of boxed pies on the kitchen counter. After delivering them to the SUV, she packed the pottery mugs and tankards. She then went back inside for the box of bubble bread. She found there were two large boxes. "Tess is selling the dickens out of the bubble bread."

Michelle exclaimed, "Unbelievable. Tess called to double the order. She's selling it right off the café's display shelves, as she puts them out."

Ricki rushed past the women. She quickly gulped down the food, then grabbed her cup of coffee and downed it. "Ready."

"You're looking dapper," Bryana commented.

Ricki's shoulders lifted as she stood. "You said I got to make an impression on our customers."

Michelle's quick glance at Bryana barely tapped her. "Any customer in particular?"

Ricki had taken the box from Bryana and made her way to the SUV.

Michelle's shrug was one of futility. "I'm not getting my questions answered today."

"See you later, Michelle," Bryana said. She kissed her spouse's cheek.

"You didn't answer if you thought it was going to be okay. Are we going to be able to save the farm?"

"Michelle, life is a difficult prospect. Maybe there's some logic to how a creator makes a world, dispenses fortune, and experiments with us. It's like we test the land. We take vacant, crusted fields and determine their future. We allow fields to lie fallow. We cultivate them when we believe it to be time. We rotate crops. And we can't predict anything at all with any certainty."

Bryana looked out the kitchen door across the rolling greenery, the meadow, and the small lakes. If the wheat was a bumper crop, she would not only be paid what Billy Dreher had agreed to, but the bonus would be a tidy sum. If the hay was mowed, and there was an excess, there would be additional money from that as well. If this patch of earth they owned was lucky, they would make enough to get them through.

The thought remained. Year after year, her father had tended the land, yet storms, insects, and an assortment of other misfortunes had put Anthony and Victoria in debt. And now she understood the peril involved when the gamble was against fate.

Just as her parents had taken their stewardship over the land seriously, Bryana knew the land required reverence. She probed the contents of her heart. During the last years of her father's life it had all gone wrong. Her eyes flickered, watering.

Michelle's voice interrupted her thoughts. "Well, I believe we'll make it be okay."

"Some legacies are more wonderful than others. Chance," Bryana ratified.

Farming and pottery were both teachers of chance. The potter shaped earth into contours of beauty. It was left to the love of those born of earth to till the landscape carefully. One of the connecting links of humanity was love of home. This had been her parent's home. The textures of the land, as well as life, were universal. She was determined to begin an internet study about farming. Fate selected the where, when, and why of life. She had to be a quick study and learn what her father's lifetime had taught him.

And how could Bryana possibly answer a question about life in Buffalo Plains? People like the town's folk, and the Rolands, were not so easy to interpret.

Tolerance, she speculated was formed with balance and fragility, but also required accuracy. It was very nearly incomprehensible to believe these people who were blessed with earth, a solar system, and a universe, didn't understand, nor did they appreciate, tolerance. It was overwhelming to believe that all the mystery sprouting from previous discoveries had not taught people how to accept, and not to neglect one another. Magnificence was ignored. Bryana wondered if her anger wasn't making her ignore the better parts of what she had been blessed by. As well as the area's fine, decent, and truly loving people.

On the trip into Buffalo Plains with Ricki, Bryana's mind rushed to digest the thoughts. She was glad the conversation between her and Ricki was sparse. Finally, on the outskirts of Buffalo Plains, Ricki gave a sigh. "Think they'll be anymore shootings near your property?"

"If Tank could line up every Sapphic in the world and execute them, he would. And he'd have a cheering section. But I don't believe he's purposely trying to harm a dog. And with us it's as though he wants to joust. Make us miserable. After all, he thinks years ago I attempted to sully his mother. So he has it out for me. But the hunters had harassed my father for years. They'd come on our property, shooting, swearing, littering. However, I don't believe Tank relished the idea of bothering my father. With me, well, he relishes tormenting me." Her words were terse. "They enjoy witnessing our pain."

Ricki's eyebrows arched. "Why did Tank's mom accuse you?"

"As I've said, it was complex." Bryana halted a moment. "Sarah's accusation was that I came out to her. Sarah was engaged. She told Vince. That's why I'm worried about your being around Gloria. I don't want it blowing up on you. Or on us. It's the one thing that would force me to send you back with L.J. I won't have Michelle subjected to additional hatred. She'd lose the café account as well. Just don't even think of Gloria."

"You gotta admit Gloria's got a body that would excite a stone."

Bryana chuckled. "Just keep your rocks in your pocket."

"Scandal in Buffalo Plains. But with Gloria it isn't as if she's engaged to some land baron, slash, financier, with all the power. Her mom runs a café in a poor befuddled town."

"Gloria is a prize, so her fans would be aiming for you. It would change everything if you screw this up for us."

With a slow, teasing cackle, Ricki said, "When I was a kid, I was told to ignore hecklers. The one bit of wisdom my mom left me with. When I was about five or so she took me to kindergarten. I can remember her squeezing my hand when we passed by a bunch of neighborhoods boys. They were calling her names. Whore, drunk, druggie - all the names that fit her. And that was when she told me to ignore hecklers. She was in prison by the end of the school year. I was in the social service's maze for a while."

"What happened to her?"

"Musta died. That's what one of my foster parents said. I wished I was the one dying, but no luck. For a while I ended up with an aunt. I figured it would be better. But she was a hood rat, and never choosy. One of her creep boyfriends pestered me. That's when I got tough. This one guy was terrible. I stabbed him when I was about twelve or thirteen. Too bad it didn't kill him.

Stabbing him, even in self-defense, was my introduction into juvie. After that I hit the streets. I hated the world so I was soon back in jail. I'm not proud of what I've done in my life. And I won't make excuses."

"You're trying to get it together now. Now is what matters." Bryana pulled off the side of the road onto a small exit. The vehicle slid to a stop atop gravel. "See that wheat? It's just the right shade."

"For what?"

"Come on," Bryana got out of the SUV and made her way to the side of the field. She leaned and pulled several handfuls of wheat heads. She separated the stalks from the spikelets. She crumbled the grassy cape husks from the nuggets of green wheat seedlings. As the grain fell into her palm, she examined it. "Perfect. Not too ripe. Nice and soft."

"Perfect?" Ricki looked bewildered. "A bunch of weeds."

"Wheat. Green wheat, and just about to turn gold. You're going to like this." Bryana rubbed more of the wheat heads between her hands and dislodged many of the small kernels. She then whisked off the chaff wrappings. Her hand swung up to her mouth, and she began to chew. "Gum. Chewing gum. Very, very refreshing. Growing up, we used to chew wheat gum whenever the season allowed it. I still do."

Ricki tried it. Her frown deepened, and then lifted as her lips burst into a smile. "Wow, this is good."

Bryana handed the young woman some sheaves of wheat. "There you go. A couple of packs of free gum. Ignites the sensations."

"Yeah. Does Michelle and L.J. know about this?"

"Sure. They chew it whenever possible. The crops dictate how ready the wheat is, so it isn't an all-season fix. The wheat in this field is perfect. I'm a devotee of it."

"Thanks for showing me." As she chewed, Ricki's lips automatically lifted to a smile.

Bryana's gaze scanned the crystalline sky. She pointed out the wild sunflowers at the rim of the road. "Sunflowers are the state's flower. This county is named Tinpsila. That's the Lakota Indian name for sunflower. When the Lakota tribes roamed, there was more wildlife. There was an abundance of white tail deer, mule deer, antelope, and elk. The skies were filled with bobwhite quail, pheasants, and water fowl." Bryana paused. "The Native Americans fought to keep their land. Their property was never assigned to any one person. It belonged to them all. And they probably chewed the wheat gum just like we do."

Feeling torn inside, Bryana wondered if she had any right to the deed for this land. Now all she could do was to fight to see that it was regarded with complete reverence. And fight for her right to live in Tinpsila County.

Chapter 15

Bryana drove the SUV into town. Both women were silently preoccupied. After finding a parking space in front of the Brass Rail tavern, Bryana muttered, "Let's get this over with, then on to see if the Buffalo Plains heartthrob is at the café. Gloria is certainly eye-candy, however, remember, its no-touch candy."

Charlotte Gottschalk waved the women in. "Got your check ready. Sorry to hear about your dog. Will she be okay?"

"No way of knowing yet. But I hope so," Bryana answered.

"A few of the hunters were in last night. When Tank came to town to pick them up, he told us all that you called the sheriff on him. But Tank *handled you women*. My cousin's kid is as big a jackass as his old man. And Vince is a total jackass."

"One of the hunters shot my dog. Tank is paying for the vet bill. But Idgie could have been killed. I worry about the Roland kids. Tank says I should watch my dogs, and Alice would watch the kids."

Charlotte's eyes shifted uncomfortably. "Between you and me, most of the time she's in no condition to watch anyone. Says she takes meds for her headaches, but I've heard..." Charlotte's fist went up to her mouth as if she were tipping a bottle. "Well, she's often got that little vodka-sodden slur. Then there's her wobbly, sugary smile. I can tell she's doing something. She goes from flighty, to messed up, to semi-conscious."

"Michelle suspected she might be..." Bryana repeated Charlotte's motion in the air. "Imbibing. Maybe Sarah can help her."

"Sarah. Jeezus, Sarah is too busy campaigning against you. She claims you're stirring trouble for her son. I saw her on the street early this morning. She warned me."

Bryana leaned nearer. "Warned you?"

"Yep. Said I shouldn't be selling your mugs. Some of the fucking hunters go back with full sets of the mugs, and Sarah claims I'm dancing with the enemy by encouraging you and supporting your business. I told her I'm making a good percentage off sales, and I'm not going to stop selling them. She said she'd see about that and huffed off. I'm sure I'll get a visit from Cousin Vince soon. He'll piss and moan."

"And?"

"And I'll tell him to go fuck himself. 'Cause I don't need his sermons. And if I wanted Sarah's lectures, I'd go to a university." Her sputtering converted back into a grimace. "Tank and Vince both make my skin itch. Even when he was a kid, Vince was obnoxious." She spoke his name as if she were spitting the word. "What a prick."

"I don't want you falling out with your family because of doing business with me."

"Bryana, they aren't family. I'm the black sheep. That excludes me. They treat me like a tramp. For years Sarah didn't even acknowledge me. She married that pious pisser and she became his duplicate version. If I were her, I'd rather be molested by a cage of gorillas than marry Vince. The thought of Vince deflowering anyone makes me gag. And Sarah is definitely a gorgeous woman. She could have done better."

"I hope you'll be careful. Vince is on the City Council. In fact, he's the leader of the town tribunal. You might find yourself charged with not obeying the city ordinances."

"Naw. Tank needs somewhere to take their clients," she broadcasted with a sweep of her arm. "He needs this bar as a bit of hometown mystique for the hunters."

Bryana suggested, "It's also his bank. How about if you need a loan?"

"I'll go next door to Payton. I've slept with the president of the Payton Bank. Left him smiling for life," she explained with a loud howl. "Hussy as I am. Sarah once called me a floozy. She told me I had no business acumen like the rest of the family. But this place is making money. So I must not be too ignorant."

"Char, just watch out for the Rolands. They can make your life miserable. I'm a good example of that."

"Sarah's a gossip. Her club women probably knows all there is to know about you. Shit, she lives for all those old crocks. She has undoubtedly told her group of gadabouts all about how my indiscretions blacken the family name. But I only consider it advertising." Charlotte's laugh lifted like an elevator. "The old biddies will complain about me to their hubbies. The husbands will beat a track down here to the bar. New customers!"

Bryana and Ricki were still giggling as they headed across the street to the Buffalo Plains Café.

When they entered, Ricki placed the box of pies on the counter. "I'll get the other boxes," she said as she turned to go out the door.

Tess greeted Bryana then quizzed, "Didn't your dog have some trouble?"

"One of Tank's hunters shot Idgie," Bryana answered. "She was on our property."

"Not the story I got. Sarah Roland was in earlier."

"She wasn't there. I was." There was an edge to Bryana's voice. "And Idgie was downed on my property. Michelle removed a bullet from her leg."

"Sarah said Tank told her your dog was on their property, and attacked a hunter. He shot."

"Either Sarah or Tank hasn't got the story straight. And I know Tank had the story straight because he's paying the vet bills. Idgie has never gone off property. And she's never, ever attacked anyone. If she would have seen the hunters, she would have dashed home. Just as we found her, pointed in the direction of our house. She was obviously trying to outrun the crazy hunters next door."

"Sarah tends to take Tank's side." There was a moment's silence. Then Tess cleared her throat. "Sarah seems to think I shouldn't sell your bakery goods."

"It's your business. And if you have a loan with Buffalo Plains Bank, I'm sure Sarah and Vince will make it their business."

"I know what you're saying, Bryana. I don't plan on cutting off your orders. Lots of repeat business. I'm only telling you because of something she said."

"Yes?"

"She asked if your premises had been inspected by the state food inspectors. I'd call that a very subtle hint of her intentions."

Bryana swallowed hard. She had a sinking feeling inside. "Thanks, Tess. Sorry if I was a little sharp. I just found out from Charlotte that she also had a threat from the Roland clan. Sarah warned her to stop carrying my pottery."

"What did Charlotte say? And please don't tell me in her exact language."

With a glint of amusement in her eye, Bryana answered. "She declined Sarah's request. And I don't use much of the same language Charlotte does."

"I would hope not. She's got a foul mouth and a bad reputation. But for whatever reason, I still like the woman. When she comes in mornings for a coffee and pie break she always makes me laugh. Even if sometimes the things she says are very off-colored."

As soon as Ricki had completed loading the bakery items, she sat. Tess poured her coffee. Very nonchalantly, yet purposely, she asked Ricki, "Did Gloria tell you about the Art Fair being on Saturday and Sunday?"

"She didn't mention it," Ricki replied stealing a quick glance at Bryana.

"They'll be blocking off the street, and setting up stalls. Bryana, you ought to bring your pottery and set up a table. Bet you could sell some of your work. I'm going to be glad for the boost in sales from having all those people walking by."

"Sounds like an excellent idea. Thanks for mentioning it. Don't you think it's a good idea, Ricki?" Bryana questioned sternly.

Ricki mumbled, "Yeah." Her eyelids nervously batted as she looked away.

"In fact, we'd better get home and pop some clay into the kiln." Bryana marched to the door then turned. "Thanks, Tess. Thanks both for the information and for continuing to market Michelle's pastry and my pottery. We appreciate your patronage."

The minute they stepped outside, Ricki stuttered, "I'm just talking to Gloria on the phone every so often."

"Ricki, I've got all kinds of troubles. Money troubles. Keeping my pets and livestock safe. Storms. Now we've got to get licensed to bake on our property. I don't need to worry about you, too. Tess has an observation tower keeping track of her daughter. And her little conversation just now was to let me know she knew about your phone call. It was to put me on notice."

"I'm not laying her."

Bryana swung around, facing Ricki. "And don't. Unless you want to move and find another job. Just don't! And as long as you're around me, understand I respect women. So learn it now. You *do not lay* women. And you never share sexual expressions with someone you don't feel amazingly wonderful about. And you respect that act, just as you respect that woman. You make love with someone. You do not *lay* them. That is what insecure, immature jocks do to impress their buddies."

"I shouldn't have said it. I do respect Gloria. And respect love. I'm not sure I've ever loved anyone until I got here. I'm not sure I even knew anything about love until I saw you and Michelle."

Bryana wanted to continue her tirade, but Ricki's eyes had flooded with tears. "Don't mess up. Just don't. Please."

As Bryana whirled back around, she was standing face to face with Sarah Roland.

It shocked both women. Sarah's strawberry blonde hair had become gray at the sides and temples. It was styled in medium-length waves. Her lustrous green, nearly aqua eyes had been perfectly made up, yet seemed to hide a tired secret. Dullness nearly extinguished the once expressive bright sparkle. All excitement seemed gone. The woman was medium height, thin, and attractive. Her mouth opened then clamped shut. Both women's eyes held a lingering gaze.

Bryana rapidly moved out of her way.

Sarah scoffed, "Trying to replicate the perfect gentleman?"

Pain instantly covered Bryana's face. "You're married to the perfect gentleman. I'm just being kind."

Sarah's eyes narrowed. "Kind! Pestering my son is your idea of kind?"

"Sarah, one of the hunters shot my dog. It was on my property." Her heart was racing, and her mind seemed clouded as she continued looking into Sarah's eyes.

"Lies. That's all that comes out of your unscrupulous mouth."

"We both know that isn't true."

"Just leave my family alone!" Sarah's words were insistent. The biting intonation echoed as Bryana turned quickly.

She walked to the SUV with Ricki following after her. Ricki asked, "You okay, Bryana?"

"Yes." She opened the door then turned back to Ricki. "Why?"

"You looked like you wanted to slam your fist into the door."

"Now you've seen my angry face. You don't want to see it again." She turned the ignition key with a vengeance. "And now you've also met my biggest mistake."

"One of my pals used to have a saying I kinda liked. It's about a person being proud of her own droppings. Well, that's what I thought when I saw Sarah Roland. A real snob."

Bryana gave a sharp chuckle then her mood returned to pain.

Ricki was wise about reading expressions. She sat silently on the ride home. She was glad Rolf Jarvis was standing in the driveway talking with Michelle. She quickly excused herself, saying that if they were going to be ready for an art show, they would need to throw clay, dry clay, glaze clay, and bake it. The young woman nearly ran to the studio.

Rolf welcomed Bryana. "Hey, you need to get a six-shooter for Idgie so she can fire back next time."

"There better not be a next time," Bryana issued her warning. As she examined Idgie, she saw the dog's brace had been reworked. Idgie went to her side. Bryana knelt, taking Idgie in her arms. "She's standing and walking better now."

"I opened up the sides of the brace, it was way too small. Put leather and soft lambskin padding around the leg, then buckled her up. When you dress the wound, make sure you leave enough space for your thumb to reach inside the brace that's over the wound. Needs more air to heal."

"Thank, Rolf," Bryana said with a nod. Tufts of sheepskin edged the brace. "Idgie looks more comfortable. She's such a love."

Rolf rubbed his chin. "You're dogs aren't the usual farm dogs."

Bryana explained, "No. Not hybrid. They're our first non-blends. One of our friends ran a poodle and schnauzer rescue. Talked us into taking one then the other. To me a dog is a dog. And no dog deserves to be shot."

"Makes me wanta to go over and pound Tank," Rolf said with a husky fist lifted. I can't stomach that guy. And his whiney wife."

"Now they're going to try to shut down our bakery business," Bryana divulged.

"What?" Michelle nearly shouted. Her face was flushed.

"Seems like Sarah Roland paid a visit to both Charlotte and Tess. Both told her to get lost. Tess told me Sarah inferred the state inspection agency would be looking into our license."

"For selling homemade breads and pies?" Michelle yelled.

"Yes. We need a business license and we'll need one from the state's food inspection agency."

Rolf clapped his burly hands together. Before Michelle could say anything, Rolf jumped in, "You're in luck. I know the people at the agency. Worked with them when Ella and I were getting into our home enterprise with selling buffalo meat. And Ella's goat cheese. Didn't know it 'til I applied, but I'm even related to one of the big shots. I'll give him a call this afternoon. See if he can get things in motion for you."

"You're the best," Michelle exclaimed.

"Yes," Bryana agreed. "And in the meantime, I'll go into the town hall and get a business license for our pottery, bakery items, herbs, and veggies. Then we'll have a sales number to include our taxes quarterly. Makes it better than estimating at the end of the year. Probably saves money since I'm squeamish about owing the government. I'm sure I'd overpay."

"Just remember," Rolf said with a huge grin, "grocery items don't need a sales tax. Just what profit you make off 'em. If it's like the buffalo trade, it's precious little to compute," his sputter and goodbye was heard as his Ford truck rolled away from the women.

"Licensing," Michelle said with a deep inhalation. "I'd forgotten about that. We've been so busy with everything else."

"I hadn't forgotten," Bryana admitted. "I was waiting for the time when a final decision about staying was made. I guess we just made it. I'll return to town and apply for the license and business name applications. As an umbrella name does Dawson and Hays suit you?"

"Yes," Michelle agreed with a grin. You sure you don't want Hays and Dawson?"

"Let's go alphabetically." Bryana walked back to the SUV. She felt the gravel under the tires as she drove down the length of driveway. During the fifteen-minute trip to Buffalo Plains, Bryana's thoughts were how cornered she now felt. She wanted, above all, Michelle's happiness. With a sudden recall, she felt how secure her life had been. Now, it was all up for grabs.

She viewed the cuticle of sunflowers bordering the county road. She thought about talking with Ricki about the flowers. She failed to mention that sunflowers reached for the sky, and for the sun. For all they were worth, they reached and stretched. The bright golden faces turned, following the sun throughout the day as they made their way. Bryana squinted. Words snagged in her throat when she tried singing along with a cowboy song. The words forming were stained by her emotion. There was the hollowness of wondering where to go next if they didn't make it. Or if Michelle was unhappy.

Her own face was a mask of bitterness. Her expression reflected her spirit. She could remember being happy - safe. But events churned, and questions regarding their future were being slung at her mind. Her dreams had collided with a dismal reality. Wanting, as well as planning, for a retirement of ease, and security, was not to be. It would be hard fought, and perhaps harder won, if they were even to be able to exist through this unknown. Tears swamped her eyes then drizzled down her cheeks. She tried to pull up the memory of clasping Michelle that morning. Inside Michelle's embrace was the only place Bryana now found comfort. Even that was another question.

Chapter 16

Bryana had not expected so many tented stalls at the Annual Arts Fair. Between wandering artists and strolling shoppers, the street was filled. As if the town had brightened itself, colors popped from stalls, flags, and signage. During early hours of the morning Bryana and Ricki had set up their stall in the closed-off main street of Buffalo Plains. They'd placed their pottery on card tables and planks that resting on crates. Deciding to leave Idgie behind with Michelle and L.J., they had brought O'Keeffe. The poodle sat patiently, behaving as passersby visited, bought pottery, and sometimes petted O'Keeffe.

Bryana had talked with Ricki earlier over breakfast about not having contact with Gloria. And absolutely no intimate contact of any kind. Ricki had agreed, and while setting up their art fair booth, reiterated that she would behave.

Bryana attempted to cheer up the conversation. Small talk was never easy for her. "Good crowd this morning."

"I'm not crazy about these people," Ricki whispered. "Small towns creep me out."

Amused, Bryana said, "Cities sometimes creep me out."

"I'll bet this town hasn't got one single mezzanine level."

Bryana leaned back against the canvas of the folding lawn chair. "Not much fancy in these parts, but I care about this town because it's my hometown. And they had a mezzanine in the old movie theater. It's been closed up for years. A sign of the times."

"Glad I didn't live back in those days. I like modern. A dance room filled with women. An auditorium cheering for concerts. Things going on."

"The lure of the crowds," Bryana said with sarcasm. She then thought about the modernity brought to clay by Ricki. Ricki's work was dynamic. It was precise. Bryana thought about her own work as sculpting a part of nature. She would take designs from dried creek beds where soil erosion had splayed lines. She attempted to make the lyrics of her soul a visual. Ricki's free-style work was more colorful than Bryana's. And just as she'd been influence by the younger potter, Ricki had toned down many of her color schemes that blared out too loudly and discordant.

Bryana picked up a plate that Ricki had created. "You did an amazing job with the contrast. I really like the wineberry, peacock blue, and seafoam colors against the brick-colored background."

"Yeah, it's a little muted. I held back on hitting the color too hard. This gives the plate a certain tenderness."

Bryana agreed, "Yes. Somehow it seems you're letting your soul become visible. Color is already the loudest voice of pottery, you've softened it in a loving way. Excellent."

Ricki was introspective for a moment then said, "I still like my wild smack-down colors, but now it's like I'm going from hard rock, to a quiet love song."

Catching the implication, Bryana changed topics. "Hope we sell lots of our trinkets. Whatever we don't sell today, L.J. said she'd take back to Denver with her tomorrow. She plans to return here next weekend. I sure appreciate her help. Yours, too."

Ricki leaned against a light pole. "L.J.'s a good woman. Found me where I'd been lost at the side of the road. Figuratively. And she took me in."

"She sure seems to relate to the folks around here."

"L.J. said she'd talked with one of the hunters yesterday when she was horseback riding. She said he told her that he felt badly about how some of the hunters reacted to the dog shooting. Tank boasted that they only got five points for shooting a dog. And for weeding out the lesbian nation next door, ten points were offered. The hunter said he didn't abide by that kind of talk. And he wasn't a fan of Tank's. L.J. claimed the hunter didn't seem to be an unreasonable guy."

"A guy who calls himself a sportsman and goes hunting on a stocked pasture isn't my idea of reasonable. And the hunter is supporting Tank and his miserable business. How atrocious to make a joke of injuring a dog!"

"L.J. told me that the hunter won't be back next season. He was putting his firearm up."

"He was probably infatuated with L.J.," Bryana joked.

In the momentary quiet, Bryana's thoughts rose above the festival's empty chattering. This was her town, yet she felt adrift. There was a harshness of not belonging. Since being outted by Sarah, her life in Buffalo Plains was that of visitor – an unwelcomed visitor. Sadly, she loved many of the people. She admired their spirit, and their fight to survive. Being outted in such a vicious way seemed so much worse than a small glitch. Bigotry was ultimately a reason she was losing everything now. She was certain her parents, although loved, had been shunned. That had not only emptied the coffers of her parents, but also hers and Michelle's. The productivity of everyday of her entire life was now seeping away. Disappearing down a drain of hatred.

She felt worse about Michelle losing her future. Her lover had always been a sacred part of Bryana's.

Throughout the day sales were brisk, and both women chatted with customers. Most were friendly towards the women, and interested in the pottery. From time to time Ricki disappeared, but had potty break excuses, and taking O'Keeffe for her walks. When she returned, she threw herself into selling pottery. Bryana suspected Ricki might be meeting Gloria on her breaks, but didn't mention it.

Bryana heard the familiar ragged laugh of Billy Dreher. Her neighbor to the north made his way to the stall. He had changed from his normal overalls into freshly laundered plaid shirt and denims. The man of over seventy wore suspenders, and a belt. His bushy grey hair stuck out of the battered western hat. Beneath his feathery eyebrows, his constantly suspicious olive black eyes formed a squint as he greeted her. "Figured I'd be seeing you here," Billy said as he lifted up a tankard. "They got these here tankards at the Brass Rail."

"Yes. For the time being," Bryana said. "There was some trouble with Tank Roland, and everyone is being encouraged not to do business with me."

"The hell you say. Tank troubling you, eh? I heard about your dog."

"I called Norm when a hunter shot my dog. My dog was on my property. Sarah is now on a campaign of shutting down my pottery sales, and Michelle's baking."

"Sarah never has seemed like a happy person. Not deep down. Worse since she married that tight ass," Billy observed. "Even when she was a kid she was never happy the way you were. You'd come over and help my missus. God rest her soul. You and Mrs. Dreher would milk those goats."

"I recall she taught me to make goat cheese." Bryana's smile was one of remembrance.

"Yep. But Sarah would trail along and do nothing but moan. Tank's a louder moaner, but he got her temperament."

"I always thought she was nice," Bryana said with regret.

"She got worse when she married Vince. Mrs. Dreher knew people. She used to say love is the glue of life. Well, Sarah got herself glued to Vince, and she really became miserable. Marrying a fella like Vince Roland would make anyone as snarly as a mean ole coyote."

Bryana recalled the little girl companion she knew. Sarah's shyness made her appear to be unhappy. The girl Sarah never spoke unless spoken to, nor would she go out of her way to talk with anyone unless she liked them. But Bryana knew her friend as being enthralled with the farm. Sarah saw splendor in nature, animals, and would often laugh at Bryana's antics. "That was years ago. Guess we all see people in differently. Maybe all folks are an acquired taste." She glanced away, then asked, "How's the wheat?"

"If the weather holds, it's gonna be a bumper crop. Won't make the two of us rich, but it will sure help fill our coffers for the year." Billy gazed upward. "Glad the clouds haven't parked overhead in a while. Gives us a chance. It would be great if the crop came in with good prices."

"It would be wonderful if the crop came in, and with good prices."

"Yep. Land can be harsh before the harvest. But so far we're ahead of the pests, the weather, and the grain prices. Looking good." He paused, replacing the tankard. "That woman visiting you, L.J., chatted with me. She says the crop looks beautiful and is like an exquisite woman." He chuckled. "She's a character. Sure can ride her horses like a pro."

Bryana laughed. She turned to share a smile with Ricki only to notice her young student wasn't around. "L.J. grew up on a horse ranch down in Florida. Horses and cattle actually. She learned to ride before she learned to walk."

"Said she's going on back to Denver tomorrow, but will be returning often."

"Yes. She'll be helping out weekends. Help us get caught up. We've been getting behind with our chores."

"The other one, Ricki. Is she sticking around over winter?"

"Probably. To give us a hand. And I'm teaching her pottery technique. She's a good kid," Bryana defended. "A city kid."

"I knew she wasn't from these parts."

"She's a tad rough on the exterior, because of a terrible childhood."

"Like you said, folks are an acquired taste. Friends are like wheat. You keep the grain and toss out the chaff to nourish tomorrow. It's all perishable in the end."

As he walked away, Bryana interpreted his words. He was suspicious of Ricki. She was city. Brash at times, she looked and dressed differently. Before being distracted by several customers, she had looked around the market for Ricki.

Relieved when she saw Ricki coming from across the street with two lemonades, Bryana was also guarded. The lemonades were in Buffalo Plains imprinted paper cups. Her eyebrows lifted. "I wondered where you went. We have cold ice tea in the cooler."

"I was thirsty for lemon."

Bryana took the lemonade Ricki offered. "Was Gloria working with her mom?"

"Yes."

"When your response is monosyllabic, I worry."

"She's twenty-one. I'm twenty-two. We're both of legal age."

"Age isn't the problem. Perception in this small town is the problem. Gloria is ready to graduate after summer school. Tess said she just needed a few hours of classes. But trust me, it doesn't make it alright to hit on her."

"How about if she hits on me?"

The moment of silence was probably making Ricki think how it would be inconceivable to Bryana. That wasn't the case. "Maybe it's time you think about going back to Denver." Her words were brittle.

"Whose side are you on?" Ricki questioned.

"I'm siding with my salvation. With everything Michelle and I have worked for. An entire lifetime of hard work is in jeopardy."

Ricki threw down the small coin apron she'd been wearing. "Fuck it all." Ricki walked away, her anger flaring. "Just fuck it all."

"Aren't you going to help me pack up?"

Ricki stormed away without answering. Bryana began wrapping and packing the pottery. After about fifteen minutes, she stopped. She'd heard the scuffle of Pete Myer's boots as he ran towards the alley across the street. Some instinct directed her to follow him. Her feelings had been correct. She heard Tess give a keening wail. In the alley behind the Buffalo Plains Café Bryana heard voices becoming more clamorous. As she turned the corner, she saw Tess screaming at Ricki and Gloria. Her heart sunk.

"What the hell's goin' on?" Pete demanded.

"I came out to check on what was taking Gloria so long…" Tess caught her sob and her voice trailed. "Those two. Arrest her." She pointed towards Ricki. "She's a pervert."

"Mom, you can't have someone arrested for kissing," Gloria countered.

Ricki glanced sideways to see Bryana approaching. Her eyes lowered. She became white. "Mrs. Walters, it wasn't anything…" she began.

"You get out of this town. We don't want your sort." Tess's hysterics exploded when she viewed Bryana. "Bringing your scourge into this town. Shame on you."

"Tess, I apologize for Ricki's actions. I had her word that she wouldn't cause trouble. She'll be leaving to return to Denver in the morning."

"Bryana," Ricki argued, "why are you going against me?"

"You broke your word to me."

"It was my fault," Gloria screamed. "I'm tired of this pretense. That's the real lie. Pretending to be accepted. Mom, it was my fault. If Ricki goes back to Denver, I'm going with her."

"You need to graduate," Ricki bartered. "Then decide what you want. I'll wait for you."

Tess pulled Gloria's arm. "You get back inside. Finish your few weeks of classes. By then you'll be over this crush."

"Do as your mother says," Ricki encouraged. "My life has been one mistake after the other. Finish school."

"I'll finish," Gloria said through her tears. "Then I'm moving to Denver." Storming away, Gloria slammed the door.

Pete's hands were on the shelves of his hips. "You aren't nothing but trouble, Bryana. I ought a throw that punk in jail for disturbing the peace."

"I'm less happy about this than you are." Bryana reached for Tess's arm. "She'll be leaving in the morning. I give you my word. And my word means something," she said loud enough for Ricki to get her drift.

"I don't want more problems," Tess said. "Let's just forget it. No charges, please." She was clearly embarrassed. She glanced away. Flinging hands up and down before burying them deeply into her apron pockets, she uttered, "It's over now." She turned to Bryana. "I don't hold you accountable," she said slowly. "You and Michelle have been great to work with. That girl. She's trouble."

"She's had a difficult life," Bryana began.

Pete broke into the conversation, "Don't start that crap with me. Bad lives don't make people act indecent. Mrs. Walters here don't deserve *your* problems."

"My problems," Bryana said with a glare, "are no longer a crime in this country. I'm not sending Ricki back to Denver because she committed a crime. She's leaving because she made a promise to me, and she broke it. Bigotry and intolerance are stupid. And stupid converts to hatred. I'm not apologizing for what I am. I'm not sending Ricki back because of who she is. *You got that?*" she asked as she pressed nearer Pete's face. "We authenticate our human qualities by how we treat one another. Not by who we love."

Pete backed up as Bryana passed him. He yelled after her, "We don't want these kinda brouhahas in this county. She's not accepted around here."

"She was accepted by me until she broke her word." Bryana whirled back around. She moved towards Pete and stood nearly toe to toe. "And you are a blustering, bigoted disappointment to your uniform. Your father is decent. A couple weeks ago, you started in on me. Saying how I'd let down my parents. They would have rather had a good-hearted lesbian than a prejudiced, close-minded screw-up like you."

Tess quickly said, "Let's drop this before the whole town gets in it." The few people and Pete disbursed.

To Tess, Bryana apologized, "I truly am sorry if anything I've done has brought problems for you. We are all the collateral damage when our lives meet up with hatred. Check out what the Bible says about the evil of hatred."

Tess waved her hands. "I know what the Bible says. And my kid was good until I let her be a cheerleader in high school."

"A cheerleader?" Bryana frowned. Her head tilted in disbelief. "What did being a cheerleader have to do with it?"

"She got all uppity and snotty, so I suggested softball to her."

Bryana nodded in silence. Her eyebrows lifted in disbelief. She walked away, not wanting to turn around.

Ricki had finished packing up the SUV. When she saw Bryana, she got into the vehicle. Bryana said, "Thanks for getting the pottery in."

"Just glad we sold so much. Less to pack back up. Bryana..."

You're going back to Denver in the morning. I expressly instructed you not to mess things up for us. We trusted you. Now you've called attention to all this in a public display. Michelle and I do business with that woman. Or we *did* business with her. Now, who knows? What I do know is that you promised me. I had your word."

"I'm sorry. She flirted around, and then I flirted around with her. One thing led to another. I didn't seduce her. Or bring her out. She's been out since she started college. She told me."

"What you did with her isn't why I'm upset. You broke a trust. You betrayed me. And you had fair warning. Do whatever you want, but don't implicate us. We have enough problems, Ricki. We don't need this, too."

Ricki's head dipped. "That's fine. I'm tired of all these rules and regulations. All these bigots. Fuck 'em all."

"That's your answer. Rather than being an example to change the rules, you want the rules changed for your benefit. Damn it, I want to alleviate this mess I'm in." She looked up as they entered the driveway. "See that barn roof. I want to crawl up on that roof and re-gild the worn weather vane. Paint it as bright as the center of the sun. I can't. I'm limited. There are things in life we can't do. Restrictions. We've got to live with them. We can't risk other people's livelihoods without consequences. We can't break our word without it costing the trust that we garner. And we can't always reconstruct the world as we would like it to be. Michelle and I have worked our entire lives. And we're broke. Sixty is a hell of a time to begin again. And that's what I'm doing to that fine, loving woman." Bryana's eyes begin to fill.

"I'm sorry," Ricki apologized with a droning whisper. "I'm sorry. Is there anything I can do to make it up?"

"What you've done illustrates a disregard for everything Sapphics are fighting for. We need restraint, and we need the respect of those who hate us and vote their hate." Her glance strayed. "Alley fights are a thing of the past. Or should be. We need to demonstrate our responsibility and honor."

Ricki's face was pinched; she put her head down in her hands. Tears sprung through her fingers. "I never wanted to hurt you, Bryana."

After the SUV eased up to the garage, Ricki got and opened the trunk. Bryana barked, "I'll tell Michelle and L.J. you'll be returning to Denver. You get the pottery loaded into L.J.'s Jeep."

Bryana looked in the kitchen then decided L.J. was probably riding one of her horses or might be in the barn. As she entered she saw only Michelle. Before she could begin, Michelle exclaimed, "Good news. I trapped the tortoise shell cat. She came in here to deliver her kittens. Look, a nest of mewing newborns." Michelle pointed down to the corner of the enclosed stall. "After the kittens have finished their nursing cycle, we'll get the mama fixed and set her free again. There wouldn't be any way a shelter could find a home for a feral cat. But if we keep enticing her to hang out around the barn, she might just stay out of danger's way. Maybe we can find homes for the kittens. I'll begin working to tame them."

Another expenditure, Bryana thought, then corrected herself. It would save both the mother and the kittens, and there was no price on that. And her lover was happy about the kittens. Problems and pain seemed etched in the crevices of the entire future. Pensively, Bryana said, "Michelle, we have a problem."

Michelle glanced at her spouse as she closed the stall gate. "No sales?"

"We nearly sold out. The problem was that Tess found Ricki and Gloria behind the café in an embrace, slash, kiss. Created a scene, and naturally Pete got into it."

"That dries up bakery and cafe business with Tess."

"A good probability, yes. And Ricki will need to leave with L.J. in the morning. I gave my word. And unlike Ricki's word, mine is good. She is no longer welcome on this farm."

"Bryana, they're kids." She took Bryana's hand. "Raging hormones. What did Tess say?"

"She took it better than I thought. She said she had no problem with us. Maybe we have a chance at keeping her account. But we won't have it if we don't send Ricki back."

Bryana didn't wait for an argument. She exited, and saw L.J. leading her mare back to the barn. Telling L.J. was difficult. L.J. responded by agreeing her friends had no choice but to send Ricki back. L.J., however, promised to be back the following weekend to help out.

Ricki had gone to her bedroom, and didn't appear for the makeshift dinner. Bryana went back out to her studio and began throwing clay. As she examined some of the mugs that Ricki had made, sadness came over her. Ricki had talent, and so many great qualities. And she knew she could have taught her a great deal.

When all the lights in the farmhouse went out, Bryana quietly entered. She tiptoed directly to the bedroom. Michelle was sound asleep. Bryana took a quick shower to get the clay and dust from her body.

As she slipped into the bed, her fingers traced the pillowcase that her mother had made. There were flowers embroidered, and the pillowcase edges were crocheted lace. Michelle had found a chest filled with needlework Victoria Hays had created. Michelle insisted that they use them. She'd said that the pillowcases and beautiful linens should live in today. Come alive with their beauty and usefulness. Bryana was happy that they pleased Michelle. There was so little pleasure in Michelle's life, Bryana considered.

Her eyes clamped shut, and her sleep was restless. It wasn't long before she heard the squeal of tires, and the clatter of gravel. Then there was a loud screech of breaks. Quickly throwing on her denims and a blouse, she made her way to the kitchen door. As she opened it, she saw Gloria's car.

Gloria catapulted out from the driver's side. She hurriedly went to the passenger's side. She flung open the door. Bryana approached. "What's going on?" she quizzed.

She needn't have asked. She saw Ricki's lame, limp, discordant limbs eased from the car. Her face had been bloodied, her body beaten. Blood had splattered and drizzled down her shirt. "Oh, no," Bryana murmured, taking one of Ricki's arms while Gloria took the other.

"I didn't know where else to take her," Gloria said through her tears.

"What happened?"

"A few guys saw us. Started hassling us. We only wanted to meet so we could say goodbye," Gloria said. "A couple of the guys I've seen around, but they're older than I am. And there were a couple guys I didn't know. I'm sure they were custom-cutter harvest hands. They kept messing with us. Shoving Ricki and calling us names. Ricki shoved them back, and they began beating her. I screamed, but no one heard us."

L.J. had heard the commotion. She burst through the door, cursing, "What the hell?"

Michelle then appeared. She had immediately called the sheriff's department. When she arrived outside, Ricki was on the ground, moaning. She'd brought her medic's case. As she examined Ricki, she sighed. "Looks like no bones broken, but her face is a mess." She poured alcohol on a pad and began swabbing the blood. "Ricki, talk to me. Can you tell me if your head was injured?"

"Just my face," she answered slowly moving her bloodied lips minimally. "Don't call the cops. It was a shoving match until I threw the first punch when they called Gloria a name."

Bryana stated, "They've been called."

Thankfully Norm Myer arrived. Brusquely he asked, "She going to need a hospital visit?"

Michelle looked up at him. "I don't think so. I can clean up her lacerations. She's battered, but I don't think a doctor would do more than patch her up and send her home to rest."

"I have no home now," Ricki said as her eyes clamped shut. "Only an unfriendly world." Her head sagged.

L.J. patted her shoulder. "We'll get you back to Denver tomorrow. You have a home with me there."

"Can you identify the men?" the sheriff interrogated.

"Naw," Ricki answered. "I don't want to press charges. Why bother?"

"We don't like women getting beat up in Tinpsila County," Norm answered. His brows dipped. "Women should feel safe around these parts."

Stoically Ricki said, "I didn't know who it was." She then coughed and sputtered, "No charges."

Norm addressed Gloria, "And did you know them?"

"I didn't recognize them."

Norm turned back to Bryana. "My job here is done. If she changes her mind, let me know. I'll arrest them."

"Thanks, Norm," Bryana said with a solemn nod. "I believe you would."

He pointed to Gloria. "Unless you're planning on staying, I'll follow you home and make certain you get there safe and sound. Your mama's probably worried about you."

Gloria went to her car. "Ricki," she yelled back. "I'm moving to Denver when I graduate. Wait for me."

"I'll wait," Ricki called to her with encouragement. "I'll wait."

L.J. and Michelle helped Ricki inside. Bryana watched as the vehicles rolled down the driveway. The only sound was the snorting of engines as they moved towards the country road.

Bryana turned to see a shaft of light from the bedroom window. Tears collected in the corners of her eyes. The night felt frail, and she felt frail.

Chapter 17

It was early when Bryana crawled from bed. She pressed the crumpled sheets back. She had tossed and turned for the few hours she attempted to sleep. Although she'd hoped to be quiet enough not to rouse her lover, Michelle awoke and began fixing breakfast. Ricki could be heard packing.

The fragrance of bacon filled the house, and a wafting aroma of pancakes on the griddle blended. As Bryana sat at the table pouring maple syrup on buttered pancakes, Ricki crossed the kitchen to the door carrying her belongings.

Michelle insisted, "Ricki, you can load your things in the Jeep later. I've got a plate ready for you. Just sit down and have breakfast. When Ricki eased into the chair, Michelle looked under the patch over Ricki's eyebrow. "We'll redress your face before you leave. How's the bruised midsection?"

"Fine." Ricki was curt. There was an obvious estrangement. It disturbed both Bryana and Michelle. Ricki's usual hearty appetite was slowed by pain. Chewing with precision, she winched several times.

"Your jaw hurt?" Michelle asked.

"I hurt all over. But I been beaten up enough before. So I try not to notice. That's what you do. You pretend it's nothing."

"Ricki," Bryana began, "I wish things were different."

"Me, too." Ricki stuffed a forkful of scrambled eggs into her mouth, gulped to reduce the chewing of the food. She then stood. She grabbed her canvas bag before limping towards the door. "Thanks. Thanks for everything," she said as she left.

"Can't we let her stay?" Michelle questioned.

"Michelle, we can't risk losing everything we have. We trusted her. I told her a dozen times not to mess up." Tears swamped Bryana's reddened eyes. "If the townspeople didn't hate her before, they hate her now. She's in danger around here. Besides, I promised Tess."

L.J. came down the steps yawning. As she sat, she noticed the faces of her friends. "Look, I apologize for bringing her here. I should have known, or suspected, she might be a problem. Kids that age have firecrackers going off in their panties. Add to that, she's a kid and hasn't ever had any discipline. And maybe she never will. I'll keep her with me, and maybe she'll turn around."

"L.J., we didn't want for it to turn out this way," Bryana shook her head. Her eyes were beginning to tear. "I was hoping we could influence her. She's a good worker. She helped with the tornado cleanup. After helping the townspeople, she acted as though she was invested in the good of the community. I believed she'd turn around."

"Maybe she will," L.J. said as she began to devour the eggs, bacon and flapjacks. "I hope she will."

"And I'm sorry," Bryana said as she cleared her throat. "I didn't want to let *you* down. It was a favor to you. And if the situation here was different, we could take a chance. We have no more chances left. Her staying would endanger us all."

L.J. blew into the mug to cool the coffee. She then took a quick sip. "I know. I'll be back next weekend to help you out. The women at the shop can deal with Ricki for a couple days. We'll try to prop Ricki back up. But none of us can afford to risk our tranquil golden years bailing her if she isn't prepared to change."

Defending Ricki, Michelle said, "From everything I've heard, she has changed. She's drug free. She worked her ass off. And she's got a sweetness about her with the animals." Her jaw clamped tightly for several moments. "She's in love. And it appears not to be one-sided. That's not a crime."

L.J. rubbed her eyes. Her hand lingered on her temple. She questioned, "Do the two of you think Gloria will head for Denver after she graduates?"

Michelle and Bryana explored one another's faces. Both nodded affirmatively, simultaneously. "I imagine she will," Bryana guessed. "Gloria isn't as she's perceived to be by the townspeople. She isn't a fickle airhead teasing the boys. She just doesn't want them. When she touched Ricki's face last night, she'd made her determination."

"I never saw myself as having a home for runaways," L.J. spoke softly.

Bryana clenched her fist several times, as if exercising her hand. "I never saw myself becoming homeless. And that's what we're facing. We're in our early sixties. Starting over isn't as much of an option." Her voice reflected a foreboding.

Michelle acknowledged, "I suggested clemency. But I guess I know it isn't realistic. Not for us. Not for her. I agree it's too dangerous for her in Buffalo Plains. If she were to stay, some of the bullies would no doubt start taunting her. She'd get knocked around. Or worse. There is so much animosity and Ricki is taking the brunt of it. Remember what happened to Matthew Shepard. We aren't safe at all. They've joked about shooting us. They could have killed Ricki. We're dealing with liquored up hunters being riled by the Rolands. It isn't safe."

Bryana added, "Yes." Her contemplative frown lingered throughout a long pause. "I know Gloria loves working at the café. Ricki was getting along fine with working on the farm. In the best of worlds, Gloria could finish school, work with her mother. And Ricki could work here throwing clay. They could live a nice, loving life together in the sweetness of a small town. Be like the kids we never had. And would have liked to have had."

Michelle picked up her plate and carried it to the sink. She turned with a sudden exposed anger. "It would be nice. But it can't happen. I'd hoped things were changing with this new generation. I'd hoped maybe it might help by being out, by leading an exemplary life, and walking in Pride marches."

"It has helped. We've got to believe it has," Bryana disputed. "It just hasn't helped Buffalo Plains yet."

L.J. pushed her empty plate away. "Your breakfasts are terrific. And I've met your neighbors. It is changing."

"Just not fast enough for Ricki," Bryana said. Her words sounded like desperate angry thuds.

L.J. laughed, "Don't count her, or us, out. We can't lose our resolve, and we sure as hell can't lose our belief things will improve." She stood, hugged her friends, and spoke. "Look, I'll be watching after Ricki. She'll be okay. Well, we'd better take off. The Colorado state line isn't that far, but the outskirts of Denver are a long couple hours."

"Thanks, L.J., and your horses will be fine," Bryana promised. "We'll say goodbye to Ricki, and then I'll milk the cows and get the milk cans down to the mailbox."

L.J. frowned, "I was wondering where you took the cow's milk surplus."

"Fill the cans and take them to where they'll be picked up by one of our neighbors. They have the dairy equipment to pasteurize and all. A small dairy farm. They have a herd, and then pick up from the neighbors. We get free dairy products, and make a little money on the side. See, that's what I mean. Out here in the middle of nothing, we all need one another. We can't afford to antagonize each other."

"Too damn bad your neighbors to the west don't know about that."

"They'll eventually find out," Bryana forecasted.

The goodbyes began stiffly then Ricki crumbled into Michelle's arms. "I'm sorry, I let you down," she said with a sob. She looked at Bryana. "And I let you down most. And I owe you so much. Sorry I messed up."

Bryana's smile indicated she understood. She then rumpled Ricki's hair. "I hope things turn out for you. You're a good person, Ricki."

When they saw the Jeep pull onto the country road, there were no words between Bryana and Michelle. Both women simply went about their chores independent of conversation.

Bryana took a moment to lean against the corral rail post. Mornings on the plains were euphoric. Sunshine hugged the blond meadow fields. A gust of hot wind would assist in drying the wheat for harvest. Tears brimmed in her eyes. She considered life here would be lovely if the women weren't under constant barrages from the west, and if their finances weren't overwhelming.

For Bryana surveying the land was an act of love. Many considered the levelness of the plains territory to be uninteresting. She loved the sun-drenched horizons that reached forever. And the dots of different color were extraordinary. She remembered the artist Gauguin's quote about color being a kind of music. The Kansas plains blended with the easy lifting wind to become a fully Technicolor lullaby.

Observations were memories coming alive across the plains. Farm life was much more difficult when pioneers braved the land. Bryana thought, we are passengers on this planet and the trip is our time. We, she considered, are the caretakers. She felt to be falling back in love with the landscape. If not for the problems, her little corridor of life would seem perfect. Solemnly, she considered the many times since her return that she had fallen back in love with the farm.

Her saving grace was that she had never fallen out of love with Michelle. And yet, she wondered what the residual feelings about Sarah might be. Bryana had worried about that for decades, and it never resolved itself. She had some spiritual belief that it would all be okay. That was the way of life, she mused. Miracles are. They just exist.

No matter what faith, belief, or theory about earth, the very complexity of earth's formation had to have been a miracle. Bryana recognized that when she worked.

Michelle patted the mint and herbs as if they were a symphony of inhaling grandeur. The wildlife astounded her with not only their resilience, but their intensity.

Bryana's whimsical grin creased the corners of her mouth. Then it had converted back to a dour, sad expression that broke when a flock of birds lifted in the shape of a V. They landed in the thickets surrounding the far eastern pond. Those birds knew where they were going. She knew at this moment they sensed danger. There was more safety for them on the farm's eastern side. But if she and Michelle couldn't save the farm, there would be no safe area for the waterfowl.

She twisted her head to view the other small pond. The crick in her neck was from sitting over her potter's wheel. It was another reminder of her age. All the work would be worth it if the farm could be saved. The women were working for the wildlife, and themselves. It was so there would be a safe haven.

A flash of yesteryear visited. Bryana thought of the large pond with such love. When she was a girl her father took her rowboat fishing. Her mother would fix sandwiches and iced tea for their lunch. Bryana and her father would spend hours fishing, and laughing. Now, she thought, it would be nice to have the time to fish. She headed towards the studio with her memories somewhat lifted.

By early afternoon she needed a break, and Bryana returned to the farmhouse. She inhaled the cinnamon fragrance. "Smells luscious."

"Tess called."

"To cancel her orders?"

"No. To place an additional rush order for pies and bubble bread."

"Ah ha, that's why the fragrance of cinnamon is in the air."

"I'll have everything completed later this afternoon. Would you mind dropping the order by? Oh, and while you're in town, maybe you could take Idgie by the vet for an exam."

"She's doing great with her revised brace. I just hope it will heal properly."

"She might surprise us with a good vet visit this afternoon. Do you mind running to town?"

Bryana's grin stretched across her face. "You mean you're sending me to face Tess, *and* to get any bad news on Idgie's leg?"

"That's right, soldier. Marching notice." Michelle laughed. "If Tess was troubled by us, she wouldn't be calling in an order." Her arms enclosed Bryana. "You might not get scolded too badly."

"She likes the money she's making off the bubble bread. But I'll get an earful, I'm sure." Bryana kissed Michelle's temple.

"Maybe. Idgie is rocking around like a hero. Still a little gimpy, but she's running nearly as fast as O'Keeffe. I saw them this morning. The brace revision seems to be helping."

Bryana sighed. "When they're out, we need to watch them every minute."

"We keep better track of our pups than the Rolands do of their children. I saw little Jon and one of the girls out by the fence. I gave them some bubble bread. They're not bad kids. Jon is sweet when I'm handing out bubble bread."

"Let's not encourage them to hang out. Next thing Tank and Alice will accuse us of overloading their kids with glucose."

"It isn't the kids' fault. And they said they were hungry. I don't think Alice fed them lunch. When I asked what they had for lunch, they shrugged their little shoulders."

"Michelle, why do you always see the good in people?"

"Maybe that's what they show me."

"Tank and Alice?"

"Tank is terrified he isn't going to make himself a man in his father's eyes. Alice, well, she's sort of a victim trying to escape. I believe pills and booze might be her crutch. And the kids are enduring it all."

Bryana concurred, "You're probably right."

"People around here are mostly kind and good-hearted. Like your parents."

Bryana's nod was neutral.

Chapter 18

Until mid-afternoon, Bryana worked glazing and firing pots. When she glanced at her watch, she realized she needed to get ready for her trip into Buffalo Plains for two stops she would rather not be making. After cleaning up, she hauled the bakery items into the back of the vehicle then carefully helped Idgie onto the blanket-covered backseat. She then drove cautiously, with as few bumps as she could manage, into town.

Grappling with her dislike of confrontation, she figured she would get the bakery goods delivered first. Tess was huddled over the counter sipping coffee. She looked up with eyes circled in red. "What a night," she muttered. After pouring a cup of coffee for Bryana, she sighed deeply. "What is Gloria thinking? She doesn't look like a..." she paused, reconsidering what she was about to say. "You know, a gay woman."

"She doesn't look androgynous like Ricki, no. But that means nothing. People are what they are."

"She's doing it to pay me back for being a strict mother, or maybe because I worked when she was small."

Bryana reached then brought her hand back to surround the coffee cup. "Tess, think about it? What benefit would there be for her to pull a switch inside her and *become* gay? I don't blame you for wanting her to be straight. Being lesbian is a difficult life. But if it's what you are, it's impossible not to be yourself."

"She played with dolls when she was small."

"Gender identification is so bogus. Look, Tess, I can imagine you're fighting this because Gloria is your child. And I'd do the same. But there just isn't any benefit for a person *selecting* to be lesbian. You come in to this world tainted with original sin, that's bad enough. But the indelible *sin* is being born how you were born. Homosexual. So you become a sinner. Then, add to that, you become a criminal in some people's minds. And when I was coming out, we *were* criminals. Thankfully that has changed somewhat."

"I've never chased anyone out of here 'cause they're gay."

"And that's good. But some people do chase gays out. And think about it? You become alienated — often from your family and friends. People you've loved all your life. You get ridiculed. You get harassed. Being straight is easier. *Unless* you're Sapphic. Then it becomes impossible or becomes a mistake. How you handle this is up to you. You've devoted your life to raising a daughter. And she's a good kid. It would be sad if you were to lose her now."

"You think she's going to leave after she graduates?"

"I don't know. I just don't know. One thing I do know. If you turn your back on her, you'll both suffer."

Tess stood. With her counter towel, she roughly swabbed the Formica top. "I'm suffering plenty right now. What if she sticks to this? I wanted grandchildren. I worked when Gloria was growing up and never got to do all the things with her I wanted. My mom took care of her, and I figured I'd be able to have lots of grand-parenting time. Now what?"

"That's still possible. But if you insist she deny who she is, it is probable that she'll be unhappy. No matter how many children she has." Bryana thought about Sarah. She imagined Tank had brought very little, if any, happiness to Sarah.

"What did your parents say when they found out?"

Bryana breathed in deeply. "We never really discussed it. I'm certain they knew, and they accepted it."

"And what about Michelle's parents?"

"Her father died when she was a child. Her mother, Jersey, was supportive. When a couple of the rough juveniles snickered and called us names, Jersey faced off with them. She told the boys to shut the — well, she told them to shut up." Bryana grinned. "She told the mouthy kid she would turn his testicles into wind chimes."

"Oh, my," Tess stammered.

Bryana explained, "And when Michelle suggested we deny it, Jersey wouldn't let us hide who we were. She said we shouldn't let society make us artificial people. Don't become castaways because folks with an inferiority complex didn't approve of us. We should ignore the bad, and appreciate the good people. For years gay people have hidden. We've dressed to please others. We've even used encrypted passwords to know one another."

Tess said with a sliver of hope, "Maybe my Gloria will change back."

"Maybe. But in all honesty, it isn't probable. No more probable than if you were to change to being Sapphic."

Looking embarrassed, Tess paged through her checkbook. Hastily, she signed a check for the order. She handed it to Bryana, along with another order. "I'm sure blowing through that bubble bread. It's improved business. They come in to buy something off the bakery counter, and end up having breakfast or lunch. Tell Michelle thanks."

Bryana smiled as she tipped her head. "I'll tell Michelle."

Walking away, she felt sadness. Her feet were heavy, as if she were wading through rubble. By the time she reached the SUV, Idgie had fallen asleep. Bryana hated to turn the ignition key and wake the schnauzer. Starting the car, she rolled the windows back up and put on the air-conditioning. Idgie's head remained down, and she continued sleeping.

As Bryana approached the vet's office, she roused Idgie. "Time to check out your leg, girl."

Thankfully, it was a good report. There was some damage, but the veterinarian's opinion was that it would heal nicely. There might be a slight limp, but nothing that would impede Idgie. His final admonition was to keep her out of bullet range. Dogs should not be targets. Then he amended his words to add, "No creatures should be used in a killing game for sport."

He mentioned that he'd received a check from Tank Roland. That meant if there was permanent damage, Bryana would have legal recourse. Tank had accepted responsibility by making the payment. And follow-up appointments would be paid by Tank.

Bryana told the doctor about Sheriff Norm Myer's directive. There was little Norm could do about Tank's business. But he could and had insisted Tank pay all damages. The vet said he would be carefully watching Idgie until she was completely healed. And he would be sending all-inclusive invoices to Tank.

Once home, Bryana reported the good news to Michelle. The orders for pies and bubble bread were safe. Idgie's recovery looked good. When they were about to be seated, there was the sound of a truck pulling up. "Just when everything was looking positive. What the hell does Tank want?"

Michelle looked out. "His grimace could be a Halloween monster's mask."

Both women stepped outside. "What now?" Bryana asked as her fingers tightening into fists.

"Why are you women feeding my kids?" he stormed with his excessive jowl sputtering.

"Michelle gave them bubble bread. They said they were hungry. For god sakes, Tank, this isn't the kids' fight. They're hungry little kids."

"I don't want you feeding them. Jon told me you gave him candy bread. He can't keep his trap shut. Blabs like a woman."

Michelle stepped towards him. Her eyes burned with anger. "You are an absolute pig. You're a sexist. Your business is a disgrace. You're off partying and drinking with your *clients*. And you and your wife are woefully neglecting the kids."

"You deviant! Don't dare start with me or my family!" His serpent-like glare was pure rage. "Damn you two dykes to hell." He paused as his anger accelerated. "You'd better watch it. You saw what happened to the city dyke. Got the crap beat out of her."

"Word got around quickly," Bryana spat back at him. "Those men were waiting for Ricki. Since you know all about this, you probably hired a couple of the local hooligans and some harvest hands from the southern counties."

"Watch your accusations!" he bellowed. He gritted his teeth into an enamel scowl.

"And you watch yourself! Your lynch mob mentality may not be a thing of the past, but more people are finding it repugnant," she shouted back. "Now, get off our property. And stay off. Keep your hunters out. If I see anyone from your side of the fence on my land, I'll call the law immediately."

"I'm betting," he said with a look of glowering satisfaction, "you'll get a slow response. My daddy had a word with Norm Myer."

"Norm is more honest than you think. And he tries to keep Pete honest."

"My daddy opens his wallet and we'll see whose side the Myers' take," he snarled.

A chill ran through Bryana's body. She knew from both the boast and the threat that Tank, and/or Vince Roland, had been responsible for Ricki's beating. Tank savored Bryana's anger. His eyes glazed when he bragged how Ricki had been pounded. Now his eyes shone with a haughty, menacing gleam.

Tank slammed his truck's door. The husky truck roared down the gravel road. Clouds of dust lifted until it was as if smoke was burning from a huge fire. Michelle neared Bryana, and took her hand. "He is such an ass."

With turbulence erupting inside, Bryana swallowed. "He had Ricki battered. He wants to demolish everything we have or care about so that he can satiate his greed by getting this land. His father doesn't like losing. And Tank doesn't like disappointing his father. You had that description on point."

"Well, try as they may, it hasn't impacted our business. And our hound is recovering. So the day hasn't been entirely awful."

Bryana's laugh began with a chuckle and then became a roar. "You're beginning to sound just like your mother. Even a horrible threat comes out okay."

"Jersey would have also added a song between her cheers." Michelle looked around then her eyes filled. "I miss Jersey. I miss her zany craziness. It always fit every situation. I miss your parents. What was it about the people of their generation? If news wasn't good, they would even retrieve news from the past that was. Jersey once told me not to be too pragmatic. Then she laughed and said to cancel that bit of wisdom."

"Because she wasn't pragmatic?"

"No," Michelle sputtered. "No, because she said she couldn't spell *pragmatic*."

"She could have spelled *practical*."

"She could never have lived practically." Her head dipped. "Bryana, do you think Tank will attempt to harm us?"

"We've got to be diligent in watching our animals. And the western border of our land. Tank and Vince are cruel. Diabolical. Money buys favors."

"Why don't you include Sarah? She's also attempting to ruin our business so we'll leave the area."

Bryana walked towards the door. "Maybe she should be included."

Michelle followed. "You're still giving her the benefit of the doubt?"

"Once in a while your optimism brushes off on me." She reached back to take Michelle's hand. She kissed it tenderly. "I miss Ricki."

"I hope she's doing okay."

"L.J. will make sure she is."

"I'm grilling herbed chicken, corn in their husks, and potatoes. Let's chow down."

"And desert?"

"A cherry or apple pie might just be cooled to the correct temperature by then." She gave Bryana an inviting embrace. "Come on, my mellow artisan. Let's have dinner, followed by pie a la mode. And since we have the entire place to ourselves, we can snuggle in early."

Bryana's skin rippled slightly. They'd promised over thirty years ago they would remain bonded throughout eternity. Fortune, she acknowledged, was important in love. And that was magic enough, no matter what maelstrom might happen along. Or might be happening inside her, she deliberated.

Chapter 19

Both dogs had followed Bryana into her studio that morning. As she sculpted undulating indentations with serrated tools and imagination, the pots began to form surface designs. When she threw or worked the clay into shapes, she often wore tight latex gloves to keep her hands from cracking. The constant stress and dampness was hard on the skin. With the large volume of pottery she produced, she needed to be protective. But sometimes, she allowed the skin of her hands to touch the clay. She relished those times.

She also felt passionate about the glazing process. Colors intrigued Bryana even when she was a child. Recently she'd started the Tierra Sunrise collection in an attempt to exact the yellow and pink-orange color combination of the Kansas sunrise. The glazes needed to be calibrated to gently move from one color to the next. Although she knew she could never encroach upon the perfection of nature's morning horizon, or twilight's pastel, she replicated it as best she could.

Rows of leather-dry mugs, plates, goblets, and pots lined the shelves. Another set of shelves were filled with teapots and decorative pots. Touching the leather-dry clay reminded her fingertips of gliding over silk.

As always, at the end of each day, she would do a check of the work. She examined the clay to make certain it passed her strict inspection. She would run her fingers over the objects. Each of her mugs was carefully, and exactingly, held by Bryana to make certain the handle was comfortable.

She enjoyed shaping raw earth into contours of beauty when she molded the creative pots. She found a mutual equation was true in both tilling the landscape and forming pottery.

Time with the wheel allowed her mind to wonder. She thought about how lovely the final stages of summer would be. She hoped there would be a bumper crop for all the farmers in the area. While the tornado had ravaged some of the crops to the south, it had spared the crops surrounding Bryana and Michelle. If Billy Dreher's wheat crop became golden, and was successfully harvested, it would temporarily ease some of the financial problems of the farm.

From there her thoughts turned to autumn's prospects. They would be busily digging the root crops of potatoes, carrots, and onions, as well as hanging twisting chains of garlic and peppers. Gunny sacks filled with produce would be placed in the root cellar. Grain and corn would be ground into sacks of flour. Michelle had already been talking about new varieties of whole-wheat breads she planned to bake. The corn would be used not only for cornbread, but also chicken feed over the winter months.

That was if things went according to plan, she considered. Her father always insisted they live in the present. Crops raised on the stretching plains were dependent on good fortune. And Anthony Hays didn't believe in counting on good fortune. He was a lifetime farmer and he knew looming vulnerability, as well as the triumph of success. Every season was up for fortuitous grabs.

Her father had been a good farmer until the stretch of unfortunate weather required that he borrow money. At that point interest seemed to eat away at all the profit. In his elderly years, it was more difficult for him to deal with running the farm. As if falling deeper in a bottomless pit, the debt continued to compound. There were also her mother's medical bills.

Bryana's concerns soon returned to the immediacy of making the farm profitable. If the crops were good, she would consider planting a small crop of soybeans on the barren land west. The patch of earth had been a fallow thirty acres. If soybeans could be produced, it would add to their financial stability. She had ideas, but they were empty illusions until they proved viable and lucrative.

Her arms and back began to ache, so she would switch work. Remembering L.J.'s request for a few more terra cotta bas-relief pieces, she turned off the wheel. She went to a waist high bench.

Placing the terra cotta clay down, she began working the inside, bringing a third-dimensional scene of mountains. L.J. said mountains always sold quickly.

By noon she needed a break. Lunch would provide it. Sitting across the table from Michelle gave her the mental and physical timeout she needed after working all morning. There was tranquility within the kitchen.

Before they'd finished their chicken sandwiches, potato salad, and iced tea, Bryana heard a loud knock on the front door. She snuck a peek out the window. "It's Norm Myer."

Michelle frowned. "I didn't even hear him drive up. Even the dogs were quiet."

"I remember he was in the Marines. He probably knows how to silently advance on the enemy." As she swung the door open, she asked, "Norm, what brings you out here? And to the front door?"

"A complaint," Norm blurted.

Bryana rumpled her hair in the gesture of impatience. "Let me guess," she said as her arm lifted to invite him inside. "Was it perchance Tank and Alice? Those people feed on conflict."

"They're saying you enticed the kids to the fence." Norm's stance was usually one of shoulders back, lifted highly. Now they were hunched slightly, and his eyes darted from the ground to the women's faces. "Claims you're giving them food that could be tainted."

"What?" Michelle's voice was packed with anger. "Those children were standing at the fence while I was in the garden. They yelled out they were hungry. They told me they hadn't had anything to eat. Their mother was *sleeping*. I gave them some bubble bread."

Bryana defended loudly, "Michelle would never hurt anyone, Norm, especially not a child. You know this whole thing is bogus. Tank is stirring trouble. He came over with his usual bravado to shout at us. I told him to leave the kids and dogs out of it."

"That was one of his theories. It was retribution for the hunter shooting your dog."

"No one takes it out on children," Michelle argued.

Fidgeting, Norm said, "Well, this is just a warning. Both Tank's family and you two – stay away from one another. I'm tired of being called out here. I got other business to take care of. We don't go for all this haggling. The department isn't cosmopolitan enough to serve as a therapist for disputing neighbors."

"Norm, we lived in Denver for over three and a half decades, and only once called authorities. That was for an armed robbery. It isn't that you're not a delightful guy," Bryana half joked, "but we don't need to see you twice in one week. When my dog is shot, and a woman is beaten, I believe authorities should be contacted. Am I wrong?"

"No." He reached the door then turned to them. "Bryana, we go back a long way. I've always admired and respected you and your family. Good people. Tank has always been a problem. When he was a kid, a teenager, and even now. I'm the first to admit he gets free passes. And as for Pete paling around with Tank. I've talked with him about it. Pete's not a bad man. He's influenced by a friend."

Bryana glanced away then offered, "No. He's your son, and you're not a bad father. And not a bad friend. I'm just frightened that you're being influence by money and power."

"Come on, Bryana, I'm attempting to be neutral. And as for Pete, he just wants to be a good friend to a loser. I tried to teach my son loyalty. Even now, I'm trying to set an example for him. Show him I'm loyal to my friendship with you, Bryana. I made it clear if he finds the young men who assaulted Ricki James, he's to bring them in. I can't get criminals to court without witnesses, but I can make it uncomfortable for the suspected perps. But I need identifications by the victim. Until, and if, the witnesses come forward, I can't do any more than that."

"Ricki's had enough trouble in her life. She doesn't go looking for it. And Gloria is aware of the Roland's powerful fist on this community." Bryana's message was clear.

"Let's try to diffuse this feud before people need to take sides."

Bryana swallowed away her thoughts before they became angry words. After Norm left, Bryana went back to her lunch.

Suddenly, she pounded the table. Coolly she remarked, "He's covering his ass. How flipping loyal is that? He hates Tank and his benefactor, Vince. But he needs Vince's support."

"Politics is politics. At least with Norm we have a chance of justice. Anyone else would probably be worse."

"Lesser of a thousand evils." Her gaze strayed. "I have always loathed Vince. And now I can't stand his repugnant son. Even my dear friend Norm seems tainted by them."

Michelle corrected, "I wouldn't put Norm in their category."

"I'm beginning not to see a difference." She lowered her glance as she stabbed at her potato salad. Her words were riddled with a painful skepticism. "I can't tell you how terrible that makes me feel."

"Bryana, Norm could have arrested Ricki for fighting even when she was battered. Pete could have arrested her for disturbing the peace. He didn't because he knew his father wouldn't allow it. Just now, both of us could have been arrested for trying to poison children. It could be *much* worse."

The telephone rang, interrupting Bryana's meditations. When she answered, she heard L.J.'s voice. "Are you and Ricki alright?"

"We're fine. Her bruises are turning weird colors," L.J. teased with a laugh. "Ricki wanted to apologize again for causing you problems."

Bryana could hear the muffled voices in the background. "Ricki wants to say sorry," she whispered to Michelle.

Ricki's voice was contrite, and soft. "Hey, Bryana, I'm sorry for putting you in a spot. L.J. talked with me about it. You and Michelle have so much to lose. And I'd feel terrible if I was the cause. I know you gave your word to Tess. And I gave my word to you. I made you look bad because I wasn't trustworthy. I promise, I'll never let you down again."

Bryana replied, "You're a decent person, Ricki. And we appreciated your help. Glad you understand our decision."

"I wouldn't have let you down for anything unimportant. I've never been in love before. I'm in love with Gloria."

"And how does she feel?"

"She loves me."

Bryana paused. "Ricki, you're both young and confused right now. Her feelings could change."

"But we could ignore how we feel and lose the love of our lives."

Bryana's eye closed. She opened her mouth to speak, but words came as if in slow motion. "All I'm saying is, please be careful."

"I'm sure she loves me. She's even got an on-campus performance set up for me at her college." As if the line had gone dead, there was silence that prodded Ricki to explain. "Payton College has an arts program for performers. Pays two-hundred bucks. Gloria took a demo CD I had with my songs on it for them to listen to. They want me to open for some singing cowboy. He's on the chart. Anyway, it's settled. This weekend."

"But where would you stay? You know you're not safe here."

"At Gloria's dorm. For the weekend. L.J. said we could drive Friday afternoon, and she would take me directly to the dorm then she'd come back to your place."

"What if you got picked up by Tank's friend while you're going through Tinpsila County? I'm certain Tank was involved in your attack."

"Gloria said that Payton is in the county next to Tinpsila. L.J. said she'd drive the long way, far south, and wouldn't even be going through Buffalo Plains, or Tinpsila County. Then on Sunday, she'll come directly to Payton, and back around the south side."

"I hope you appreciate her," Bryana said with a chuckle. "She's going out of her way for you. Literally and figuratively. She knows you're a good kid, too."

Ricki's voice was apprehensive. "Will you come to see me?"

"Of course we will. We wouldn't miss it."

"I have another favor to ask. I don't have a guitar. Gloria said she could scrounge one up at the dorm, but I was wondering if I could..."

"You can borrow my father's Martin. You made it sound alive again. And you have new strings."

"Hey, thanks. I'll dedicate one of my songs to you."

"I'd like that, Ricki."

"I'll write the song myself," Ricki said. "Oh, and could you bring me some bubble bread and a pie? I loved that chocolate pie."

"I think Michelle can be persuaded," she answered as she handed the phone to Michelle.

Michelle had been leaning over Bryana's shoulder to listen in. "Ricki, it sounds great. And I'll bring a few pies for the dorm. It's good advertising to give samples. Are you okay?"

"Yeah. I'll be fine now. I was afraid you and Bryana would still be mad at me."

"We were a little disappointed, but you'll make us proud."

Michelle continued talking. Bryana hoped there would be no problems. She hated to think of taking Tess's order in the next day. If Tess had heard the news, she would not be pleased. Finishing her iced tea, Bryana stood. It was slow and as if there were weights on her shoulders again. However, she lectured herself, it was a free country. Ricki had a right to perform anywhere she wanted. L.J. had the right to drive wherever.

Still, there was some unknown addendum. The what-ifs ganged up on her.

Before she had much time to explore her concerns, Rolf Jarvis arrived. "Bryana, my pal at the state's inspection agency said someone is being sent out here to do a surprise inspection later this afternoon. To give you your permit or not. Usually they make appointments."

"We don't have any violations that might be a problem," Bryana stated.

Rolf agreed, "I know. I've been in your kitchen before and it's spotless, but you might want to keep the dogs out of sight. I know Michelle said she never cooked with them around, but out of sight is out of mind, if you get my drift."

"That's easily done. I can put them in the studio with me."

"If there's any chance they might bark, I could take 'em over to my spread."

"Thanks, Rolf. Maybe it would be best. In case."

"What made them decide on a surprise inspection of our little in-home bakery?" Michelle questioned as she approached.

"Think of a man important in town. Someone who could get the agency's attention. Vince Roland is my guess."

Michelle gave a swat in the air with the tea-towel she was holding. "Mine, too."

"Come on, Idgie," Bryana called. She watched Idgie's lumbering trot. Then she whistled for O'Keeffe. Both dogs were confused when Bryana instructed them to hop into Rolf's truck. They knew Rolf but had never been to his farm. "Just for the afternoon, girls. Think of it," Bryana said to the dogs, "as a summer camp experience. I'll come get you later. And don't chase any buffalo."

"They'll be fine. Ella and I will see they learn some camp songs," he said with a laugh. "We'll keep them inside so they don't try to escape and return home."

"Thanks, Rolf. We appreciate your friendship."

"We need to stay tight. We're all out here in the middle of nothing."

"And we need to be able to depend on one another. Wish my other neighbor could realize the importance of village life."

"Tank thinks like his father. They never think they'll ever need anyone," Rolf said. "And they may be right. But God help 'em if they're wrong." He got in his truck and waved back at Bryana and Michelle. "Prepare to get back spoiled pups. And, I've got some buffalo jerky to prove it."

The women laughed as they returned to the kitchen. "We're sold on Rolf," Michelle said. "Now the dogs are going to see how nice he is."

"They may not want to come home."

"I think they will." Michelle picked up a roll of paper towels and tossed them to Bryana. "Probably won't need cleaning, but let's give 'er the once-over. We need to remove every speck of dust."

"You keep the kitchen more antiseptically clean and the utensils more sterilized than an operating room."

"Where do you think I got my Mrs. Clean training?"

As Bryana sprayed disinfectant then wiped, she answered. "Probably not from Jersey."

"Mom thought a dust rag was a dirty dress. And a mop was a corner decoration."

"But she knew how to create fun. And happiness." Bryana saluted. "Let's get this place shined to a glow."

"Make Victoria's Pies and Pastry go down in history," Michelle said staunchly.

They had hastily named their newly formed business when they'd applied for the permits. Bryana and Michelle joked that it sounded like a law firm. But Dawson and Hays was only a company name. Under the umbrella were the trade names of Victoria's Pies and Pastry and Bryana's Trinkets and Treasures. Michelle insisted the pastry business be named after Bryana's mother.

After the two male inspectors had gone through the kitchen, and adjoining rooms, carefully, they gave their decision. Victoria's Pastry officially passed inspection with flying colors. The inspectors actually did wear white cotton gloves. When complete, the inspection warranted a handshake, and a small piece of paper that could be placed on the window sill.

Bryana had left to pick up the pups, and when she returned to the house with the two dogs, she sensed the joy. The women decided to have a glass of wine, and even gave O'Keeffe and Idgie an extra-large portion of dinner. Rolf and Ella had spoiled the dogs, and in addition, sent home a bag of buffalo jerky for them.

There was a temporary kind of happiness that had once existed each day. The inspection, and getting the permit, was a victory. Bryana enjoyed viewing the gleam in Michelle's eyes each time they were near.

The soul was a vessel, Bryana thought as she looked across the dinner table and into Michelle's face. That vessel is filled partially with one's own qualities. And life fills in with many other elements. When filled to the brim, the vessel reflects a soul.

"Bryana, Bryana..." Michelle attempted to get Bryana's attention.

"Sorry. Just contemplating life."

Michelle laughed her melodic laugh. "Sorting your philosophy?"

"Probably. But we really need L.J.'s psychological input when it comes to philosophy."

"L.J.?" Michelle questioned.

Bryana's laugh boomed. "Last time I asked her about happiness, she told me happiness was the *babe-fest* between birth and death."

Chapter 20

Light from the window brightened the bedroom. Bryana and Michelle had snuggled in bed longer than usual. But the mellowness of wine had allowed a good night's sleep. They reserved wine and beer for special occasions, so after two glasses of celebratory wine the previous night, tucking in early was a treat.

Both had awakened to the passionate desire of love sharing. Although the morning began later than normal, they quickly caught up to speed. Cackling hens evacuated their nests of straw when Bryana gathered eggs. She then scattered more ground corn and grain for them. It was her final chore before creating pottery.

Gazing up at the morning's hot, humid Kansas skies, Bryana wiped the perspiration from her temples. After loading both kilns, she spent more time than was necessary weeding the garden. The still weather was appreciated, but for most of the morning Bryana had considered the thought of confronting Tess.

Wind began to lap at her legs. The timing for soft winds was perfect for the ripening wheat fields. Tender warm breezes dried the wheat grains. The golden yellow colors increasing the chance of making the harvest before rains or hail could destroy the crop. This crop was nearing perfection, and the combines would soon be rolling.

These thoughts gave Bryana hope. But then her concerns looped back to the potential problem of the Buffalo Plains Café. Speculation about what Tess might say was not conducive to her creativity when Bryana went into her studio. The parable about good pottery inviting tranquility was true. However, it wouldn't completely shut down the frustration of what Tess might say.

Bryana showered to get ready to deliver the pastry. She also wanted to drop some mugs off to the Brass Rail. She debated with herself about which delivery should be first. She decided Charlotte might lift her spirits.

Bryana would take in a platter decorated with playfully colored buffalo, deer, and wild fowl. She'd been experimenting with the majolica form of pottery. She liked painting animal designs. Bryana was most challenged by the variety ceramics offered. When her arms became tired of throwing pots, she would change to slab work. The one thing that never changed was her relentless passion for clay. She found the complexity of clay and paint offered enough variform and color for several lifetimes.

If Charlotte agreed to sell the large platters, it would be another form of revenue. If not, Bryana thought, oh well. As her father always said, "Ask anything you want. People can say yes, maybe, no, or hell no. At least questions usually get answered."

She flashed a grin into the mirror when she was done brushing her teeth. Tess hadn't canceled her orders yet. And she might well know about Ricki's performance. It was a quandary when it came to how she would react upon learning of the young lesbian's return. But since Ricki was probably only going to spend the weekend, Tess might not even be aware of it. However, if she knew, and Bryana didn't mention it, it could indicate some duplicity on Bryana's part. Either way, Bryana wasn't happy about the prospect.

Throughout her life she'd worked hard so that one day she might prosper enough to relax. Now it seemed all for naught. She picked up the keys and leaned to kiss Michelle's cheek. "I'll open up the SUV and load up." As she stepped from the back porch, she bellowed, "Oh, no. No."

Michelle burst through the door. To the side, where the delicate herbs garden had been growing, were tracks. Mint, basil, and an assortment of other fragrant herbs had been pulled. The lavender was limply leaning. Beside them a small figure stood. Michelle's hands went to her cheeks, "Oh, lord! Jon what are you doing here?"

Nonchalantly his little hand reached for another bush of lemon basil. Michelle grabbed her cell phone and began dialing.

"Leave that plant alone," Bryana gruffly ordered.

He glanced at the ground then pulled his hands back empty of the ravaged herb. The women examined the damage done to the herbs. He had pulled out over a fourth of their herb garden. Within moments, Alice was dashing across the field towards them. "What now?" she screamed.

"You son has just pulled up about a fourth of our herbs. He was not enticed over here to ruin our herb crop! I can assure you," Michelle charged with angry restraint.

Alice yanked the boy's arm. "Jon, did you come over here and destroy these plants?"

"The girls wouldn't let me play with them," he broodingly answered. "It smelled nice over here. It smelled like candy bread. So I come over here. I pulled these weeds so they'd give me candy bread."

Embarrassed, and stunned, Alice stuttered, "He gets away so fast. We'll pay for the damage." She explained both Jon's and her culpability. "I don't know what gets into him."

Bryana glared. "I just don't want the law coming to my door accusing me of enticing a child. You know we would never harm children."

"I told Tank he was going too far. I know Jon wanders. He never gives me a minute's peace." There was a slight slur, as well as the expression of hopelessness. "Let me know the cost." With rage, she grabbed Jon's arm. "I'm going to lock you in your room. That's what I'm going to do with you, young man."

Bryana interrupted, "Alice, punishing the boy won't help. It hasn't helped yet. I know you and Tank hate us. And we aren't fond of you either. But Jon is a five-year old. He isn't involved. Instead of being unpleasant with one another, maybe we can try civility. If for no other reason than for the children, we should stop the bickering."

Michelle added empathetically, "And your children are welcome to come over as long as they respect our property, the livestock, and our dogs. Maybe sometime when he gets bored he could come over and watch me make pies. Or Bryana make pottery. Take some of the pressure off you."

"Tank wouldn't allow it. I'll keep them home. Jon, do you understand you are never to come here again?" A vacant expression told her story.

"But I want some candy bread."

Michelle started for the door. "Would it be alright if I gave him some?"

Alice pulled him away. "No. We're not encouraging him. I'll have Tank buy some at the café. Jon's not coming here, and that's final."

As Alice towed the crying boy, his tantrum exploded.

Michelle knelt trying to press some of the rooted plants back into the soil. "I'll get what I can back in. Water them good. I'll dry and store the ones without roots."

"Premature harvest, but we can at least save some of the plants."

"Yes. And at least we handled the scene with some decorum. I thought with Jersey raising me, I came from a dysfunctional family." She looked back up at her spouse. "You go on. I'd rather replant the entire garden than face Tess this afternoon."

"Saving the good jobs for me, huh?" Bryana asked with a smirk.

"Go. Dawson and Hays is depending on you."

"See you later. I love you," Bryana said as she slid into the driver's seat. As she drove, Bryana thought how lovely it would be if the children from next door could visit them. She could teach them about throwing pots. Maybe interest them in pottery. And they could help with baking, and learn from Michelle. The children would enjoy it, but probably not as much as she and Michelle would. Learning, being taught, was part of Bryana's youth. Those were the childhood memories that counted most with her.

The trip into Buffalo Plains went by too quickly. Bryana wasn't prepared for possible combat with Tess. Her first stop would be to the Brass Rail. Charlotte Gottschalk's bracing laugh would cheer her.

"Bryana," Charlotte called to her when Bryana entered the bar. Charlotte drew a beer and placed it in front of her. Bryana had placed the cardboard box of mugs on the bar.

Bryana sat on the stool, and with a quick sip, thanked the bar's proprietor "Good suds. It is hot out there. I got the outside chores done earlier."

"Heat's good for the crops, dries that wheat out. But it's hell on my body." Charlotte cackled, "Crap, I'm a hot-blooded broad, and break out in a sweat mid-winter. But this hundred-plus degree shit is too much for me. I got the AC blasting in here."

"Feels good to me."

There was a brief pause before Charlotte commented, "Heard your little acolyte got her ass whipped."

The cool beer slid down Bryana's throat. "News travels."

"No one's going to file a complaint. Bet my rat-ass cousin and his asshole son appreciates that."

"You also think Vince and/or Tank had something to do with it," Bryana questioned.

"Do apes scratch themselves? Hell, yes, they had something to do with it. It's a warning message. Tank brought a couple hunters in here this noon. The small tavern experience. Anyway, we served 'em up buffalo burgers, and unfortunately Tank didn't choke on his. He told me about the assault. Thought it was funny how the dyke got her comeuppance for messing with a hometown gal."

"I'm amazed we haven't been chased out of town with pitchforks," Bryana lamented.

"Most of us wouldn't tolerate it. Bryana, there are plenty who hate. But most of us just live and let live. One thing you got saving you is your other neighbors. Their crops planted on your land are safe. Tank isn't going to do anything to Billy's wheat, or Rolf's hay. Renting out the land was a smart move on your daddy's part."

"When Dad couldn't take care of it, he decided to do the share. The percentage was smaller, but the risk was minimal. No grain elevator storage fees, no cost of labor and harvesting. Seed, fertilizer, and all are costly. My father was old school. He had usually planted a quarter section in wheat, and another hundred and sixty acres in corn and alfalfa. When Mom died, he began easing up on his work load. We still do the side-crops of herbs and veggie gardening."

"They say there's been a renaissance in family farming. It would be nice. But flipside, we got the land barons like Cousin Vince. He wants to gobble up your farm so Tank can expand his business of killing helpless animals. Just another corporation pandering to lazy hunters. Vince is salivating for your property."

"I won't sell to him." Bryana took another sip. Then she continued interrogating Charlotte, "So do you really think he instigated Ricki getting beaten up?"

"I'm sure. Vince keeps his head down. Doesn't go to the bank often. Only shows up at the City Council meetings once a month. Delegates. He even delegates his dirty tricks to Tank."

"And Sarah."

"She's like his cleanup crew. Wipes his ass," Charlotte's lusty laugh filled the entire barroom. "Sends her in to threaten people not to give you any assist. Hell of a note, because people saw how you and your band of merry women helped out when the southern strip of our town got hit by the tornado."

"Everyone doing okay now?"

Charlotte leaned near, "From what I hear the insurance companies aren't doing much, if anything. It's a crime. Fucked by mother nature, then by the money-grubbing corporations. But the initial help was what was needed most anyway. What the townsfolk put back together. And you and your women helped."

"No matter what we do, it doesn't seem like it will be enough. Our dog gets shot. Their kids come over to our property, and we get reported for having enticed them."

"I heard about that from Tank, too. He was roaring. Said he didn't want his kids around perverts. Only the dumbshit called it *pre-verts*."

Bryana shook her head and snickered. "And Jon was over just this morning tearing out a quarter of our herb garden. He'd have leveled it if we wouldn't have discovered him. We called Alice. She came over to rescue him from us pre-verts."

"Tank was a little shit when he was a kid, too. I even felt sorry for Sarah. But she spoiled him just as much as Vince did."

Bryana began unwrapping the platter. "Before I forget, I made this platter. I thought maybe the hunters would be interested. Or the townspeople."

"Hey, I like it. Maybe customers would like taking home a nice gift for their wives. And I like this myself. What are you asking for it?"

"I thought maybe forty dollars. I've got more time into platters."

"Fifty is better," Charlotte computed. "And they're worth it. It's huge."

"Good suggestion. Look, I'll bring another one to town next time so you can keep one for your own."

Charlotte chuckled loudly, "Thanks. I guess you already got an agent, or I'd apply for the job."

"Agent? You mean Michelle?"

"I mean L.J. That woman could sell snow to Santa."

"She's selling some of my slab work – the bas-reliefs, and large vessels to art shops now. And you're right; she can spin like a pro."

"Hope she doesn't make you too rich. First thing, you'd wanna up and move away."

Bryana contemplated the prospect of making enough to move away. She felt torn. "I'm not sure I'm the type to be rich."

Charlotte's boisterous chortle rolled. "Me either. You know the old saying, if you're not going to be honest, you might as well be rich. Cousin Vince is an example of that theorem."

Bryana finished the glass of beer. "Thanks, Charlotte, I always enjoy coming in. Good luck with the platters. Well, my next stop is the café."

"Better fuckin' you than me," she said with a bob of her eyebrows. "Tess is the stodgiest woman I've ever met. I told her to smile more and she might hook up with a nice old farmer."

Grinning, Bryana gave a wave. "That's not probable."

Chapter 21

As Bryana crossed the street, she acknowledged that she was constantly experiencing some feeling of being emotionally tattered. She opened the back hatch of her SUV and carefully lifted the first box. As she entered the café, she noticed Tess's penetrating eyes.

Tess blurted, "Did you hear the *latest*?"

"Give me a clue," Bryana wisely requested. Her nerves were raging torrents of stress.

"Your friend is entertaining at the college. Tomorrow night! Gloria set it all up. And she tells me I can't do anything about it." Tess's eyes broadcast sorrow and defeat. "And she's right. She's of age."

Bryana fumbled as she carefully placed the box of pies on the counter. "I heard that tidbit of news, yes. Sorry," she commiserated. "I have no say in it either."

"A tangled situation," Tess said with a sigh of exasperation.

"Do you want me to get the bubble bread box inside, or take the pies back?"

"I'm not blaming you. And like I said, we sell that bubble bread like crazy." Tess reached across the counter to hand Bryana a check and an order form.

With an emotional load off her shoulder, Bryana retrieved the huge box of pastry. When she reentered, Tess had placed a cup of coffee on the counter. As Bryana sat, she uttered, "Tess, if it's any consolation, I understand how you feel. I know you have Gloria's best interest at heart. I don't know where we go from here either. Ricki didn't ask my permission. She isn't staying out at the farm."

"I know. Gloria said we're all against them. Even you and Michelle."

"Maybe it would be wiser if we would accept them."

"Accept them! Accept that! God is against it. The Bible is against it."

"Actually, the Bible doesn't have anything to say about Sapphics. However, short hair on men was a sin back in biblical times. And many other sins mentioned are now small infractions of the past. I always believe that if we are in the image of God, then we must think in a God-like way. If I took God's place as an almighty entity, I would change with the times. If it were a proven fact that sexuality is determined by DNA, I would take that into consideration. And it has been proven. My thoughts would be far more favorable to the reality of nature. Homosexuality has been found in over four hundred and fifty species already."

"And they say homophobia is found in only one, I heard that," Tess replied. "But the holy words..."

"The Bible was pretty much a cut and paste job through the centuries. Even the accounts of the various writers differed. It certainly wasn't three-dimensional, tangible information. Look at how Mary Magdalene was portrayed?"

"That was changed back how it belonged. Jesus never said she was a whore."

"But originally the scribes, or whoever, got it wrong. They might have gotten other things wrong, too."

"Jesus doesn't get it wrong."

"That's what I'm saying. The people who transcribed, translated, and *edited* it might have gotten some of it wrong. And later some of the popes were pretty shifty. They would rewrite to self-serve their beliefs with a handful of passages that weren't what Jesus would have wanted. I believe Jesus was a magnificent prophet. He was enlightened about the analytical messages of good and evil. He was one of the very first feminists. He advocated for women, and they were part of his ministry. I don't believe Jesus was a hater."

"I just know there's hope for you yet."

Bryana grinned. She watched the expression on Tess's face thaw. "I'm not saying what's right and what isn't. I'm only saying how relationships matter. Love matters. There's an old saying about it doesn't matter who you love, or how you love, but *that* you love."

"I'll never approve of sin. And abominations."

"Michelle's mother jumped around with religion. Church of the week, Michelle called it. Anyway, when Michelle was getting into her adolescent years, Jersey picked Catholicism as her spiritual flavor of the month. Michelle said she didn't know if she should aspire to be a saint or a Sapphic."

A laugh forced its way from Tess. "And she didn't pick saint."

"She had no choice in the selection. She *is* Sapphic. That's how she was created. And I'm not so sure she isn't somewhat of a saint as well. I know she's the truss that holds up my life."

"It's just so unnatural. You really believe Gloria isn't going to come around?"

"Life is short. True love is never long enough. When you fell in love with Gloria's father, would you have given him up? Would you have *come around*?"

A light, long ago extinguished, seem to flash for a moment. It was of passion, memory, and lost love. "Nothing could have kept me from loving that man."

The next few moments were still. Intensely profound. Bryana could see it in the way Tess's inelastic, taut frame appeared to ease into a yielding shrug.

Bryana broke the silence. "Are you going to Ricki's performance?"

"I wasn't invited."

"Would you like for Michelle and I to pick you up. I think it would mean a great deal to Gloria. And to Ricki."

"I won't be a party to this." Tess resumed her inflexibility.

"I know one thing from experience. Parents will make every attempt to influence their children to take an easier, more acceptable road. As I mentioned last time we talked about it. I wish I could tell you what you want to hear, but she probably isn't going to outgrow it. It most likely isn't a phase. Even if Ricki is out of the picture, Gloria probably won't be what you want her to be. Not if it's how she was made."

"She was made a girl."

"She was made a human being. Tess, consider it. Why would anyone elect to be gay or lesbian? A major part of the world is against you. Being straight is a luxury and who wouldn't rather have a luxurious life than be Sapphic? Trust me. You've witnessed what Michelle and I have been going through. Ricki was beaten, and she's been kicked around all her life. She'd rather have luxury than liability. And being gay, regrettably, is a never-ending liability."

Tess looked up at the ceiling. "And if she doesn't change, I'll lose her. If I don't accept Ricki, Gloria will go traipsing off to Denver. You really don't think she'll ever change, do you?"

"Do you?"

Silence filled the room. Tess gazed blankly across the room. "I love my daughter."

"I know. Gloria knows." Bryana went to the door. She turned back. "Let me know if you change your mind about attending the performance." The bell that was attached to the door gave a reverberating jingle.

When Bryana arrived home, she reported how Tess was upset, but not at them. She understood a parent's helplessness when a child becomes independent. Michelle suggested they take L.J.'s horses for a ride. Exercising the horses, she claimed, would also be a welcome break for the women.

The women agreed they wouldn't be getting the horses lathered up, as L.J. often did. The workout would be mild. But the horses would get some exercise. As would the women. Bryana rode the less tame of L.J.'s horses. Several times the horse lurched, and Bryana needed to calm the filly back down to a manageable gait.

They chatted as they rode, with horses ambling, the perimeter of their farm. Bryana watched the horizon's setting sun. The dogs had been allowed out, and the freedom of wide open territory excited them. O'Keeffe took long leaps into the air, while the brace was encumbering Idgie's leg and prohibited any excessive exercise. As she limped behind the horses, Bryana commiserated. "Don't worry Idgie, you'll be healed up as good as new in a few weeks."

"Not quite as good as new," Michelle disputed. Her jaw tightly clamped. "And I saved most of the herbs that were pulled out with roots, so we didn't lose as many as I figured we would. It did needlessly add to my work load."

"Our life here would have been tough enough without the added burden of the Roland clan. It seems as though things just keep intensifying." Her words were choppy and her voice tentative. "And I don't know how to make it better, Michelle."

From off to the side came voices and laughter. At the fence, leaning near to watch the women were Nita and Letty Roland. "Freaks!" their screams taunted. "Daddy says you're freaks," Nita accused.

Her six-year old sister added, "You are *bad freaks*. Evil sinners. Freaks of nature. And we'll tell our parents if you try to hurt us." With sing-song tempo, the girls hollered, "Freaks! Freaks!"

The girls had always talked with Bryana and Michelle before. They'd asked questions about the animals. And simple questions about what the women were doing as they hoed. Now their words were hostile, gloating, and vile.

The women traded glances. O'Keeffe began to charge towards the children with a curious gait. Bryana called, "Home, O'Keeffe." The poodle's midair leap brought her down. She spun around. Then the dogs obediently followed the women back to the farmhouse.

As the women dismounted, Bryana issued a huge sigh. Without a word, they removed the saddles, bridles, reins, and bits. After stabling the horses, they quietly walked towards the farmhouse.

"It's so sad, so very sad," Michelle said sorrowfully.

"You know the old farm expression about being able to fix anything with baling wire? All the baling wire in the world can't fix hatred."

"Harming a child has never, ever occurred to me," Michelle said with dejection. Her eyes were cast downward as she fought back tears.

"No." Bryana wiped her own tears away then reached to dry the tear sliding down Michelle's cheek. "Nor me."

Chapter 22

The following day had spun quickly towards evening. With only the two of them, the workload seemed impossible to complete. By the day's end, they were ready to clean up for their drive to Payton College.

"Nice to put on dress slacks and a fancy blouse," Michelle said as she slid her arms into a burgundy blouse. "It's a shock to look down and see something other than frayed denim cuffs."

"I know you miss getting gussied up the way we used to do for our date nights in Denver." She chuckled then added, "I remember when you'd take things from your closet and examine them. You'd say, 'What would Jersey wear?' before finalizing your fashion decision."

"And you rarely cared, as long as your outfits were clean and covered your privates."

Bryana gazed at Michelle. "You look lovely tonight, my adorable woman. You always look wonderful, but you're really sparkling tonight." She embraced her lover then spoke, "I'll get Dad's guitar in its case and take it out to the SUV."

"By the way, you look sexy all dressed up, too." Michelle's expression made Bryana smile. "Save some energy for later."

"You got it. I'll try not to worry about Ricki being up on stage. I'll try to keep thinking about energy retention."

"I always hold back enough energy for later. To please and be pleased by you!" Michelle grinned then added, "I worry about Ricki's performance, too."

Bryana lifted the guitar case onto the bed and opened it. "I'm sure Ricki will be great. Yes." Bryana paused, contemplating. "I wonder if we should have stood by Ricki and kept her here with us. Regardless."

"She broke her contract with us, knowing it endangered us all. And it would have made you break your word to Tess."

"I know. But it would have been nice to stick up for a sister."

"We made the decision we needed to make. We stuck by her until it infringed on our word to someone else. As much as I care for Ricki, she broke her word to us."

Bryana settled the Martin guitar into its case's nest. It fit perfectly in the cradle of a gold-colored, plush-lined interior. She remembered how both her father and Ricki had reverentially lifted, touched, and played the guitar. "And you were right, she apologized."

"Bryana, sending her away was partly for her protection. Ricki was badly beaten. We couldn't ignore the potential of more violence against her."

"Maybe we could have protected her in some way."

"If we could have, we would have." Michelle grabbed her shoulder-strap purse. "Let's go before we're late. You'll need to get the guitar to Ricki before she goes on. It probably needs tuning."

By the time they reached Payton College's small auditorium, the plan had been in place. Michelle would get front row seats saved, and Bryana would take the guitar to Ricki.

With unfounded optimism, Michelle saved seats for Bryana, L.J., Gloria, *and* Tess.

Backstage Bryana handed the guitar to Ricki. She hugged the three women. "Michelle is saving seats for us."

L.J. nodded. "And I need to talk with you later about making more of the terracotta bas relief works. Have a special order for you. A large unit. I told the woman I'd need to make a special trip to Kansas to pick it up for her. She pulled out her credit card." L.J. burst out laughing. "Couldn't pay me fast enough. So, I'll need to take it back on my next trip here. Also, I have another couple of art shops in downtown Denver wanting to carry your *artwork*."

Bryana's smile was visible in her eyes. "Artwork. I think of myself as a pot thrower. A slinger of mudpies. So I'll happily be devoted to art shops." She grinned widely. "Funny about life. What if the farm becomes financially viable because of pies and pottery?"

"Wouldn't amaze me," L.J. encouraged. "Just remember, I'm the middle woman."

"That's something I could never forget," Bryana playfully acknowledged. "So get out there in the audience, and get your seats. I'm right behind you."

Both L.J. and Gloria gave their good wishes, before leaving to take their seats.

"Thanks for letting me use the guitar," Ricki said to Bryana. "I know how special it is to you."

"Ricki, *you are* also special to me. And to Michelle."

"I'm plenty nervous. I've never played in an auditorium. Even a small college auditorium. I've only played coffeehouses and little clubs."

"You'll be great. Remember what I told you when your apprenticeship with me began?"

"Yeah. You said to make each mug or pot special. Like I was making them for my best friend."

"Like they were gifts, yes. I always believed the clay I threw would become treasures. And it's the same when you're singing. Sing your songs as if they're treasured gifts to each audience member."

"I'm not that great a singer or a songwriter. But I can play the heck out of this guitar. I'm not under the illusion I'll ever end up a star. I'm not such a great performer."

"If you're going to be a star performer, you've got to begin by considering the audience your friends. Because if you do that, they *will* be your friends. Even when you played for us, I noticed you went into another world. You were distant – alone. Bring the audience into your world, that place where you travel when you sing. Bring them along."

Ricki's lips turned upward at their edges. She embraced Bryana, her head falling on Bryana's shoulder. When she pulled back, she said, "Bryana, I'll try it. I'm usually frightened. I take myself to a safer place. Like I need to be isolated."

"Those people out there have gotten dressed, walked or drove here, and they're sharing their time with you. Giving their time. Time is their life. They want to see you."

"I'm only the warm-up act."

"Ricki, I've heard you. You're much better than the starring act. And the audience may never have heard of you, but they came early to see you. If the main act was all they wanted, they'd have had an extra half hour to themselves. This is your chance to thank them for being here. And it is their chance to become your fans. And friends."

Ricki's smile bloomed. "Thanks, Bryana. I love music. And I love Gloria. I've written two songs for her. It's like I write the lyrics, but she's the song."

"Share the lyrics with the audience. Now, tune that guitar."

As Bryana left, she heard Ricki complete a run of chords. Back in the auditorium, she took her seat. Ricki had just been called to the stage and was testing the microphone. Through a side view, Bryana saw in her periphery – Tess Walters. She waved at Tess. Then she watched for Gloria's expression when her mother eased her way through the row. The mother and daughter hugged.

Because of a huge smile on Ricki's face, Bryana was certain she had seen Tess arrive. Ricki's songs were being shared. Rather than with her dispassionate withdrawal, Ricki opened up and involved the audience. By the end of the set, she stood to loud applause, whistles, and cheers.

"She's really good," Tess commented. "I'm amazed."

"Me, too," said Gloria. "She was better tonight than I've ever heard her. I guess because she wasn't nervous."

"Maybe she was just *giving* her songs tonight," Bryana offered.

Chapter 23

When the concert ended, Gloria, L.J., and Tess, went backstage to get Ricki. Bryana and Michelle were uneasy about leaving the farmhouse unoccupied for too long. They were walking through the parking lot when they saw Charlotte attempting to catch up to them. She yelled, "Bryana. Girl, slow down."

"What are you doing here?"

"This is how I get some of the bar's entertainment. I need to get out of that bar once in a while. A good excuse is looking for talent. Look, tell Ricki to call me about playing at the Brass Rail. Maybe she'll bring in some of the younger crowd. Pay isn't great, but the singers usually get lotsa tips."

"She is excellent," said Michelle enthusiastically. "Ricki is staying at Gloria's dorm, but we'll get the message to her."

"Great. I see Tess is coming to terms with it." Before the women could respond there was a blaring horn several cars away. "Hell, Sylvester is over there honking. Tell her to call. And get me half a dozen platters. I got orders for them." Charlotte scurried across the lot shouting, "Sylvester, I'm gonna loop that goddamn steering wheel around your pecker if you start that honking business with me."

Michelle gazed over at Bryana. "Ricki has had a world of pain in her past, but maybe things are changing for her. And you've got platter orders."

"Yes," Bryana replied. "But it looks as though our luck isn't completely improving." They were walking directly towards Sarah and Vince Roland.

Vince Roland's shoulders squared. Mid-sixty, he'd kept himself in shape. He appeared dapper in his perfectly tailored suit. Arrogance showed with his steeply tall frame. Perfectly groomed, his glossy, graying black hair was short and neatly trimmed. Staunch lips were set more resolutely than a statue's. His most prominent feature was his ink-dark eyes that were issuing skittering glances in all directions. When they settled, they reflected a menacing, threatening gaze.

Sarah immediately appeared haughty and contemptuous. Her head prominently held high, she moved to the side away from Bryana and Michelle. Vince was not moving. There was an upward curl of his lips when he asked, "How you gals finding farm life? Ready to move back to the smog and filth where you belong?"

"Vince," Sarah half whispered, yet with deference to his authority.

"That's alright, sweetheart," he chided, "They don't mind answering a couple questions. Maybe they're ready to do some business with us. With our son."

"We *gals* aren't doing business with you or your son," Bryana curtly informed him. "In fact, you and your son are the last people on earth we'd ever consider doing business with. My father didn't want his treasured land to become a corporate wildlife killing business. Your wildlife habitat caters to non-sportsmen. The hunter's shooting-gallery game is cruel, heartless, and ugly. They pay huge prices for their wall décor and bragging rights. Meanwhile neighbors and their livestock are endangered. And even your own grandchildren are imperiled."

"You leave our grandchildren out of this," Sarah vehemently hissed. "You're jealous you have no family. So leave mine alone. I've heard about you're tempting them with your bubble bread."

"We weren't enticing them when Jon came over and pulled out a quarter of our herb garden," Michelle charged.

Bryana added, "And certainly not when your granddaughters stood at the fence and called us freaks." Her eyes narrowed. "Do you think we're freaks, Sarah?"

Sarah's facial feedback was blank. Her mouth froze.

"My wife doesn't answer to you," Vince bolted forward, nearly in Bryana's face. His truculent eyes were emblazoned with hate. He snarled, "You two *are* freaks of nature. Queers. Abominations! That's what you are."

Bryana's glare intensified. She was looking straight into Sarah's face. "I guess I don't need an answer from you, do I?"

When the Rolands had hastily retreated, Michelle and Bryana climbed in their SUV. Michelle questioned, "What was that all about?"

"Nothing." Bryana's face became more enraged. Her hands shook, trembling from anger. "Nothing any longer important."

"Fine," Michelle murmured. Her chin plunged into the cup of her hand, as if she were considering the evening's events. "I just have the feeling that seeing Sarah really bothers you. Do you want to tell me why?"

Thoughts looped as if they were wild, babbling conversations. "How should I be feeling? The woman has ruined my life. And your life as well."

"I don't consider our lives ruined. We're together. Jersey used to say that when two people are in love, every day is like a big hug from heaven. What's really wrong, Bryana?"

"I told you. I've got a right to be angry."

Sensing Bryana's need to think, Michelle looked out the window as Bryana drove.

Bryana knew Michelle wanted her to explain, but she couldn't. Decades ago, Sarah had made her feel like damaged goods. When Bryana left Kansas it was as if her heart was nothing but wreckage.

Finally, Michelle said, "Bryana, grumpy doesn't suit you."

Annoyed, Bryana cursed, "I'll be fucking grumpy if I want to be."

"Do you still have feelings for Sarah?"

Confused, Bryana, balked at the inference. "I'm hurt that Sarah betrayed me. I'll always be hurt. We leave a part of ourselves behind with everyone whose lives we touch. And each person leaves a portion of themselves when they touch our lives."

"You know you can tell me anything."

On their drive through Buffalo Plains, Bryana asked, "How about we stop in at the Brass Rail for a quick brew?"

"Great. We can give Charlotte Ricki's cell phone number."

After the women entered, Bryana wrote down Ricki's number and gave it to Charlotte. "Nice of you to give Ricki work."

"She was terrific," Charlotte replied. "I'm betting she can bring some youthful business in. We'll see. The kid still had some markings on her face from that attack. Tank had something to do with that. When I asked him pointblank, he told me no and said I should mind my own fucking business."

Bryana lifted the beer Tess had placed in front of her. After a sip, she said, "He did it. Well, he hired thugs to do it. Maybe on Vince's orders. We saw Vince and Sarah in the parking lot at the college."

"And they said?"

"We didn't talk about the attack. He seemed impatient to talk me into selling my farm to him or Tank. I explained that wasn't happening." Coolly, Bryana repeated, "Never going to happen as long as I'm alive."

Charlotte lifted her shoulders as if perking up her breasts. Then with a raucous laugh, she gave a fake shimmy. "And Vince isn't getting my tavern as long as I'm alive. He thinks you'll roll over. So you might as well have saved your breath. That fucker wasn't listening. He never hears the word no. Even his own mother said he badgered Sarah into marrying him. He's used to getting everything he wants. We need someone to stand up to the Roland's power and wealth. Vince is planning to pass on the battering ram, and the bullying manual, to Tank. Another generation of greed, hatred, and crooked deals."

Bryana's jaws tightened. She replied, "We all know Vince and Tank are both rotten to the core. Vince continues to roll along as if he's infallible."

Charlotte drew a beer then took a huge gulp. "Everyone's terrified of him. He's been in control of the town for so long. You have something he wants. And to be honest, he thinks he'll have the support of the town because you're lesbians. I'm sure he'll have some of them backing him for that reason. But not most. I know the hearts of the many. They don't scream you down with their opinions, like the bigots do. They're tolerant. Loving. It's the loud-mouthed bullies that make the noise."

"Charlotte," Michelle questioned, "why can't those people realize we aren't harming anyone?"

"Vince with his churchy holier-than-thou crap is just another form of control over the people. He isn't representative of the flock. His contributions influence people. That's all. But most of 'em don't give a damn about Vince."

Bryana swallowed as she looked away. "His hatred and bigotry has trickled down to Tank. Now, another generation," Bryana said with a defeated sigh to punctuate her statement. "Tank's daughters are now screaming their hatefulness over the fence. Calling us freaks. Tank wants us to feel the need to hide. If we experience enough fear, maybe we'll sell and get out of his backyard. Give him the property he lusts after so he can expand that lousy killing business. Those hunters don't come after meat for their table. They come to kill. Not as sportsmen, but in some macho urge of pretense. From the unfair and unethical hunting devices they use to call the prey, to high power rifles with scopes, it's all set against the animal. Wildlife."

"He's always been a bully." Charlotte rolled her eyes. "They want to make this the hunting capital of the Plains. I always figured Sarah would balk at it. She must cringe when she sees what's happening."

"I would have thought. She never was intolerant back when we were in high school."

"Obviously you didn't know she was homophobic when you had your little talk with her. Or whatever."

Bryana's eyes clamped shut. "She's sure as hell homophobic now. Right in there with those money-grubbing, land-grabbing, power-hungry..." She hesitated a moment before continuing "They want our property. And they'll do anything to get it. And yes, our being Sapphic helps them."

"Even after the Roland family gets what they want, they'll just pick out another minority, target, enemy." Charlotte continued after a swig of beer, "Someone has to stand up to them. But I don't know who. You two have so much against you because you're easy victims."

"We're only easy if fear makes us cave in," Michelle disputed. "And we're only victims if he wins."

Charlotte roared. "You're not only the best damned pie maker in the county, you got a good head on your shoulders."

Bryana's lips opened then shut again. Finally she said, "I worry about Ricki being back. And if she works here a night or two a week, she's putting herself at risk."

"You're right. I haven't thought that through," Charlotte said as her eyes squinted with concern. "That butch looks like she could be a real slugger if she was on an even playing field."

"Tank doesn't believe in even playing fields," Bryana interjected. "Four husky men beat Ricki."

"Okay, we can protect Ricki. Sylvester lives half way between here and Payton College. I could give him an extra few bucks to pick her up, and return her after the performance. I'm sure we can figure something out while she's in Payton."

Bryana explained. "But after seeing Tess is accepting, I'm thinking Ricki might be able to come back to our farm."

"You aren't concerned the locals might give you problems if she does stay with you?"

"I think it's time to address fear," Bryana answered. "The only one we made a promise to was Tess. And she's becoming accepting."

Michelle lifted her beer to toast, "Let's lighten up the dark ages. Time to grab fear by the throat. Storm the Bastille. Conquer Waterloo."

"Yeah." Charlotte's glass lifted again. "Fuck the weasels."

Michelle choked on the beer as she laughed. "Yes, fuck those weasels," she repeated.

Bryana chuckled. "You tell 'em, Michelle." She then became somber. "I hate using Ricki to get the barometer reading on the hearts of the citizenry," Bryana said. "But I doubt I'll be able to talk her out of a paid gig. And she'll undoubtedly want to spend her time at Gloria's dorm until the term is over."

"If anyone's up to the challenge, that kid is," Michelle said with confidence.

Bryana added with a brooding tone, "*If* it's a fair fight."

"And it's likely there will be a fight. I'm sensing that Ricki would like to relocate to Kansas for good. Tess understands if Ricki stays, Gloria might stay as well. Tess has always dreamed of handing down the Buffalo Plains Café to her daughter, just as it had been handed down to her. Maybe something great can come of this," Michelle said optimistically.

With an astringent tone, Bryana said, "If they stay, Ricki and Gloria will be in for the same crap we've been taking. A life full of multiple wild fires. I pity them."

"That's why we've got to try to make it better. Set a positive example."

Bryana questioned, "How the heck are we going to do that?"

Michelle hesitated a moment. "Kindness is my only answer."

A sharp snicker escaped from Charlotte's lips. She wound her churning lips into a secret, "Kindness *and* a batch of tough dykes might be a better answer. Have you seen that college women's softball team? Big bruisers."

Chapter 24

L.J. had decided to spend Friday night in the dorm since it was summer school and there were lots of vacant rooms. Ricki's new friends insisted she stay. Saturday morning L.J. gathered a few slices of pie and some bubble bread that Michelle had sent for the dorm. She stormed into the small bakery near campus with Michelle's pastry. After chatting with the manager, and allowing him to sample, the bakery became Michelle's first Payton customer.

L.J. called Bryana and Michelle immediately, telling them she had an order for Victoria's Pies and bubble bread. She also informed Bryana and Michelle that she intended to call on a bakery the opposite side of town, and add another new customer. She would phone them if she got new orders from that bakery.

Michelle had been rolling dough when she'd called. After hanging up, she relayed the news to Bryana.

Bryana questioned, "Can we handle more customers?"

Michelle laughed. "Sure. I'll do a second shift. If L.J. gets the other bakery to give us a try, it will mean the delivery trip to Payton is more cost-efficient."

"Even at that, the petrol is expensive."

"L.J. factored it in to the quotes she gave them. Added an extra buck per unit. That should take care of it. Said she'd take her commission out in trade." She quickly corrected, "Not with me. With pies and other pastry."

Giggling, Bryana shook her head. "L.J. is outrageous. She told me she has her father's business acumen."

Michelle sputtered, "What she has is pure balls. That special order fresco you did of the soccer players - I can't believe she charged over a hundred dollars for it."

"That made us an extra fifty. She astounds me. She doesn't blink an eye when she quotes a price."

"So have you got your expensive clay baking done for the morning?"

"At a hundred, I'd better get some extra bas-relief done now. They won't be ready for her to take back with her this trip. They take longer in the kiln. But when she returns, she can pick them up. I don't mind using the kiln space when she charges a C-note for them."

The remainder of the day and the next morning, both women busily worked on their tasks. Michelle increased her baking quantity, and Bryana tirelessly continued filling orders.

L.J. arrived early, and had completed most of the chores. The women agreed to take a couple hours off to ride horses. Bryana and L.J. rode Brandy and Sherry. Michelle rode the slower, aged, and cantankerous quarter-horse, Pierre.

For an hour a steady stream of gunfire was coming from the western quadrant of the Roland property. The women commented on the hunters busily shooting what Bryana called 'bucks in a barrel.' The white-tailed deer were no match for the half dozen hunters with scopes, high-powered rifles, and confining fences.

Because O'Keeffe and Idgie were accompanying the three women on their ride, they decided to keep away from the dangerous western border. The women rode slowly, so Idgie wouldn't stress her leg.

When they neared the fence, they saw Rolf Jarvis. He spotted them as he pitched a bale of hay. "All quiet on the western front?" he asked.

Bryana halted her mount, and answered, "So far. But I'm thinking it's only a matter of time until the Roland team stirs something up. We ran into Sarah and Vince at a college program."

"He'll rile something," Rolf muttered. "What a pompous, arrogant ass Vince is. But he'll have us all out of here before our toes point upward. Billy's getting up there and maybe his kids will want to take over the farm. They probably don't want to fight to keep land. What the taxes don't steal, corporations like Vince's will finish thieving. Ella's nephews are coming out next summer.

Maybe we can interest them in working for nothing in the buffalo trade."

Michelle commiserated, "I hate the thought of family-owned farms dying out."

L.J. dismounted from Brandy. "Y'all know if everyone stuck together and fought, there might be power in numbers."

Rolf sauntered to the fence, took off his hat and wiped perspiration on his face with a large handkerchief. "Roland runs the money. He owns most of the stock in the grain elevator co-op. The bank is his. The city council. He picks us apart one loan after another, one harvest after another, one miserable trick after another. How do we fight it?"

"One buffalo at a time," L.J. responded.

Rolf chuckled loudly. "Hell, yes."

Bryana's shared her thoughts. "They've tried to provoke us. Tried to harass us. I just don't know what else they have in mind for us."

"That Tank is a snake. He'll come up with something. Until then, my herd is increasing, the crops look good, and we ignore the Rolands. As best we can."

"But they aren't your bordering neighbors," Bryana said with a scowl. "They'll come for you after they roll over us."

"Come on, Bryana," L.J. objected. "Darlin', let's get some spunk a-going."

"That's right, put on those stomping boots," Rolf said with a strong fist in the air. "Spunk!" He invited, "Come on over for a brew and a buffalo burger. That'll cheer you up. And as you see, my bison are pasture-fed. No feedlot fattening for my herd."

Michelle nodded to Bryana. "Sounds good."

Rolf took out his cell phone and called Ella. "We got some down-in-the-mouth women out here on the range. Think you could wrangle up a few buffalo burgers and some cold beer for us?"

From his phone the women could hear Ella's sweet voice laughing the scales. The women followed after Rolf, for a wonderful lunch prepared by Ella.

Rolf and the women gathered around the picnic table for a feast. Ella had made her specialty buffalo burgers, potato wedges, freshly picked beans, salad, and beer.

L.J. continued complimenting Ella on the burgers. Better than any she'd ever had, she praised. With each mouthful of the burger, blue cheese, mushrooms, and sauce, she gave an orgasmic moan of pleasure. It delighted them all. Bryana had relished seeing Michelle relax. Things had been so tense, even the pleasures and a few moments of fun seemed a treasure.

After, the women went back to the farmhouse and stabled the horses, Bryana was still considering how rare the good times were now.

Although it was good to know they had friends, both Bryana and Michelle were unsettled about their plight. After their face to face meeting with Roland, they understood from the treacherous gleam in his eyes, he had determined to be victorious.

There would only be one winner.

Chapter 25

The following morning, L.J. had packed her Jeep with pottery, and the pastry orders she would take to the Payton bakeries. She was going to drive first to the university dorm to check if Ricki wanted to return to Denver with her. Ricki's last decision was she would stay with Gloria because Charlotte had booked her to entertain at the Brass Rail midweek.

Bryana hugged L.J. "Drive carefully, and tell Ricki if she wants stay with us here, she can."

"Separating her from Gloria is not going to happen," L.J. said with her firm voice.

"Tess doesn't want to lose her daughter."

"Last night Ricki told me that Tess talked with Gloria about what Gloria wants. After their little talk it was decided that when Gloria has finished college, Tess wanted both Gloria and Ricki to move into Gloria's grandfather's house. Tess hadn't sold it when he went into the hospital, thinking he'd improve. But he hasn't and won't. So she said the kids could move in there and watch the place. Gloria could work full time. Ricki could do work on that house, as well as the odd jobs for you, as well as her pottery."

"Ricki puts her heart into everything she does," Bryana said.

"I'm sure they'll probably drop by before Ricki's performance. She mentioned Gloria said she could borrow her car to come help on the farm while Gloria studies and goes to classes. Ricki also said she could work on getting a greenhouse built."

"She didn't mention it to me," Michelle said. "But it certainly sounds nice. Now that Tess is coping with everything, well that's all we're concerned about."

"Ricki misses the animals. Especially the dogs. Wanted to do a little physical labor. And toss a few clay projects. I told her I'd order gobs of those medallions she did last time. She pressed clay about silver-dollar size, made her designs then put a couple holes in the top to hang a chain or a cord of leather. Made a great necklace. Some of the kids in the dorm were wearing them."

"I saw those," Bryana said. "I wasn't sure they would sell. Great colors and designs. Maybe she'll be able to make enough to give her some cash."

"I'm sure she'll trade her construction skills to pay for the clay and the kiln time."

Bryana laughed. "Hey, that's my contribution to her rehabilitation. Besides, those little medallions don't take much clay or much room in the kiln."

L.J. slipped into the Jeep. "When I told her we nearly sold out, she called them her little trinkets. Said you made the treasures, and she made the trinkets."

"Trinkets and treasures are interchangeable. It depends on circumstances," Bryana said.

"Meaning?" L.J inquired.

"It all depends on the valuation ascribed the object."

"I've got no earthly idea what you're talking about."

Bryana's eyes dimmed. She shook her head. "I can't explain it." As if catching herself, she paused. "Nothing important. Anyway, Ricki underestimates her skills as a potter," Bryana said. "As well as an entertainer."

"I agree. I won't make it back here until next weekend, but if you're going to the Brass Rail to see her perform, tell her I'm thinking of her. Wishing her luck."

"We're definitely going," Bryana replied. "If anyone gives her any crap, Michelle will act as a bouncer."

L.J. roared. "We all know who the bouncer is amongst the bunch of you. Charlotte and her mammoth boobs." L.J. giggled. "Baaaa…"

As L.J.'s Jeep navigated down the driveway, Michelle grinned at Bryana. "You realize she's correct."

Bryana responded knowingly, "I realize L.J. watches out for breasts."

The women worked on their chores until noontime approached. Bryana had spent part of the morning feeding the livestock, and cleaning up after them. She'd worked the remainder of the morning in her studio.

At noon she returned to the farmhouse. Michelle was in the kitchen. She was wringing the tea towel in her hands. From the look on her face, she was visibly shaken by something. "What's wrong?" Bryana questioned.

"Good news and bad news. Both bakeries called. They loved the product, and ordered more. Bad news is that the bank's vice-president called. There's an outstanding loan. The note has just come due. Apparently your father had taken out one additional loan before he died. For twenty-five grand. I think it's a mix up of some sort."

"That's not possible. You had all the bills gathered up. A couple old grain storage bills. The implement notes. There was no outstanding note with Buffalo Plains Bank."

Michelle repeated, "The vice-president, a Chad Donovan, says he has a note. And he's insistent that we take care of it *immediately*."

"Okay. Let's not panic. It's got to be a mistake. I'll get ready and go into town. Check it out."

Michelle put down her embroidered tea towel. She offered, "Maybe I can go with you. I'm a little stronger in the accounting department."

"How about your baking?"

"We can drop what I have off at the Café. I can finish the rest tonight."

"I would appreciate the company. You're the computing whiz."

"Bryana, when we went through probate, there was no outstanding loan to the bank. I don't believe your father took one out while we were here. What would he have done with the money? And why wouldn't he have told you?"

"He was over ninety and might have forgotten." Bryana seemed perplexed. "But where would he have spent it? Where would he have put a twenty-five-thousand dollar check?"

"There's got to be a paper trail of some sort." Michelle's perplexed facial expression was contorted. "It hadn't been placed into his checking account. He banked at the Buffalo Plains Bank, and surely wouldn't have a checking account anywhere else. Your father wasn't the kind of man who would have carried a check for that much around with him for weeks on end. And certainly not cash. I don't get it."

Bryana reeled around. "We've looked in every crack and crevice of this farm when we searched for any additional outstanding bills. The bank notes were all carefully stored in the metal safe with Dad's will. Carefully stored and bundled. They were each stamped as being repaid. " Her hand quickly reached to her forehead and her fingers then spayed wildly across her head. "No, I don't understand."

After a hasty shower, the women drove into Buffalo Plains. Pensively, Bryana entered the bank after Michelle. When they were seated, Bryana commented, "I can't imagine what this is all about. Obviously Vince had it planned. His smug look showed how confident he was that we were in trouble. And he took no time in slapping us with this."

The tall, middle-aged man appeared, extending his hand. "Chad Donovan. We've met before, right after your father's passing," he said to Bryana.

"Yes. I recall. At that time there wasn't any outstanding loan. Also, no notes in probate."

Donovan took off his eyeglasses. He rubbed the bridge of his nose, before nervously twirling the glasses. "An oversight. It had been made out to his farm's incorporated name, hence it wasn't pulled up when there was a probate search. It recently came to our attention."

"Aren't their banking regulations prohibiting this sort of thing?" Michelle queried.

He carefully replaced his glasses. "I assure you, it is absolutely a legitimate debt. Obviously, we apologize for any inconvenience. The note was signed, and funds credited to your father's account."

"Our records don't show that."

"Well, Ms. Hays, the posting into his savings account was on the date the note was signed by your father. He had two accounts, you know."

"Why would he have two accounts?" Michelle asked.

"In this case, I assume, it was a slush fund. Payments were being made to a second mortgage for many years. There was only an outstanding balance of the twenty-five- thousand dollars when Mr. Hays borrowed on the farm to pay it back and close it out."

"I hadn't heard of a second mortgage," Bryana disputed.

Donovan leaned forward in his huge desk chair. "We have the paperwork available for you to see. I'm assuming your father wanted to close out the second, and because it was only twenty-five-thousand, decided to take an additional loan to clear it up." As he stood, he said, "I'll get the papers."

Bryana shook her head. "This is crazy. Why would Dad have bothered?"

Michelle sat up, leaning towards the desk. In a hushed voice she said, "Something isn't ringing with any clarity. The only reason he might have signed anything, would be if they called him to come in and they had him sign multiple papers. Thrown an extra couple in for good measure. Papers he wouldn't have carefully examined before signing. Maybe they told him the loan would be at a lower rate of interest. Your father didn't care about the trivialities of finance. But there's something crooked going on."

When the folder of papers was produced, both women examined them carefully. The paperwork seemed to reflect what they'd been told. The signature looked authentic. Bryana asked for copies of the transactions, and Donovan immediately supplied her with them. It was as if he had been certain she would request them.

Bryana held the paperwork tightly "Thank you. I'm going to have it examined by an accountant, or possibly an attorney. If it is a legitimate debt, it will be a few weeks before we can pay it. The wheat crop looks as if it's going to be good, so it shouldn't be a problem."

"Well, actually, Ms. Hays, there is a problem. The bank president has decided to call the note due immediately. It is overdue, and he has the authority to call it in. Which means within five days, including today, it must be paid."

Bryana objected. "We just found out about it."

"Yes, but as you see, it *is clearly* overdue. And we've deferred payment until Friday, end of business day." He stood and held out his hand.

As the women walked back to the SUV, Bryana felt her knees weakening. "We don't have twenty-five grand. We've paid so many of the bills, and loans, there is nothing left. We're selling pots and pies to meet our day-to-day expenses. Twenty-five-thousand isn't the end of the world, but its money we don't have."

"And I don't see how we can get it five days. Even if we had time to sell some things off, what would we sell?"

Bryana reached for the SUV's door handle. "Exactly, what the hell do we have to sell that would bring that kind of money? We're scraping by, barely."

"Land is all we've got." Michelle was resolute.

"Michelle, the land is the collateral. If we don't meet that loan, they'll *take* the land."

"First things first. Let's have an accountant and lawyer eyeball this file."

"I'm relatively certain even if it is bogus, Vince Roland and company have everything in order. And my question remains, how do we raise the money in less than a week? We've borrowed and loaned L.J. over the years, but she mentioned she's over-extended months ago. Now, by acquiring the horses, plus the economy's hit on the shop, I'm sure she hasn't got any extra funds."

"She would help if she could, I'm sure," Michelle added. "There isn't much cash around. Everything seems to be undervalued. Vince Roland knew we're strapped."

Bryana covered her eyes. The grip of shock was squeezing her. Words plunged out, as if being spat, "Of course he did. Knowing that by calling in the loan now, we wouldn't have the money until after harvest. That's why the rush. And it's pretty damned obvious we aren't going to be getting an extension loan from our town bank."

Michelle balled up her fist. "There's got to be something we can do. What about Payton Bank?"

"Maybe we can rub up against the president of Payton Bank," Bryana snickered. "It worked for Charlotte to get her loans."

"Her knockers are humongous, and she knows how to flirt and *deliver*."

Bryana turned the ignition key. "I suppose our boobs aren't great collateral."

Michelle chuckled. "So what's your next best idea?"

"We could go to Payton Bank and put the farm implements up for collateral. Paying the loan to the local bank, then decided how to pay off the Payton Bank. It would give us some time."

"Bryana, Payton Bank will check our credit with Buffalo Plains Bank. You know what a mess that would be. And it would undoubtedly take more than a week. Vince Roland would see to it that it would be slowed down. Besides, we still have implement payments. The newer equipment isn't even ours, free and clear."

Pulling out onto Main Street, Bryana drove slowly, as if to assimilate all the events as she drove. "The one thing I thought we had was the land."

"And if we have a note against the land, even though the land is far more valuable, they can take it. Now we really know the meaning of dirt poor."

Bryana tried to keep her eyes on the road, but the vision began to swim from behind the tears. "Michelle, I don't know what we're going to do. If they begin foreclosure, it would cost us dearly. Everything."

Once they arrived home, they called the accountant Bryana's father had used for years. He was probably, they surmised, on the Roland payroll. He told Bryana that if the bank had produced the information, it was correct, and she should just pay her debt.

The next project was to find an attorney. There were no appointments open for the several she called. The one helping put together the Hays probate declined, saying he knew very little about checking bank records and less still about bank fraud.

Bryana leaned down to hug Idgie. Her face pressed against the schnauzer's fur. "This is it."

Michelle took out her cell phone again. "We'll keep phoning everyone we know in case they know an attorney willing to help us."

After a dozen calls, Michelle replaced her phone carefully in her pocket. She entered the parlor where Bryana was diligently searching through the desk. "I've called every attorney both here and in Payton. One attorney, Paul Brody, stumbled a little. As if tongue tied. He finally said something like that had happened to another person. One of his clients. At the time, he wished he could have looked into it. It sounded fishy. It was the Schumacher family. They own the implement and hardware store."

The creases on Bryana's face deepened. "I know Eric Schumacher, and I could call him. The thing is - would it be worth our time and effort for an investigation? I'll give him a call, but right now it seems more vital that we come up with the money."

"I called L.J. first. She can get us ten grand by tomorrow afternoon. Billy Dreher said he's betting on the bumper crop. Until then, he can't pre-pay us the entire amount. But does have five-thousand he can come up with to help. That's fifteen, but it ends the prime possibilities."

Bryana considered the predicament. "Selling ten-thousand dollars' worth of anything we have around here still seems impossible."

"How about we lower the increments we ask to borrow. We have a firm fifteen-thousand. Let's make a list of all our friends and acquaintances over the years. Anyone who might have a thousand we could borrow for a couple weeks."

"Do you have any idea how humiliating it is to ask people for money?"

"Bryana, I'll call a couple of my friends from the hospital where I worked. Times are tough, but maybe they can swing a loan. It's only for a few weeks until we get the grain check."

"Harvest is about a week away. It could still storm, and then what? We become deadbeats. Homeless deadbeats."

"We'll find a way to pay our debts. We always have." She coerced, "Come on, Bryana, it's all we have and it's worth a shot." Bryana jotted down a few of her friends, then handed it to Michelle.

"I'll call them for you," Michelle offered.

While Michelle continued making calls from the kitchen, Bryana went into the parlor and carefully dialed Schumacher Implement. She presented her dilemma to Eric and was astounded when he explained the exact same thing had happened to his family when his mother died. Although the family hadn't disputed the loan, they had questioned it. They were told by their attorney it was probably going to cost more to bring a suit than it would be worth. Eric said his brother and he had closed their account with Buffalo Plains Bank. The experience had left a terrible taste in their mouths for all things Roland and all things bank. They were certain it was not on the up and up.

After hanging up, Bryana rushed into the kitchen. She reported what Eric had told her. The women were more certain than ever the claim of a loan was fraudulent. Bogus documents. Exasperated, Bryana murmured, "We're still basically at the same place. All the fees would be taken by attorneys. And there isn't time."

"I don't suppose there is. I got two-thousand from our neighbor at the old house. And two-thousand from a doctor friend I worked with in Denver."

"You're not calling Denver our home now. You didn't say back *home*." Bryana questioned, "Does that mean you're resigned to believing this is our home?"

"My home is wherever you are. So this is it," she said with a lift of her eyebrows. "And the Kansas pink and yellow horizons at sunset are like no others. A thousand shades. They remind me of a giant peace rose blooming across the edge of earth."

"You have fallen in love with Kansas?"

"Bryana, I've always been in love with a Kansan." Michelle embraced the Kansan she loved. "Yes."

Chapter 26

Although a constant barrage of calls was being made throughout the next two days, there was little progress. Bryana and Michelle were still six-thousand away from the amount needed to save the farm.

One thing had come to light. Billy Dreher had mentioned it to one of the neighbors east of his farm. When Billy called, very nearly apologetically to Bryana and Michelle, he mentioned something he'd heard may not be important. His neighbor told him about the same thing happening to Tom Haskell's family when his father died. Again, Roland and Donovan were involved in finding the missing loan papers. And Haskell's father had mentioned how he'd needed to sign so many papers when he was last in the bank. He was told they were non-disclosure forms.

After Bryana phoned Tom Haskell, she was more convinced than ever that the loan had been fraudulently devised with the goal of taking their farm. In fact, Haskell had even called the small weekly newspaper when he found out it had also happened to Gina Hamersmith's family. The newspaper, being funded by a large advertising contract with Roland's various enterprises, countered by calling the story unreliable. Without media backing, and legal attention, the speculation was thwarted.

Bryana's next phone call was to the only person with any authority she felt she *might* be able to trust. "Sheriff Norman Myer, please," she requested when she reached the county sheriff's department.

"Norm here," his husky voice responded.

"This is Bryana. I have something confidential we need to talk about."

There was silence on the other end of the phone. He then said, "Bryana, I know your neighbors are from hell. And I don't like it any better than you do…"

"Norm, this is much bigger than hearing Tank's hunters with their dreadful gunshots all day long. This is far more serious. But I need to see you when I tell you. I could always read your expressions like an open book when we were growing up. I've got to know you're on my side."

"Bryana, if I come out there again, Tank will only start up with something else. Is everyone on your place okay?"

Bryana answered tersely, "Yes, we're physically okay. But we need to talk. Please, Norm. This is *very* important."

"I'll meet you somewhere."

Bryana gripped the phone. "Look, if you're frightened of losing Roland's backing, then I'm wasting my time. I'll take it directly to the state attorney's office."

There was a brief pause. "I said we could meet. And I'm not afraid of Tank or Vince. I just don't want them taking out retribution on you."

"I hope you're telling me the truth, Norm. Look, we're going to the Brass Rail tonight to see Ricki perform. How about before that? We could meet somewhere."

"The old Stuart place has been vacant since they lost it last winter. It's in foreclosure now. We can meet there without being spotted." With a moment of hesitation, he continued, "Bryana, this is where you usually tell me not to bother. Are you okay?"

"I'll be there at seven. It's still light outside then." With reluctance, Bryana added, "Norm, I need to trust you."

"Seven. Bryana, I am on your team. I've been on your team for decades. I'm not a fella who changes teams mid-game."

As she hung up, she thought she'd heard a believable, sincere response in his voice.

She told Michelle, "We can meet Norm at seven. Before we go to Ricki's show."

"Will it do us any good?" Michelle inquired with reluctance.

Bryana turned, facing the wall. She saw her mother's favorite plaque. On it were written the words: Toss a little seasoning into food and life. "Maybe."

The women finished their chores, showered, and dressed to go into town. Michelle had carefully typed out the information on the loan note scheme. She included names, phone numbers, and verbatim reports, single spaced, on one single page. Eric Schumacher, Tom Haskel, and Gina Hamersmith had all experienced the same strange emergence of a loan they knew nothing about. Attorney Paul Brody was dubious about the loan. But didn't have enough actual evidence to refer to it as being fraudulent – only highly suspicious.

Bryana pulled the SUV onto the small dirt road leading up to the Fred Stuart farmhouse. She smiled slightly.

"You're smiling?" Michelle questioned.

"The meeting place. Fred Stuart and his wife lived here. This vacant farm is in foreclosure, and is about to be turned over to the bank. Roland will take over ownership. The farm's auction advertisement from the bank won't be dispersed. Roland will place the lowest bid. He's buying all the property surrounding us. Or stealing it. He's squeezing us out."

"He's *trying* to squeeze us out," Michelle corrected.

"I'm smiling because on this very land, we are meeting to attempt to get the theft ended. Wouldn't it be superb irony if this was the turning point that would show what a crook Roland is?"

"I'm not saying it's a probability. But it is possible," Michelle said with a laugh.

"I'm hoping probable."

Sheriff Norm Myer had viewed this as important enough to have changed out vehicles. He drove his own compact Ford, Michelle had noted. "Does it mean he doesn't want to appear official when he blows off this information?"

"I'm guessing he already knows it's important. He's attempting to protect us from being harmed. If anything comes down, he doesn't want us in the crossfire."

Michelle took Bryana's arm before she exited the SUV. "Are you sure?" Michelle asked. "I honestly think we could be in danger if Vince Roland discovers we've got all this information."

"I'm as certain as I can be. Do you want to come?"

Michelle handed the paper to Bryana. "I'll wait here."

Bryana met Norm midway. His heavy plod was uneasy. He held out his hand to shake hers. "Bryana."

"Thanks for meeting us, Norm." She quickly handed him the paper then systematically explained the information she had."

His blanched face froze by the time she'd reached the third name on the list. "In court they call this a preponderance of evidence." He exhaled loudly. "Okay. Here's what we do. Don't tell anyone else about this. Sit back and wait."

"I don't have time. My note is due Friday or Roland throws the farm into foreclosure. If I don't hear from you by Friday morning, I'm taking it to the district attorney. And higher."

"Don't take it anywhere. Listen to me, *you can't* say anything to anyone. Not the district attorney. No one. Just drop it. Let me handle it. Please, Bryana. Trust me." Concern covered his face.

"Can I trust you?" she asked. His eyes blinked. She saw a glint of pain. "Well, can I?"

"Yes." His hand reached up to his hair, and he scratched the side of his head. "Please do as I say. It's more important than you know."

"Norm, I mean it. I'll take it to the Supreme Court if I have to."

"I'm going to take care of it. Don't interfere."

"If…" she began her follow-up threat.

Through clenched teeth, he growled, "Listen, damn it. You don't know what you're dealing with. I know where the bodies are buried. I know who to talk with about this. And who won't take it back to Roland. You don't know."

She wanted to persist, but saw the anger in his eyes. "Don't let me down, Norm."

He turned quickly, folding the paper twice and placing it in his shirt pocket before he reached his car. Once in the driver's seat, he looked back at Bryana. His nod to her was both a goodbye, and a stern warning.

When Bryana got into the SUV, her eyes watered. "Michelle, I'm not certain what to think about this. He told me to keep quiet about it. He said we don't know what we're dealing with. His words were like a precursor to doom."

"Enough people probably already know. By now it's been stirred and things are coming to the surface. If Vince or Tank harms us, the people we've talked with about it will eventually say something."

Bryana's face tensed. "Or they might take it back to Vince. I'm not certain what to do."

"For now, let's go enjoy Ricki's show. Have a brew. Try to relax."

Chapter 27

The trip to the Brass Rail was silent. Each woman was considering their problem from their own vantage point. Saving the farm was paramount. But they were two days and six-thousand dollars away from buying off the immediate danger.

The Brass Rail was filling quickly with not only the regulars, but also a younger crowd from Payton College. Ricki and Gloria spotted the women, and went immediately to give them hugs. Ricki said, "Glad you're here. Gloria has a message from Tess."

Gloria began jabbering quickly. "Mom heard about your difficulties. She says she wants to pre-pay for her next orders. She gave me a check for you. She was going to try to come, but my grandpa isn't doing too great. We're going over to the hospital after Ricki's done." Gloria delved through her handbag, and finally pulled out a crumpled check. "One-thousand dollars."

Both Michelle and Bryana hugged her as they were handed the check. "We'll tell her when we see her. But thank her tonight for us. And we'll be praying for her father."

"He's tough, and promised he'd make it to see me graduate. So I think he'll be around awhile longer," Gloria said with an enthusiastic tone to her voice. "At least I hope so."

Michelle smiled as she put the check inside her bag. "We appreciate it. That's a lot of Victoria's Bubble Bread."

"Tess sells lots of it," Ricki said with a laugh. "Anymore it seems like she sells a bubble bread order with each cup of coffee." She frowned then spoke pensively, "Oh, and Bryana, Charlotte said to come back to her office when you get here. Don't worry, I won't begin without you."

"You'd better not. We're diehard fans. Your first Kansas fans," Bryana said. "I'll be right back." She had never been called back to Charlotte's office, slash, stockroom, and when she ducked into the small room, she hoped she had the right place. "Ricki said you wanted to see me."

From behind a small marred desk, Charlotte pointed to the guest chair. "Yeah. Have a seat."

"Cramped quarters," Bryana observed with a laugh.

"Don't mind the cramped quarters, but the desk is a little small to get laid on." Her husky laugh filled the confined room.

"Not big enough for a mattress."

"Bryana, when I'm getting banged, I'm not thinking about my back's comfort." Again she roared, and Bryana followed suit. "Hey, Eric Schumacher was in this afternoon. I told him about Ricki playing, and he immediately put the two together that she'd been at your place. I told him you'd be in tonight. Well, he gets this look like someone stepped on his wanger. I pick up on some problem, and you know how I am with shit I don't know about. A dog with a bone." She was tickled by that line. "Or a boner."

"I know you appreciate having the scoop," Bryana joked.

"Anyway, I finally got it out of Schumacher. He told me about the *loans* and it didn't surprise me a bit. Vince Roland has always been a crook. Now he's a richer crook. Anyway, when Eric found out you'd be in here, he said to give you this. And you're not to worry about catching up on the implement payments until you get square."

Bryana looked at the check for a thousand dollars. "This is really kind of him."

"Yeah, well, he feels the same way the rest of us do. We all hate Vince, and want him to fail. You women don't hurt anyone. You always took care of your parents, and this town revered them."

"We'll pay everyone back as soon as harvest is completed. And if the wheat field gets leveled by a storm, it will be a long wait." Bryana computed. "Tess prepaid for bakery goods, and that brings our tally up."

"I heard the amount was twenty-five grand."

"Yes. Friends have been so good. We're now about four-thousand shy of the mark. Maybe the bank would settle for most of the money."

"Don't count on it, Bryana. We both know it isn't money Vince is after. He wants your property."

"Tank used to keep the hunters away, but now he's obviously encouraging them to fire towards our farm. The gunfire has accelerated. He's doing it to anger us, thinking we'll cave in. Of course they want the farm. Vince has probably told Tank to hassle us."

Charlotte repeated, "Hell yeah, he wants the farm. And by damn he's not going to get it." She opened her desk drawer and pulled out the huge checkbook. She ripped one check off quickly. With a sweep of her pen, she filled in the figures then signed it. When she handed it over to Bryana, she reaffirmed, "That fucker isn't going to win this time. Here's your four grand. I told you before, we need to collectively stand up to him."

"Charlotte, this is a gamble. I don't want you to lose your money. And if the crop doesn't come in, you'll be awhile getting this back. You work hard for your money."

"Naw, I *play* hard for my money."

Bryana extended the check back to Charlotte. "I can't take this much money. I know everyone is struggling. If the crop fails...."

Charlotte pushed Bryana's hand back. "You take it. The crop isn't going to fail. And if it does, you pay me off in pottery. Bring me some tankards. And I'll need a steady stream of those platters. I been selling them to the old duffers who need to give their wives a present when they come home with beer breath. And if the crop is a bumper crop like they're saying it will be, we'll get our money back. A deal?"

"A deal. Thanks."

"My real payoff is seeing Vince Roland finally lose."

As Bryana walked from the office that had a small *party* desk in the center, she felt the warmth of friendship. Bryana remembered one of her father's favorite sayings. We're all born cantankerous, self-centered, and greedy. The worst of the bunch are the people who stay greedy. Bryana added her own take. The best of all are those who become kind, loving, and generous. She now knew she was *among many* of those people. They were her neighbors, friends, and people she barely knew.

Ricki saw her, and stopped her warm up of various chords. After playing the first set, she joined Gloria, Michelle and Bryana at the bar.

"Terrific," Gloria toasted her. She handed Ricki a long-necked beer. "Charlotte just said she wants to find some more dates to book you. Everyone loves the way you've weaved music from the sixties through to this year. And they loved your songs. Look at this crowd."

"This is like a dream," Ricki murmured. Her head sunk downward. "I never figured I'd be in Buffalo Plains, Kansas, playing to a standing-room only crowd."

Michelle shook her head, acknowledging Ricki's point. "Did you see the regulars cheering? Not just the youngsters like you. Those of us a little past middle-age are clapping our hands off. I'm proud of you, Ricki." Michelle hugged her shoulder. To prove her point, she nudged the bar patron sitting beside her. She asked, "Don't you like this singer?"

He nodded, tipping his hat. "You bettcha."

"And she's got an amazing voice?" Bryana encouraged him to say more.

"You bettcha. But I come in here mostly 'cause of my mom."

Michelle asked, "Why because of your mother?"

"I was off outta Tinpsila County when that tornado edged town. It messed up our place. My mama was in trouble, scared and all. She got trapped in the house all night. She tells me the next day a woman and some young gal saved her. The young gal was tall and had short hair standin' up. She come in to get my mama. Stuff started falling, but the young gal kept a coming for my ma. Pulled my mama outta the rubble. I figured it was this here Ricki who was the one who helped my mama. That makes her a mighty fine friend."

Tears formed in Bryana's eyes. She'd remember Ricki crawling through the debris to rescue an elderly woman. And Ricki sang old classics to calm the woman. "Yes. Ricki is a mighty fine friend."

By the end of the night, the women dispersed. On the trip back to the farm, Bryana and Michelle called L.J. to relay the success of the performance. Also to tell her they'd raised the money to pay the loan. It was a happy moment in an otherwise unhappy time for the women. However both women were well aware of fate's fickleness.

On the trip back to the farmhouse, they'd heard the weather report stating there was a strong possibility of a thunderstorm over the weekend. Each tried to ignore it, hoping the other hadn't heard it. But they both had.

When Bryana eased the SUV nearer the driveway, she felt her spirit go lame. She wondered why she hadn't turned the radio off when they'd started home. Although it hadn't entirely blemished the evening's bright spots, Bryana knew the truth. She had been encumbered by the sorrow of uncertainty. As if by some patchwork of fortune, the money became available due to the generosity of friends and neighbors. Now, she would be indebted to them if the crop was washed away by a storm. Pain commingled with gratitude. Heartache meshed inside hope. She knew that looping barbed wire around her heart wouldn't solve the problems she faced.

Michelle read her lover's thoughts. "At least maybe this will encourage peace in the neighborhood."

As she directed the SUV into the garage, Bryana suddenly cited a quote. "In the words of Spinoza: 'Peace is not an absence of war. It's a virtue, a state of mind, and a disposition for benevolence, confidence and justice.'"

Michelle unlocked the farmhouse's front door. She turned and frowned. "You never quote anyone other than your parents. What in the world brought that on?"

"It seemed appropriate. It's a line I had to memorize for a college philosophy class."

"Glad we had this little confab," Michelle teased.

With self-ridicule, Bryana answered, "Okay, I admit I know more about both our parents' philosophy than I learned in college. Especially your mom's unique viewpoint."

"Jersey was a sage." Michelle switched on the light, greeted the dogs, and then turned into Bryana's embrace and kiss. She held Bryana as near as she could. She whispered in her lover's ear, "Jersey would tell us to pick up our boobs and carry on."

"We'll do just that. We can't afford to ignore a proverb." Bryana wondered why she was so fortunate. Her passion for Michelle never waned. And her desire to please her spouse never faltered. Over the years, each of their kisses seemed orchestrated by fortune each time they neared. Each embrace, Bryana reflected, was a special delivery from the goddesses.

Michelle caressed Bryana's face. "Bryana, my own philosophy is that pies and wine are two of the three best known aphrodisiacs."

"That's a delicious thought. But what's the third?" She baited. "The mysterious third?"

"The correct kiss."

Chapter 28

Being awakened too early had left Bryana's energy level tipping towards the negative side. She'd heard several rounds of gunfire coming from the Roland spread. It was a given that Tank's introductory message to the each new group of hunters included some type of annoyance instructions. Hunters could successfully down game during *very* early morning hours. And naturally, he probably had suggested the side of his property nearest the Hays farm. He'd set the game cages open at the crack of dawn, and directly to his east.

Once the sun had cleared the panoramic view, the gunfire began. The hunter's boisterous yelps when they fired were also annoying. Bryana's tranquility faded as the morning became louder with gunshot and obnoxious clamoring. She turned the music in her studio up loudly while she sculpted her clay.

Get a grip, she cautioned herself. Her own anger distressed her more than the Rolands. She took deep breaths as she listened to the loud, yet mellow songs from the past. Nothing calmed her. Even knowing that she had the money ready to take in to the Buffalo Plains Bank the next day hadn't eased the distress. She felt a self-induced calm, in between calamitous gunshots that filled the skyway.

Having the good fortune to collect the funds didn't mean Vince Roland's buddy Chad Donovan wouldn't up the ante. He could have found additional *outstanding* loans. What then? It was as if they could manufacture documents at will. They'd probably had Anthony Hays sign a few extra copies of benign looking papers. Those could be dredged up and doctored to suit their needs. Vince knew how to cover his tracks with all the appropriate documents.

Anthony Hays had grown up in a generation of Americans who believed their leaders. They believed in banks, post offices, police, judges and anyone wearing an official uniform, or who had an official sounding title. They believed in decency, and truth. But this was a different time.

Throughout the day the gunshots rang, as if taunting the women. Tank and Vince might have heard about the funds being raised and decided on another fear campaign. The women had cautiously kept their livestock in the barn, and the dogs in the house. They knew the hunter's bullets would get less accurate as the afternoon wore on. The more alcoholic consumption, the less visual difference between a cow and a deer.

By early afternoon, Bryana realized she'd skipped lunch. She was not only hungry, she needed a getaway. She entered the kitchen where Michelle was busily baking. Michelle had timing down to a precise art. While pie dough was resting, she worked on bubble bread, and pie filling. While another few pies were baking, she formed and filled pie crusts.

"Are you able to take a break with me?" Bryana inquired. She poured coffee for both women and made a space at the table. In the refrigerator was a carefully covered bowl of grilled vegetables from the previous day. She placed the lunch in their microwave.

Michelle eased into the chair. "Sure. Pies won't be ready to take out of the oven for another ten." She poured cream then took a sip. "The skies look fine, so far."

Although Bryana was aware Michelle was attempting to cheer her, there was the reality of the weekend storm forecast. "Maybe Saturday's storm will pass over us. That's what Billy said yesterday when he dropped off the check for our loan. Said he had booked the harvest crews for Monday and Tuesday. A little early, he claimed, but the wheat was looking dry. While he was here he commented on the several rounds of gunfire he heard. He had no idea it was so bad. I told him it had increased."

"I'll bet he's glad we're in between his property and Tank's."

Bryana affirmed, "Oh, yes. And I'm of the opinion Billy would have lent us the entire amount just to keep us from losing the farm to the Roland clan. Tank's land abutting his isn't part of his grand design." There was a moment's pause as Bryana stirred her coffee. "All these years, I never realized how much pressure my father was under just to save his own farm. I'm certain he anguished over it."

"I'm sure he wanted to spare you. But yes, I've thought about that recently."

"Dad never complained. He just continued on with his easy going attitude. Maybe when Mom was sick he might have requested quiet on her behalf. Other than that, he probably filled his ears with cotton."

Michelle chuckled. "Your father was the finest man in the county. I'm sure Tank would have thought twice about alienating him too badly."

"Dad and Mom were well-respected in the community. We're not."

As soon as the pies were ready to be extracted from the oven, Michelle sighed. "Break is over. Maybe if the crop comes in and we pay back the people we owe, there might be some left over. I know we've got other bills, but we could pay them in increments, and purchase another stove or two. Use the metal storage area outside as our mini-factory. Build the business."

"Spoken like Jersey's daughter. She always told you to dream. And yes, we can work on the greenhouse and a bakery. If we clear out some of the farm implements to sell, it would leave the metal shed open. We're leasing out most the farmland to be planted by Billy and Rolf, so there's no need for much other than the tractor. And the tractor has most of the implement attachments we might use. Whatever money we got from the hay rake, tiller, and even that old combine, could go to bakery ovens and equipment."

Michelle kissed her spouse's cheek. "I'm glad you still believe in dreams."

"Dreams don't cost anything. And that's about all our finances can afford."

Bryana headed out towards her studio. There was a series of echoing gunfire from the edge of the Roland property. Her thoughts were that the small bakery would need insulation to silence the hideous gunshot sounds.

Suddenly she heard a piercing yowl. Looking westward, she saw Tank and a hunter running towards the field. There was a colorful, tiny pile crumpled on the ground. Tank was screaming at the top of his lungs. "Help. Help. Jonny. Oh, God, no!" He shoved the hunter to the side, as he rushed to the area.

Chills covered Bryana's flesh. She screamed towards the house. "Michelle, bring your bag. An emergency - gunshot wound." Barely audible was Michelle's response that she was coming. Bryana's legs flew across the furrowed land. She crawled beneath the barbed-wire fencing.

Shock covered Tank's face, as well as the hunter who was in a drunken stupor. His gun was pointing down, with his grasp on it tottering. He was blubbering about being sorry. And he was clearly in a drunken state.

Bryana was glad she'd neared before Tank sent the man away. She could identify him and testify to his actions and statements. When the housekeeper came rushing towards Tank, he instructed her to keep Alice and the girls away. He then told the hunter to go inside and to make certain the other hunters stayed inside.

Bryana approached Tank. "Michelle is on her way. She was an emergency room R.N. for a quarter century. She'll know what to do. Tank, listen to me," she said as the shook his arm. "Call 911. Get an ambulance out here immediately. Call 911. Tell them to have the hospital get Jon's blood type from records. He'll need blood." Tank froze. Bryana screamed, "Call now!" He fumbled in his pocket for his phone. Bryana was relieved when she heard his call. "Stay on the phone with them," she instructed.

She knelt beside Jon. Blood spurted from the wound on his neck, just above his shoulder. A pool of blood was beneath the small child's neck. She pulled Jon's t-shirt upward, and pressed it against the wound. Hearing Michelle's steps behind her, she yelled, "Neck. He's bleeding out."

Michelle slid to her knees. Flinging open the medic's bag, she grabbed a square dressing. She ripped open the package of gauze. Securely, as she moved the bloodied t-shirt to the side, she placed the patch against the wound. "This is a blood coagulation patch. It has a hemostatic agent. Hold this a minute. Keep direct pressure on it."

As Michelle was digging through her bag, Bryana reported, "There's some respiration, but it's very shallow."

209

"And the heartbeat is faint." Michelle added. Just as if she were calmly explaining to trainees, she added, "I'm now going to put a pressure dressing on top of the coagulation patch. Then slowly let's elevate the head and shoulders, placing the medic's bag under his head. It will help slow down the bleeding. I hope that the carotid artery on the opposite side of the neck will supply adequate blood flow to the brain."

"Think they'll be brain damage?" Bryana questioned as the women lifted the shoulders and head tenderly. Michelle's one hand still rested upon the wound area.

"How long will it take for the ambulance to get here?" Michelle's concern showed with her frown.

"Probably fifteen to twenty minutes." As Jon gasped for air, Michelle's glance of helplessness distressed Bryana. "Maybe less."

Michelle looked up at where Tank was in the background sobbing uncontrollably. "Tell him to wait for the ambulance down by the road. Get him out of here."

Bryana relayed the message. Tank stumbled towards the road to wave down emergency vehicles when they arrived.

"I'm not sure he'll make it, Bry. The side of the carotid artery is clipped. All we can do is try to control the bleeding with pressure. He's lost so much blood."

Bryana found herself counting Jon's breaths. Suddenly she noticed Jon's breath becoming jagged. His body began to shudder, and then a wave appeared to run through him. Finally, breath lagged to a stop.

"Quickly, hold this dressing again. Steady, firm," Michelle directed.

As instructed, Bryana leaned over Jon, and her hand clasped the top of the dressing on his neck. "Oh, God," she whispered.

Immediately Michelle, spoke, "Let's get him flat in case chest compression becomes necessary." She tilted Jon's small head back. She began CPR. Carefully, so that she wouldn't over-ventilate, she watched for a small rise in his chest. She massaged his chest for what seemed to Bryana an eternity. Within another few minutes, Jon's breath had started, shallowly at first.

"I hope his lungs aren't just spitting air," Michelle said. As she spoke, Jon inhaled slightly. "Come on, little buddy. Come on." Again there were a series of Jon's ragged breaths. "His heart is beating. Not like a drum. It's beating very faintly, but it's there." The nurse's eyes misted. "It's there."

The siren wailed as Norm Myer's vehicle spun to a screeching halt. Gravel and dust had been flung for several feet. Behind him was the ambulance in full emergency light and sound mode. The responding technicians rushed to the boy. Immediately Michelle explained her credentials, and what she'd done, and what needed to be done. As they lifted the small boy onto the gurney, she offered to accompany them. The younger emergency medic said he remembered seeing her at the hospital after the tornado. He welcomed her assistance. He then explained that the surgeon in ER was just out of med school, and could probably use an assist. Michelle glanced back at Bryana.

"I'll follow." Bryana said.

Chapter 29

It seemed as though hours had elapsed. Yet it had only been minutes since the ambulance pulled out of the driveway. Left behind were Bryana, Norm, and Tank.

Norm ordered, "Tank, you'll ride with me. First, go and see if Alice is coming, and tell the hunter who fired the shot that he is to remain on this premises or I'll add an eluding charge. We got witnesses, so don't pull a switch." As soon as Tank left, Norm asked Bryana, "Do you mind sticking around here until Pete gets here? I need you to identify the shooter."

"I'll be glad to stay and identify him while he's still drunk. Then I'll lock up the farm, and get to the hospital."

"I'll meet you there. I'll need statements."

Bitterly Bryana announced, "Oh yes, I can't wait to give you a statement. Alice wasn't available *now* for the same reason she doesn't watch the children. She's probably been medicating again. Tank is tipsy – lit up. And the hunter who shot Jon was fucking drunk. Staggering drunk. Wearing fatigues as if he just landed in Afghanistan. Earlier he was strutting around like he was a soldier. I remember thinking what a disgrace for the brave men and women who actually have courage. No bravery required to shoot unarmed wildlife and children."

"You saw him at the scene?"

"Absolutely. Afterwards, he was wandering around screaming how sorry he was. I saw his face, and I'll never forget it. And he was falling down drunk. Will that statement do?"

"Bryana, I'm on your side. You don't have to tell me what's going on in that house. Alice is oxy-ied out. She's drinking. Can you blame her for dousing the pain of being married to that horse's ass? And speaking of Tank, he's going to be charged, and this business of his is going to be shut down. I promise you. I'll see to it the charge sticks. And I'll be suggesting Alice get some rehab."

"I'll believe it when I see it."

"Bryana, I do believe the city has made you cynical," Norm said in an attempt at humor.

"My cynicism began when I returned here," she dryly replied.

The sheriff watched as Tank slammed his farmhouse door behind him. He approached and stood by Norm's vehicle. "Come on, I'm waiting," he insisted. "The bitch ain't coming."

Norm scowled as he looked towards Tank.

"You're being summoned," Bryana sarcastically said to the sheriff.

"Not so much." Norm yelled back at Tank, "You are in my custody. Shut your sorry mouth, or you'll be wearing bracelets on the drive to the hospital. You'd be in them now if I believed in cuffing someone in front of the kids." He motioned towards the upstairs window where the drapery was flagging from side to side. Nita and Letty were watching.

"Don't start with me, Norm," Tank's words were threatening.

"We've got child neglect, reckless endangerment, and many more important charges pending."

Tank defiantly leaned towards Norm as Norm approached. "You aren't going to charge me."

"Not until after I've taken statements. I've already called child services on my way here. They'll be here to assess the problems. And Pete will be along momentarily to arrest your client."

"It was a goddamn accident. You charge me or bother my client, and you're going to be losing the next election," Tank shouted belligerently.

"I told you to shut your mouth. Get in that vehicle, and do not open your mouth until we get to the hospital."

Tank began to square off.

Norm gave him a shove. "In the car. Don't give me a reason to take you in full restraints, 'cause I'll do it. You sorry son of a bitch," he said between clamped teeth. Quickly he turned to see Bryana's face painted in pain. "Sorry, Bryana. I didn't think of Sarah."

By the time the sheriff's car rolled away towards the hospital, Pete had arrived. With vibrato, he stormed the hunter's lodge. When he exited, the inebriated hunter was in cuffs. Pete requested that Bryana identify him. And Bryana sadly nodded. This was the drunken man who had shot down a five-year old child.

Pete then said they were going immediately for a drug and alcohol impairment test. Bryana felt her own hatred with her scowl into the hunter's eyes. She saw fear in his eyes as he was taken into custody by Pete. The familiar Miranda rights were hastily given while Pete placed the shooter into the squad vehicle.

Bryana slowly, deliberately, walked towards her farmhouse.

After letting the dogs out, she scrubbed blood from her hands and arms. Turning off the stove, she looked around for anything else that needed to be taken care of. She called the dogs back in, turned the lights on in case it might be dark when the women returned, and finally locked up and left. On her way out to the SUV, Bryana felt her stomach clench. Above all, she didn't want to hear bad news concerning Jon.

The trip to the hospital wasn't hurried. It was not that she wasn't concerned about finding out if little Jon had survived. She simply couldn't force herself. Certainly Michelle would remain with the surgical team until she was no longer needed,

Bryana realized there was nothing she could do. Other than wait for Michelle. Norm would be busy and would be around waiting with Tank, and she'd already identified the drunken shooter to Pete. Not hurrying seemed acceptable.

Knowing the grandparents would be arriving, and would be in the waiting room, was another reason Bryana hadn't rushed. She had no desire to see Sarah and Vince. Although it was indirectly, they were partially responsibility for the tragedy. All the adults were culpable. Everyone had been warned multiples of times. Now the worst possible scenario had happened. Bryana self-edited her thought. So far, it wasn't the worst possible outcome. But if the child didn't pull through, it would indeed be the worst.

As she drove the SUV into the hospital's parking lot, she saw Vince's Jaguar. She parked on the opposite side of the lot. Sitting in her parked vehicle, Bryana felt tears splashing down her cheeks before she knew she was crying. For whatever reason, Bryana didn't want to enter the hospital. She knew she must to be questioned by Norm. And she must wait for Michelle. But she wanted to turn the vehicle back around and return home.

For several moments she attempted to analyze her reasoning. She probed deeply into her emotional storage vault. She thought of the terror of this event. Seeing a human body fighting for life was horrendous. Feeling the slime of blood and inhaling its smell also sickened her. From the smears on Jon's small neck and face, and the squirting fountain from his neck – blood. The wound area with its tangled edges of flesh was frightening. There was a child who was not breathing, and was without a pulse. Unthinkable, she considered.

For all those years, her lover had watched life and death – pain. Bryana wondered about her own sensitivity. Had she been understanding enough, supportive enough to help Michelle get through her quiet moods?

Her eyes fastened tightly in an effort to stop the tears that were drenching her face. As if she, herself, was asphyxiating, Bryana gasped for air. Her head lowered as she sobbed against the steering wheel. Her reason was simple, yet more complex than any other emotion she'd ever had. Her sorrow was greater. She didn't want the world to lose a child. She didn't want to see Sarah. Sarah would be experiencing the pain of her lifetime. Bryana didn't want to see Sarah hurting to that depth.

Chapter 30

Bryana passed the waiting room. Inside were Tank, Vince, and Sarah Roland, along with the admittance nurse. Stationed outside the room was a Sheriff's Deputy.

With her head down, Bryana quickly made her way to the entrance of the emergency room. A tall, young physician came from the door. He went directly to the waiting area. Bryana sat on a vacant bench in the hallway.

Within a few moments Michelle exited. She slid the mask she was wearing from her face. "He'll live."

Bryana embraced her, in an attempt to comfort her. "It's okay now, Michelle. Thanks to you." With an expression of pure exhaustion, Michelle weary eyes watered then tear droplets rolled. "You said he'll be okay."

"It's just my usual post-trauma breakdown. When you know a child, it's even worse than ever. Bryana, he's a five-year old kid. We nearly lost him."

"But you didn't."

Splattered blood had caked on Michelle's shirt, as well as her neck and face. Streaks of dried orange-hued rusty red had dripped down her arms to a line around her wrists, where gloves had been worn. "Guess I look a little ghoulish," she said with a slight, forced laugh.

Bryana held her tighter. "It's all going to be okay."

Another nurse exited. "You going to be alright?" she asked Michelle.

When Michelle shook her head, the nurse added, "I remember you from when you helped during the tornado."

"Yes, I have all my certification because I'd planned on trying to get a job here. It appeared I wasn't experienced enough," Michelle said with a tone of irony, mixed with bitterness.

The nurse nodded knowingly. "Well, one thing I know. That kid was lucky you were nearby. Like the doctor said, your work was perfect. You didn't even have an ER your disposal."

"We got the blood stopped," Michelle replied. "And when his vitals stopped, we got his heart beating and breath flowing again. Bryana helped or I wouldn't have been able to do as much, as quickly, by myself."

"You're a hero."

"Most medics are heroes," Michelle said. "I did what I was trained to do. Bryana was a bystander thrown into a crisis, and she did one heck of a good job." Michelle smiled at her lover. "I'm always proud of her, but today – even more proud."

"Well, you saved his life. He'd never had made it." The nurse pointed to a door. "You can get yourself washed up there. I've brought you some clean scrubs to wear home." She glanced over at Bryana. "Looks like you'll need a change, too. I'll scrounge up some more scrubs."

Nodding, Michelle then whispered to Bryana, "I'll be back in a couple of minutes."

Through a door's window panel, Bryana saw a gurney with the child, as it was rolled across from the surgery room into a recovery room. Beneath the cover, his body seemed so small it was barely decipherable. Jon's tiny body was attached to dripping IVs.

When Bryana turned she saw the doctor, accompanied by Tank. They were going through the door into the recovery room. Tank's expressionless face appeared not to have even registered Bryana's standing in the hall.

She wouldn't have known what to say to him had he spoken. Michelle had been gone several minutes. She was undoubtedly breaking down, releasing tears she had to control while being a nurse. Knowing why Michelle was taking so long, Bryana looked back at the waiting room where Sarah and Vince were arguing. Sarah's eyes suddenly tagged hers. Bryana turned, looking back at the wall.

She felt a hand on her shoulder. Believing it was Michelle, Bryana whirled around. Her mouth bobbed for words, and then shut.

It was a tearful Sarah. Her face was drawn, aged, and her eyes were soggy with tears. "Bryana, you saved my grandson's life."

"Michelle did. I only helped."

"Thank you. Thank you so much," she sobbed.

Bryana wanted to reach out, but remained barely breathing, without a motion. "We would have done it for anyone."

Bryana looked behind Sarah to see Vince.

Vince didn't look her in the eyes, he just muttered. "We're grateful to you and your... Michelle." He sneered then gruffly said, "Makes up for what you did to my family. All these years my wife has been under suspicion for the friendship she had with a lesbian."

"Vince," Sarah pulled him by his sleeve. "Just shut up about that."

"Why, so more stories can be spread about you and the lesbian? More allegations."

"Enough!" she screamed. "They *weren't* allegations. I accused her of lying when I broke off the relationship we'd had. *That's right*. Bryana and I *had* a relationship." Sarah's eyes were fiery as she spat, "I didn't want to marry you. My parents and grandparents wanted me to marry you. I have always been in love with Bryana. Every day of my life has been filled with thoughts of her. Not you."

He jerked her arm, "You're tired, emotional. You don't know what you're saying."

"After all these years, I know exactly what I'm saying. Bryana didn't lie. She did nothing wrong. It was me. I was frightened about what society would say."

"It's okay. You had a youthful dalliance, Sarah. I forgive you. Back then, I understand you couldn't own up to it. I love you. All is forgiven."

"*Nothing is forgiven*. I want everyone to know. Bryana is no liar."

"You're Tank's mother," Vince attempted to quiet her. "What will he think?"

"Right now I don't care what he thinks. You wanted me to sign a prenuptial agreement before we married. I'm so glad I agreed. I still own the farm our son is living on. And now I'm making the rules. No more hunting club. If Tank wants to remain there, he's going to put in a corn and wheat crop. He's going to farm that land. Otherwise he can find a new home. And he's going to get his wife to rehab like I attempted to insist last year. No one would listen to me when I said hunting was dangerous and Alice was negligent."

"Sweetheart," Vince said with a sugary voice. "I stuck by you through the heartless things people said. Now I forgive you for your sins, and you must forgive Alice."

With disbelief, Sarah shoved his reaching hand away from her. "Don't touch me. Don't ever touch me again, you sanctimonious bastard. You are the most insufferable human being I've ever known," Sarah shot back.

In an attempt to thwart the conversation, Vince turned to Bryana. "Please thank Michelle for me."

"I'll let her know. Or maybe you can tell her yourself when we come to pay the loan tomorrow. That *mysterious* loan that suddenly appeared. The one you thought would topple us. And then nothing would stand between you and getting my farm. We have the money."

"What money?" Sarah questioned.

Bryana answered loudly, "To pay off the note that was found *after* my father died. The note he presented to us a few days ago for us to pay or lose our farm. Well, his henchman presented it to us. But it was per Vince's instructions."

Quickly, Vince responded, "Since all this, well…Well, I'll see that your loan is forgiven."

"Fuck you, you filthy thief. You're a goddamned fraudulent, scheming swindler," Bryana enunciated the words between her teeth. "You'll get your money. Or rather, you'll steal my money. Knowing now that it's happened to many other townspeople makes a lawsuit a probability. We'll all stand together and ask why these post-death bank notes appeared."

"What's she talking about?" Sarah insisted.

"Nothing important," he said. "Bryana, you come into the bank tomorrow and we'll take care of all this."

"I'll be there alright. And so will the others it happened to. Eric Schumacher, Tom Haskell, Gina Hamersmith, and probably many more. We'll all be there. Yes, they'll come forward with their suspicions of fraud."

Sarah whirled around. "You've been stealing from the townspeople?"

Both of his arms lifted and waved. With panic, he shook his head. "It's all a mistake."

"And you're going to give me your special indulgence. Forgive me for my *sin*."

"Sarah, I can explain..." His eyes pleaded. "I'm in love with you. I can't live without you. I can explain."

Bryana saw Norm approach. Norm's eyes held a scorching hatred. His words were directed to Vince, "I hope you can explain. Because right now, at this very moment, the State bank regulators I called in yesterday and the Kansas Bureau Fraud Division are talking with your employees. The bank examiners want to know about misappropriation of bank funds. About fraud."

"My bank employees won't have anything to say," Vince staunchly argued.

"Sure they will. I'm guessing Chad Donovan is talking right now. Smug Chad Donovan is blubbering and blabbing. He's probably making a great deal for himself. You can bet your ass he'll be talking."

Vince's shoulders sunk. As if his entire body was deflating, his steep height was diminished. "Look, I'm telling you," Vince rushed his words. His voice pitched upward. "It's a mistake."

"You think?"

"Norm, we go back..."

"Now we're going forward. Your grandson is going to be fine. Your grandchildren are going to be watched by social services to make certain Alice gets help so she can be a real mother. Your son is a completely corrupted idiot. But maybe without you pulling his strings, he might get straight. For now, he's probably going to do some time. Incarceration is a great learning curve for morons like Tank. And if you end up cellmates, maybe you can be a father to him for the first time."

"I raised him up tough. To be a man. He didn't do anything wrong."

"Tank became a man of privilege, just like you. You are all responsible for that child lying in there. He could have been killed. Don't you get that?" Norm spoke. "You all knew there was alcohol on the premise, and it was being used illegally. Tank is a criminal."

Sarah said, "Tank deserves what he gets. You have my word. There will be no hunting for recreation on that property ever again. And Alice deserves a chance to get well. She will." Her desolate eyes narrowed to loathing. "And Vince is worse than Tank. Imagine, my husband is worse than my worthless son. I was so stupid."

Norm pointed towards the door. "Vince, I'm going to give you a ride down to the bank to talk to some officials with questions. They're waiting for you."

Vince's eyes were agape with fear. "But I didn't do anything!"

Without a blink, Norm continued, "They may want to detain you. I'm warning you, the bank regulators are going to get your business all squared away. Some Buffalo Plains folks are going to be getting unexpected return of monies swindled from their bank accounts."

"If anything happened, I didn't know about it," Vince muttered. "I didn't."

"A court will determine that. For now, there may be a bank closure. You'll have attorney fees. You're going to be finished around here. Broke and humiliated. And even after all your fortune is spent, you're probably still going to be incarcerated."

"I'm not involved," Vince whined. "Can't you vouch for me?" he pleaded with Norm.

"Not in the least. Because I'm going to be getting the town's business squared away. For now, don't do anything at all I can interpret as resistance to my authority. I want so badly to bust your face and smash you to the ground."

"I don't need to go with you," Vince objected. "I'm not under arrest. Come on, for old time's sake."

"I've been ordered to bring you in. Old time's sake. I'm not putting cuffs on you. But if you resist, I'll cuff you. And I'll throw your sorry ass in the lousiest cell we have. And I'll have the State Agents pick you up there. What's your pleasure?"

Vince held the car keys out to Sarah. She grabbed them with a vengeance.

He timidly asked, "Will you please get me bailed?"

"Get yourself bailed." Sarah took a deep breath. "All you're getting from me is a divorce."

Bryana reached to touch Norm's shirtsleeve. She squeezed his arm. "You're a good man. You did take care of it. Your wife's a lucky woman. Thank you."

"I'm doing my job." Tears started to fill his eyes. He batted them dry. "I'm doing what's right. What I should have been doing all along – fighting that miserable thief."

After Norm led Vince away, Bryana began to leave.

"Wait," Sarah called after her. "I'm so sorry."

"Sorry you lied and I covered for you all these years? Sorry I took the brunt of it all? My parents suffered? Michelle was dishonored? She couldn't get a job here. And are you sorry I was called a liar to keep your honor safe? Was called a rampant seducer? Or sorry your husband attempted to steal my farm from me? What *sorry* are we talking about?"

"Everything. I'm sorry for everything. But I swear, I didn't know about the fraud. He didn't want me involve in his business. And I didn't want to be involved."

"You were his wife. You kicked me to the curb for that garbage. I stayed silent for your happiness. And you were never happy."

"Bryana, I was terrified of hurting my parents. I believed they were slowly finding out about us. That's why I said what I said about you. So they wouldn't think I was one of those women. I thought they suspected you. But when I told my mother, she was shocked. I wouldn't have needed to tell her."

Incredulously, Bryana leaned back. "You gutless wonder."

"I didn't want to be an outcast. And you were going to college. Away. You'd talked about moving to Denver. Even then. So I didn't think it would impact you."

"No, I planned on going to Payton. I talked about Colorado because I had a scholarship there. You knew that. Stop lying to yourself."

"I lied so that he would marry me, and I would be acceptable. He wouldn't have understood. I didn't want to be a freak."

"But you were exactly what I was. And you continued your charade after I came back to take care of my parents."

She covered her eyes for several moments. "You had Michelle."

"And she also took the scorn from your lies and your hatred."

"I'm sorry. I admit I made certain she that couldn't work here. I didn't want the two of you remaining in Buffalo Plains. I did it because I was jealous that she was with you. And I wasn't. I'm still in love with you, Bryana. I would go away with you this very minute. Don't you see, I stuck by him because maybe I wanted to suffer for what I'd done to you. All I know is that I have never loved any person other than you. You and my grandchildren."

Bryana ached. "For much of my recent life, I've been sad. Sad for what was being done to the woman I love. I'm beginning to understand now. Most of your entire life, since we parted, has been sadder than anything I could have imagined."

Sarah's face turned away from Bryana. "Are you going to tell Michelle the truth?"

"I promised you I'd never tell anyone. It's the only thing in all our years together I haven't told her about. I also didn't tell her you and I had been lovers because it wasn't important."

"Not important?"

"Not important to Michelle and my relationship. She never asked me details. I allowed her to assume what she wanted. Now, I'll tell her everything. But don't worry. She's a nurse. She's heard all kinds of things in recovery rooms, and never once broken a confidence."

"She sounds like a remarkable woman. And she saved my grandson's life."

Bryana took a step away. "She *is* a remarkable woman. And she's saved lots of lives. I know. Because one of those lives was mine."

"I'm sorry I hurt her, too. I hurt you both," Sarah uttered.

Without a response, Bryana walked down the corridor to where Michelle had just emerged. She'd cleaned her body and changed into scrubs. "I left a fresh set of scrubs for you, if you want to change."

"Maybe I should. Please come with me, Michelle. I need to tell you something."

Bryana's words were sometimes hesitant, but she unrolled all the vacancies of her past. After she washed up some more and changed into scrubs, she glanced into Michelle's mirrored image. She felt both remorse for not telling her sooner, as well as relief that she was finally able to unwrap the truth.

Michelle broke eye contact as she turned and leaned back against the sink. "I've always sensed a low-grade anger in you. I never understood it before. And you didn't feel you could tell me until now?"

"I'd promised I would never tell anyone. When I first met you, I didn't feel it was anything I should tell you. Then after we were together, I thought you might dump me for not telling. It was a lie, of sorts."

"Lie of omission, maybe just a tad." Michelle put her thumb and forefinger nearly together. "You just didn't tell me the entire story. But it doesn't matter. What came before me – well, that was then. You haven't betrayed our relationship."

Bryana's eyes swiftly closed. "Don't you see, all those years I've thought of Sarah. I should have only been thinking only of you."

Michelle reached for Bryana's hand. Her head went back as she laughed her throaty, contagious laugh. "And I've thought of Candace Bergen and Sharon Gless. And I sometimes pined for Meryl Streep."

Their grins broke into a chaining laugh. Bryana took Michelle into her embrace. "I take it if Meryl, Sharon, and Candace were in the mix, I would be dumped."

Michelle chuckled. "Not until after I sampled them. They might not be quite as irresistible as you are. You make my gynecological meter quake with love of you."

"And you make my world quake. I don't think there's any way I could be more blessed."

"Let's go home. I've heard enough of your worldly, devious ways. I just want your love." She paused mischievously. "And a trial date with Streep wouldn't go amiss."

"I have it on good authority – well, TMZ, that she's happily settled down."

Michelle shrugged before taking Bryana's hand in hers. "Well, then, I'll just have to settle for another amazing, arousing and gratifying, sex-fest with you."

"Bliss," Bryana murmured. "Absolute bliss." With a grin of the interior, she thought how wonderful it was that Michelle considered her irresistible.

Chapter 31

After arriving back at the farm, Bryana felt as if her soul had been set free. The full story of what had transpired between her and Sarah had been disclosed.

The women changed into their denims and farm garb. There was work to be done. They would start by feeding the livestock. As they exited the house, Bryana looked up at the top of the barn.

"Oh, my," she gasped. "I must have been preoccupied when we drove in. I didn't notice the weathervane. Ricki." Her eyes were wet as she neared the huge barn.

Michelle grinned. "Ricki and Gloria wanted to surprise you. They wanted to get the weathervane painted. Ricki called this morning and I told her you'd be in town with deliveries. That didn't come to pass. But we certainly were away."

Bryana's eyes watered. "When I was a kid the shine on the weathervane was a glint of magic. I hated when it dulled. But I couldn't imagine anyone going up on that roof. How did they do it?"

"Ricki talked a couple of students into helping her. They were rock climbers. She said they were going to attach the rope to the vane's base. Check to see if it could be secured. Then rappel up and paint. And it looks like everything worked."

"Imagine. You know, it's like Ricki is the daughter we never had."

Michelle nodded. "I was thinking that, too. We're like a family now. Ricki said to tell you that because of us, she's changed her equation."

"The half and two quarters – what she believed about people?"

"She believes more people are finer than she once believed. She saw how people helped us when we needed help. We can depend on people. At any rate, she found out she could also depend on her new friends. Even for barn climbing."

"Must have been a hell of a long rope," Bryana said with amazement. "Astonishing." Bryana's arm went around Michelle's shoulder. A moment later, Michelle was in her embrace. "I love you so much." More than either of them knew, she considered. There were no more secrets between the women. She could now enjoy the full impact of Michelle's eyes. They held the world's most magnificent gift. Bryana's own glance had often skittered, when she thought of her past with Sarah. Now, she thought only of Michelle.

"I think everything is going to be okay," Michelle said softly. "Things are turning out okay. We can grow our businesses and be safe."

Bryana had never felt more of Michelle's warmth. It traveled through her body, and coursed through her very being. Even her spirit felt heated by the woman she held near. "I'm not sure everything is going to be okay. We're farmers. We're never safe. We jump from one dilemma to another. But things are better now."

Michelle nodded, "If we made it this far, we can make it work."

As they walked towards the hill of hay, Bryana grabbed a pitchfork, "Oh, I forgot to tell you that Norm said we should come to the court house in the morning and give our statement about what happened with Jon. Then we need to go to the bank. The examiners will be there all day. They need our statements. Depositions. Whatever."

"Maybe after we go to the sheriff's and have our chat with the bank regulators, we can do our deliveries. We can deliver the pastry and pottery, and also drop checks off to all our friends who wrote them to help us."

"It will feel great not to be indebted."

"You promised me a busy, but dull life on the farm."

"It was never this exciting when I was a kid being raised here."

Michelle's laugh lifted. "But you loved it?"

"I still do. And you?"

Michelle teased, "It's growing on me. Oh, by the way, I texted with L.J. and she'll be here Saturday morning. She was ecstatic about the financial news. Early this afternoon when I took Idgie's cast off she was walking almost normally. A slight limp. I'll put her brace on when we let her outside until she completely heals. Any news for me?"

A wide-lipped smile crossed Bryana's face. "I certainly do. Rolf called while I was waiting at the hospital. The weather forecasters have issued a retraction of this week's weather. No storm clouds in sight until late next week. That's well after the harvesting of the wheat. It's going to be a bumper crop." She glanced back up at the sparkling weather vane. "That rooftop is one lovely sight."

Suddenly Michelle questioned, "You think Vince will be imprisoned for this?"

"I'm pretty sure he'll pull some time. Even if he's paid politicians and judges off, the people he's bilked are not going to be best pleased. He'll forever have the town's scorn." Her face creased into a smile. "Vince and Tank both are going to have a hard road."

"Yes, it's obvious the trajectory of his life will change. He will have lost the respect he had from the town's people. Will he lose Sarah's respect?"

"I suppose he's already lost it." Bryana didn't answer the truth. Vince never really had the respect of either the town or Sarah. Until now Vince's soul had been brined in luck and seasoned with greed. All that would change. She continued answering, as thoughts came to mind. "I'm fortunate my life has been simple. Earthen trinkets have meant more to me than the fortune of treasures. Only you are my treasure. You and all that we have here."

Smiling, Michelle lulled, "And now we will eventually have a clear title to the land."

"And bubble bread whenever we want it. Pottery serving plates. We're set."

Michelle reached for Bryana's hand. Tenderly she kissed her lover's palm. "Yes, that reminds me. When we get back from town tomorrow, I want to make some plans for two more ovens to go out in the metal shed. We've got to make certain we grow the bakery. And the pottery business, too."

"Remind me to unload the kiln first thing in the morning. Before we feed the livestock and get ready for going into town."

Michelle added, "Hope we get a little time to begin painting the shed."

"I was thinking I should begin repairing the northern fence."

Michelle paused. "Oh, and Ricki's going to help us finish the buildings, and the greenhouse. She also mentioned she could put up a little stall to sell our produce, herbs, and pies. She thinks she'll have some extra lumber. She would put it out at the end of the driveway. I'll bet Ricki can put up some fancy siding around the bakery building. Make it look like a little dollhouse bakery. What do you think?"

Bryana's innocent smirk lifted. "I think you've got plans made. It's going to be lovely. Jersey would give her stamp of approval."

"Yes. I feel safer already."

Bryana whispered to Michelle, "The wildlife is undoubtedly feeling safer."

They looked up to see if perhaps the pheasants were flying above. Maybe celebrating, Bryana hoped. But the skies were empty of birds. The wildlife festival was quiet. They were also enjoying the silence that the absence of gunfire granted. The blessed quiet, she thought.

Celebrations were often hushed when tranquility visited. But the women did view a beautiful gilded weather vane. And behind that was a magnificent Kansas sunset. It looked exactly like an unfurling peace rose.

END

About the Author

Kieran York has written mainstream works including poetry and general fiction. She is the author of the lesbian mystery series featuring Royce Madison. *Timber City Masks* and *Crystal Mountain Veils* were written and published in the mid-1990s. She also wrote a collection of lesbian short stories entitled *Sugar With Spice.*

In 2012, York's book, *Appointment with a Smile,* was published and was a 2013 Lambda Literary Society Award Finalist in the romance category. Her next novel, *Careful Flowers,* was released in 2013.

York was also a contributor in *Sappho's Corner Poetry Series – Wet Violets, Volume 2; Roses Read, Volume 3;* and the newly released, *Delectable Daisies, Volume 4.*

In 2014, her volume of poetry, *Blushing Aspen,* was published as the Sappho's Corner Solo Poets book of poetry.

Previously, during the seventies and eighties, Kieran worked as a reporter and reviewer for both newspapers and magazines and was a newspaper publisher for three years. She also wrote and performed songs with a woman's band. She has been guest lecturer and panel member at various events, including Rocky Mountain Book Exhibition, Colorado Musicians Series, Sisters in Crime Mystery Writers, and Mystery Writers of America, Inc. She is a member of Lambda Literary Society, and Golden Crown Literary Society.

She has written for *Journal of Mystery Readers International.* In addition, she has given numerous campus and coffeehouse poetry readings, as well as taught poetry and creative writing workshops.

She graduated from a Kansas University and attended Mexico's University of the Americas her junior year. She has done graduate work at the University of Colorado.

Kieran lives in the Rocky Mountain foothills of Colorado with her schnauzer, Clover. She enjoys gardening, music, literature, art, and theatre. She considers her valuables to include Clover and other family and friends, her library, her antique typewriter collection, her guitar, and her garden.

Additional information is available on her website. She has a blog – Embellish Your Smile at http://kieranyork.com.